Prey for

Survival

By

S. Bradley Stoner

Meet The Author

S. Bradley Stoner was born in April, 1949. He was raised and educated in Denver, Colorado, attending the Denver Public School system and graduating from high school in 1967. He attended and graduated from the University of Colorado (Boulder) with a degree in environmental biology in 1971. Since that time he has pursued various interests, including travel and independent study of the wilderness world and its creatures, especially in the field of predator-prey relationships. While working at a variety of occupations to sustain his interests, he has actively pursued writing as a career since 1973.

His interest in the wild world is long and abiding, having begun trips to remote areas of wilderness in Colorado with his family and friends as a very young child. Trips into the deep wilderness continue for him to this day. Active and goal oriented, he attained the rank of Eagle Scout at the age of thirteen and subsequently earned two palms, was a member of the Denver Field Ornithologists from the age of 11 until college and work stopped his active participation, and in college was elected to the Phi Sigma Society, the biological honor society, in May, 1970. Also in 1970 he was chairman of the Wildlife Committee for the University of Colorado's participation in the first Earth Day observance.

His past occupations have included stints as an investigator (he holds an approval for a private detective's license in the state of Colorado), hard rock mining, cowboying, animal health management, livestock and grain marketing, log home building, environmental consultant, and contract writer for advertising and business reports.

Stoner's other interests include photography, pen and ink art (done under the name Bridgewood), poetry (also done under Bridgewood), horseback riding and horse breaking, technical rock climbing, and of course hunting and fishing.

Library of Congress Catalog Card Number 89−040414

ISBN: 0−923568−03−4

Cover art by Bridgewood

Photo of author by Mike McCarter

PUBLISHED BY

Wilderness Adventure Books
320 Garden Lane
Box 968
Fowlerville, Michigan 48836

Manufactured in the United States of America

FOR M'GEE

PREFACE

PREFACE

THE FUR TRADE and hunt-
ing. Their roots run as deep and as long as the history of
North America. They exist still and still they are important
to the game management and economies of the United
States and Canada, despite the objections of some people.
The truth is as old as man: Older. It is a thing that simply is,
and no explanations or excuses need to be made for it.

Pray for Survival uses the fur trade and hunting as a
backdrop, but to surmise that these subjects are the sole
content of the book would be a mistake. For the book is
more about the indefinable will of man, and woman to
survive, to grow, and to learn. It is a book about love, love
lost, and a new love. A book about fear and comforting
fear. It is a book about the tearing down of false walls we
build for ourselves and about how relationships are built
when understanding is possible. It is very much a book
about the human condition and how we react to circumstances beyond our control.

PREFACE

THE FUR TRADE and hunting. Their roots run as deep and as long as the history of North America. They exist still and still they are important to the game management and economies of the United States and Canada, despite the objections of some people. The hunt is as old as man. Older. It is a thing that simply is, and no explanations or excuses need to be made for it.

Prey for Survival uses the fur trade and hunting as a background, but to surmise that these subjects are the sole content of the book would be a mistake, for the book is more about the indomitable will of man, and woman, to survive, to grow, and to learn. It is a book about love, love lost, and a new love. A book about fear, and conquering fear. It is a book about the tearing down of false walls we build for ourselves and about how relationships are built when understanding is possible. It is very much a book about the human condition and how we react to circumstances beyond our control.

ACKNOWLEDGEMENTS

WITH SINCERE appreciation to Mike and Dorothy McCarter and family for their faith, cooperation, and support in my endeavors, and to all of my friends who kept the faith.

Special thanks to Julie F. for her encouragement over the years, and to Neil Soderstrom for getting me started.

PROLOGUE

MAN IS A PREDATOR. It is a simple fact, an undeniable fact. Within the social structure, man's predatory instincts have been sharpened, honed to a fine edge, where it is only a fine line that separates the "legal" from the "criminal." In both areas his predation has been fine tuned and brought almost to the point of art. There are many levels on which it may be manifested. From the obvious to the subtle, it has become sophisticated and dangerous in practice.

Within the realm of the "legal," the most obvious example of today's societal refinement of the predatory urge is the military. Although the individual societies may clamor that an armed force is necessary for its defense, it cannot be denied that all such forces are imbued with the capability for and the motivation for offensive action. Modern forces are, perhaps, actually and potentially the most voracious collective predators that have ever existed on this earth.

Politics is simply a slightly more subtle form of predation, having in it both external and internal manifestations. Hidden pressure, economics, and personal dominance replace the more tangible teeth of the military. The chain of predation becomes more complex.

But it is in business, religion, and the social fabric of the nations of man where predatory fulfillment reaches its highest and most subtle form. Here, where preying on the fears, prejudices, greed, and miscalculations of his fellow man, he weaves the most intricate web of all. Here it is that social conscience is touted, and trammeled by the preachers of salvation, be they religious or otherwise. It is here that the individual can be broken and consumed and never have a hair put physically out of place. Subtle cruelty, sublime savagery. What happens to a man who sees the system for what it is and chooses to live totally outside of that system? To reject the society that raised him up and cast him aside, and choose to turn to predation in its most basic sense? Is it possible to run from the comforts of this "civilized" modern society of predators and return to the ancient form and still survive? To intrude on what is left of a vast wilderness that once was and hold a niche in isolation? Questions that take on complex proportions where there are not always answers, take form in the escape of a man as he begins to "Prey for Survival." Isolation ends itself, whether in the ultimate form, death, or the coming of another intruder. One can be accepted, in certain states of mind even welcomed. The other brings with it the old conflicts of domination, submission, assertion, and displacement, even those nebulous feelings of the in-between realm.

The world of nature, at once a vision of exquisite beauty and an arena of brutal savagery, is a dynamic system of delicate balances. To carve a niche within that system, it is necessary to recognize it for what it is, real and tangible, stripped of all cosmetics applied by man. To live there means that one must abandon idealistic environmentalism and practice the practical form, assume the form in which one is cast and exploit the niche. To be a predator requires an acceptance of the part, to be savage when it is required, but to be aware of the limitations of the role. Even a predator must be in harmony with his environment.

To live within the wilderness strips away all the illusions cast by certain of those in society. Those of the animal kingdom are neither evil nor benevolent, merely pieces of an intricate web of life and death, ultimately all of death. Those who claim that man must be the salvation of the wild world are not realists. The wild world will survive man, for man is an endangered species, endangered by his own methods, his own numbers. Certainly he will be preceded in demise by many of those he seeks to preserve,

but that is an ultimate fact of evolution. In the long run nature will renew herself and man's domination will pass. As
surely as moss covers the stones of ancient civilizations, it
will cover the monuments of modern ones. Nature will endure, and with her the predators, changed in form, consis-
tent in purpose.

S. B. S.

CHAPTER 1

THE FOREFINGER of his right hand caressed the trigger of the Winchester as the buck stepped cautiously into the clearing. The man's thumb slowly drew back the hammer and its click, as it latched into place, caused the buck to start, poised to bolt. In that instant the hammer fell and the report of the rifle and the buck seemed to hang suspended in the air. Then it was over, the buck came crashing to the ground at the end of its lifeless bound as the last echoes of the rifle's report faded into the vastness of the forest.

The lone figure of a man stood slowly, emerged from the tangle of willow brush, and walked slowly toward the stilled animal. Steel gray eyes peered out from beneath an old and dirty Stetson as his muddied boots felt their way along the uneven ground. Part of his mind assessed the buck, calculating the number of steaks, roasts, and the amount of jerky that would be realized. The other part played with more philosophical thoughts. How much smaller the buck looked in death than it had in life. Gone were the proud power and stateliness, the soft shine in its eyes. In their place lay a crumpled pile of hide, muscle, and bone with the wide surprised staring eyes already beginning to glaze. So it was with all creatures, thought the man, all lose the aura of greatness when death comes.

In the midst of these revelations there was a flash of white as a smile formed between the heavy brown moustache and beard, for he had triumphed. In the death of this beast his own survival was assured. He lay the rifle down carefully and his callused hand slipped the antler-handled hunting knife from its fringed sheath. In half an hour the buck was hung from a sturdy branch of a nearby pine, the

1

heart and liver lay submerged in the cool waters of the spring pool.

He washed the blood from his hands and forearms in the clear, cold water and rolled down the sleeves of his woolen shirt. He retrieved an old pipe from his shirt pocket, filled it, and clamped its heavy bit between his teeth. With the ease of familiarity, he fished out a wooden match, raked its head with a rough thumbnail, and fired the tobacco in the bowl. He rolled the smoke over his tongue, allowed it to escape and tested its pungent fragrance as it rose past his nose. He puffed slowly and contentedly, listening as the chattering of the chickadees returned to the forest.

Almost reluctantly, the hunter packed the ash deep into the bowl of the pipe and brushed the accumulation of morning dew from his had-sewn chaps. He picked up the rifle, cradling the forestock easily in the crook of his arm, made his way through the willow brush, and up the hill. It was a short distance to the place he had left his dog and horses, and he covered it swiftly.

The Paint and the bay grazed quietly in the little clearing and a giant Husky lay motionless, except for the pale yellow eyes that missed nothing, a few yards away. When the man broke through the edge of the clearing, the bay lifted its head and whickered noisily. The man walked to him, rubbed his soft nose, and said, "Come on big fellah, we've got some work to do." He grasped the halter and led the horse to the saddles. The bay stood patiently as the pack saddle was secured to his back. The man looked up as he made final adjustments to see the Paint approaching with the small, mincing steps allowed by her hobbles. The man laughed. "If you wouldn't run off, I wouldn't have to hobble you girl." Kneeling down, the man undid the hobbles and reached quickly up to grab her halter as she started to dance away. He smiled at her knowingly and snapped the lead to the halter and tethered her to a sapling. He carefully laid the saddle blankets across her back and reached for the worn saddle. It was an old one, nearly a century had passed since it had been hand crafted. The hand carved patterns that had once been the pride of some Montana cowboy were now worn almost smooth and the stamp of the maker on the fore part of the seat near the swells was but a faded oval line. It wasn't a form fitter, but its design made it a good breaking saddle and the man he had bought it from had sworn that it had been under as many horses as it had been on top of. He handled it almost reverently as he placed it on the mare's back. As he tightened the latigo, the mare turned and gazed balefully at him. "You know better than that," he cautioned softly as he pushed her nose away.

Once the horses were saddled and standing quietly, the man gave out a low whistle. The gray Husky rose and trotted toward his master, giving a deep throated growl. The dog's behavior had been carefully guided since his puppy days and by now the commands were well understood. Only this low whistle released him from his guard duty, a duty for which he would lay down his own life if it became necessary. "Well, Whiskey, did you have any visitors?" the man asked softly as he ran his hands affectionately through the thick pile of the dog's coat. "We've got a nice buck, so we ought to eat for the next few weeks. What say we go get him?"

The man picked up the bay's lead, mounted the Paint, and touched his heels to her flanks. He still had to keep a tight rein on her, for he had just broken her this summer and she was still inclined to be a bit frisky. On this fall morning, seeming to be caught up in the excitement of things, she was even more difficult than usual. The man used equal measures of rein, touch, and voice to steady his mount, but the steadfast bay gave his head an occasional toss and the lead rope a sharp jerk to show his displeasure with the spirited mare.

A nuthatch followed the little group, warning the forest inhabitants in a shrill voice. The hunter grinned at the small bit of feathered fluff, its alarm was too late for the quarry sought, and there would be no more carnage today.

At the spring the man tethered the Paint and wasted no time in securing the fallen prey to the packsaddle on the bay.

"Whiskey!" The dog withdrew a wet paw from the spring pool where he had been fishing for the heart and liver of the deer and hastily backed away. The man crossed to the pool and retrieved the organs, wrapped them in a piece of rubberized cloth, and dropped them into an open side of his saddlebags. "Hell, might have forgotten them anyway," the man grinned. "Come on Whiskey, we've got a ways to go before we get home."

The ride would be leisurely, for it was still early and there was no reason to hurry the enjoyment of a crisp fall day. He would ride quietly, stopping at the tops of hills to gaze down on the little valleys that lay below. He would light his pipe and smell the smoke that drifted back, enjoying the deep, rich lingering quality of its fragrance. Very little escaped his vision. The gray fox that skirted the aspen grove to the side, the beetle that clambered over the rotted stump, the hawk that soared far above in the clear blue sky, the rabbit that hid from the hawk in the scraggly currant bush were all observed and catalogued in his mind. These were the sights, the scents, and the sounds of the wilderness world, a complex web perceived, identified, and then put together like pieces of a jigsaw puzzle in the mind of the man. This was the world that the man had been educated to scrutinize scientifically. It was the world that circumstance had stolen from him, a world that perseverance, faith, and alienation had returned to him, a world that he loved and claimed as if it were his child, but above all else, the world that claimed him and consumed him totally.

The sun had collided with the horizon and lay fractured and splintered in the haze of evening before the man broke into a small clearing where a lonely group of buildings stood. Whiskey broke into a trot and headed for the largest of the buildings. A keen, squinted eye would have perceived the sturdy porch that fronted the man's cabin, the stack of split wood that ran the length of its south side, the horse corral and shed to the north, but it would have probably missed the half-sunken cold house where the hunter would hang his buck.

A breeze sprang suddenly from the north and hardened rapidly into a chill wind. It was not the first heralder of the passing of summer, but one like it. The man recalled that first blast of fall's northern wind, and how, once again, he had marveled at the sudden changes in his world. Leaves on the alder, aspen, willow, dogwood, and bitterbrush had begun to transform into brilliant flashes and, among the eternal evergreens, seemed to set the forest blazing. The tamaracks had begun their annual transmutation from green to gold, challenging the broadleaves to match their splendor. The elk's bugle of challenge could be heard rising and falling as they crashed down from the high country they were reluctant to leave. Each day that passed brought the increased calls of the wild flocks as they deserted their breeding grounds for more balmy climes to the south. To this man who lived by natures clock, it signalled the morn of a different day. The cold of winter was on its way and there was much to be done before its icy arrival.

The next morning the late September sun broke the eastern sky with brilliance and pursued the fleeing puffs of clouds as the man rose and shook the last remnants of sleep from his mind. He stumbled to the stove and, groping in the gray morning light of the cabin's interior, found and struck a match to light the kindling in the firebox. The flame dimmed, then flared as the fire caught with a crackle and sputter of sap. He picked up the coffee pot, filled the battered thing with water, and set it down. Reaching into the open cupboard, he grasped his last can of coffee. It was half empty. The other necessities were in short supply as well, and the man knew he would soon have to make a trip to the small town.

The town was the only link he maintained with the society of man, and he viewed even it with mixed emotions. It was a pleasant appearing little village, filled with outwardly genial people, but he remembered the pettiness, banality, and spitefulness that had lurked just beneath the surface of other towns just like it. That memory left a foul taste in the man's mind. Still, there were the necessities that he required and what the people might have thought of him made very little difference when it came to doing business, and the man he did business with he counted as a friend, perhaps his only friend. For now, there were other things that cried for the man's attention, and he gave them priority over the trip to town.

He pulled his jeans off the peg and put them on and reached for his boots. He went to the door and called for his dog. "Whiskey! It's breakfast time!" Whiskey rose from his nightly bed of old blankets and growled a friendly good morning. He trotted up to take the dried fish from his master's hand and receive the customary good morning pat. Once the dog was gnawing contentedly on the fish, the man turned his attention to his own breakfast. A man gets used to a lot of different breakfasts when there isn't a store nearby, and the liver from the buck didn't seem out of place at all.

As he washed down a stale piece of bread with a final cup of scalding coffee, the man regarded the tools of the day's labor. He reached for the bastard file in a toolbox near the door and touched up the blade of the axe, testing its edge occasionally. Finally he grunted in satisfaction and set the file aside. Keeping himself in wood was, perhaps, the most demanding and time consuming task he had. Timber had to be hauled in, using the old fashioned hitch on the bay, cut, and then split.

The hunter, turned logger for the day, had now only to split the many logs that had been tediously cut with the bow saw. He picked up his axe, sledge, and splitting wedges and stepped lightly toward the pile. Placing the first large log on the chopping stump, he set the wedge with a light tap and then swung the hammer forcefully at it. The ring of steel on steel set the local squirrel population into a frenzy of protest.

As the sun swung in its slow arc toward mid-day, the

man began shedding clothes until he stood only in his jeans and boots, perspiration gleaming on his muscular upper torso. He had a fleeting thought that all those writers who extolled the glories of such labor in the outdoor magazines must never have had to do it out of necessity. He doubted that any of them had ever laid in much more than a cord as he looked at the six to eight cords that would constitute most of his winter wood supply.

It was well past noon when the man took a break from his task for a premade meal of jelly sandwiches, jerky, and hot coffee. Whiskey ambled over to beg a few pieces of jerky and lie at his master's feet. The woodsplitter sipped the last of his coffee from the dented old mess kit cup and scratched his dog's head. Absent-mindedly, he pulled out his half- filled pipe, lit it, and began making mental notes of repairs that were needed around the place. The cabin needed some chinking replaced, the corral fence needed mending, and the horse shelter needed a few new roof boards. His mind drifted back to the dwindling supplies and he began to make mental notes of the items that would make up the list he would compile this evening. It was his habit to make the list at least a week before he went to town so that he could add those things that he might have forgotten otherwise.

Soon he was back to splitting wood, moving somewhat slower than before lunch. He was tired by late afternoon, which made the blister on his right hand even more annoying. He decided that he needed a change of pace. He took the tools back to the cabin, strapped on his pistol, picked up the buckets, and headed for the clay deposits down by the river.

The trail was narrow and winding, weaving its way through the trees and into the willow and birch that marked the edge of the flats. The flood plain of the river was strewn with the decaying bodies of uprooted trees that the spring waters had undermined, swallowed, and finally regurgitated here where the slope gentled and calmed the upstream torrent. Among the cadavers of spruce and aspen a great blue heron hunted, moving deliberately, like an old man stiffened with arthritis. Gigantic rafts of ducks and geese floated far out in the placid stretches of the river.

The man deliberately let his vision lose its focus, blurring the sparkling water, the flocks, the greens and golds of the far side of the river. Had the scene in the late afternoon sun been put to canvas, as the man perceived it at this moment, it might have rivaled the master strokes of van Gogh. There was no master of the pallet here and the soft sounds of paint-dipped brush on canvas that might have been were obliterated by the sucking and plopping of moisture laden clay.

When the buckets were full, the man toiled back up the trail and began to fill in the gaps that the harsh northern weather had eaten in the chinking. There were two more trips to the river with the buckets to complete the chore, two more visions at the water's edge, each different than the one before.

When he had finished his evening meal, and the oil lamp on the table was lit, emitting a bright if somewhat uneven light, the man sat with a sheaf of paper before him, intending to begin the list. Instead his hand and mind wandered of their own accord and the pen began to glide across the first empty page. It became an outpouring of his love for his style of life, touched on the frustrations he encountered, and ended in bitterness for the memories of the recent past. When his mind emptied itself, he reread what lay before him, calmly tore it up and dribbled the pieces into the fireplace, staring at the little flares as those little pieces of his soul that he shared with no one caught fire and turned to ash. He looked vacantly across the room for a moment, shut out the memories, wrote his list, and went to bed.

It took two more days of concentrated labor to finish the splitting of the wood. On the fourth day since he had begun this vital chore, he completed stacking it on the leeward side of his cabin. He then turned his attention to the mending of the horse corral. The corral fence was over eight feet high and built of stout spruce poles, each only ten inches above the next, and spiked to posts set solidly at eight foot intervals. It had been built to prevent large predators from breaching it to insure the safety of the horses upon which the man depended so much. As yet it had done its job, but even so a large boar grizzly had severely damaged two poles in an effort to gain entrance one night two weeks ago.

His attack had sent the horses into a frenzy, Whiskey to their defense, and the man on the run, rifle in hand. Two shots fired into the night air had sent the animal packing and a sharp whistled command stopped the Husky from pursuing a fatal course. It was the first time that the bear had visited the compound, although the man had seen track a few miles away once or twice before, and the sound of gunfire had seemed new to the animal. The man hoped it would be enough to keep the beast from returning, even though he admired the awesome grace and beauty of this powerful member of a declining race.

The man replaced the poles with those from a conservative stockpile he kept for such an eventuality. He worked with economy, both of motion and materials. The eighty penny spikes were retrieved from the damaged poles and used to set the new ones. He finished the fence and shed repairs swiftly and spent the remainder of the afternoon preparing for the trip to town, it could be put off no longer.

That evening, after dinner, he reviewed his list before going out to sit on the porch of the tiny cabin. He pulled from his pocket a small folding knife and began to sharpen its well oiled blades on a worn whetstone, gazing at the distant stars and feeling the refreshing night breeze on his face. He thought of that past day when he had gathered up his possessions, all that the bank sale had left him, loaded them aboard a small string of pack horses and headed north and into the past he idealized. The trip had been often grueling and, although he considered himself a good woodsman, he had felt doubts and inadequacies within the first two weeks. Many incidents had left him drained at the end of each day and yet he had reached deep within himself and attacked each new sunrise with renewed strength and determination and had survived the six weeks of trail life.

So, here he was about to enter his fourth winter, a far wiser man in the intricacies of survival and wilderness living. He thought of his formal education, and of his practical one, in the dynamics of a natural system, the delicate balances, and the sometimes harsh realities. He thought, too, of his role and its duality. While he still felt himself a student observer, he was also an intruding niche holder. To realize his strengths he must admit and compensate for his frailties, something difficult for the egotism of the human mind to accept, but utterly necessary for survival. Failure to recognize this basic fact, failure to act upon it would be fatal.

When he had finished sharpening his knife he turned to look once more at the stars before going in. The timepiece of the universe was still there, ticking off the seconds of eternity, the night bright and beautiful as ever. As he walked toward the open door of his cabin, the mournful call of the great gray owl penetrated the cool, crisp air. He stopped and turned, peering into the darkness of the forest. "Jedidiah Smith Marsh, the world may think you are a fool, but at least you are a happy damn fool," he said with a deep, clear voice. And he thought with satisfaction of the eyes that would watch his world as he slept.

CHAPTER 2

THE AUTUMNAL GUSTS had come too early for the four year old male grizzly, and, under the bright sun, their drying effect had shriveled the berries and fruits that constituted the greatest part of his food supply. A territorial fight a few weeks ago had locked him in mortal combat with another titan of his species. He had won that struggle, but it had cost him greatly. He bore his scars and pain in characteristic silence, but they slowed him in the hunt. When he did make a kill, it was often only enough to replace what had been spent in the pursuit and the days of emptiness. To quiet the rumblings deep within the great maw of his belly he had stuffed himself with great quantities of dry, brown grass. The noises diminished, but the hunger was not sated. He would stand wagging his great shaggy head from side to side, searching with flared nostrils for what his near-sighted eyes could not perceive. The chatter of the squirrels that ran from branch to branch, warning the forest of his presence, began to grow as an irritation in a corner of his brain.

Two weeks ago he had scented the sweet smell of Jed's horses, and an odor he did not know. The smell of man was alien to him and, while his meager brain catalogued it, he did not fear it. He calmly assessed the enclosure, standing to study it, while the horses wheeled and screamed with fear. The fragrance of that fear emboldened the bear and he advanced on the corral. Its outward leaning poles prevented him from scaling the structure, but a tentative blow showed that the structure would yield. Another, stronger blow. The first pole splintered, a second cracked. There was a sudden clap of thunder followed by a strange burning odor, the bear paused and dropped to all fours. At the second shot he had run, frightened by the noise and the flash, but he had felt no physical pain. In his first encounter with the strange two legged creature he had come away unhurt. Today all that would change.

He had come upon MacKelvy's hunting camp in the early predawn hours of morning. His keen nose sorted the odors of the camp wafting up to him on the damp early air. Among the sweet odors of fresh bacon, breads, and assorted other foodstuffs, the pungent smell of man intermingled itself. The bear circled the camp cautiously, recalling the first encounter with man. His curiosity and hunger got the better of him and he was very close to the perimeter of the camp at daybreak. He had just stepped from cover into the edge of the clearing when the burning sting of the bullet furrowed along his left hip. As his reflexes made him snap angrily at the rip, the crash of the rifle shattered the peaceful morning once again.

The grizzly crashed blindly into the protective cover of the brush as more bullets fractured among the tangle of branches. For hours he continued his flight, resting often as the loss of blood slowed him. Each time he had rested, the scent of one relentless pursuer gained on him. His keen nose told him what his dim eyes could not, move on again. The chase lasted into the waning hours of daylight and the hated scent that followed him became indelibly imprinted on the bear's olfactory memory. He had not taken any particular care to evade his pursuer, but rather chose a direct path to the depths of his territory.

Only when the bear neared his den did he take care to mask his presence. The blood had clotted in the wound and he moved carefully to avoid reopening it as he circled his home and crawled through the concealed tunnel of brush that led to the warm pit below the giant fallen spruce. There he collapsed in exhaustion. In the wretched turnings of his fever inflamed brain, the odious scent of the new enemy surfaced again and again. Within the beast grew a fear and hate that festered like the wound on his hip.

CHAPTER 3

JED AWOKE before first light, having slept fitfully. He dressed swiftly and went out into the cold, starless black of morning. His breath hung in frosty puffs as he made his way to the horse shed. He lit the wick of the lantern and called to his horses softly. When he had given them the last of the grain in the burlap sack he returned to the cabin. In spite of himself, he felt the uneasiness of excitement creep in. It had been three months since his last trip to town and he felt a slight anticipation for human companionship once more. As he finished his final cup of coffee, he reviewed his long list of supplies and checked the contents of his saddlebags to assure himself that they contained all the necessities for the forty eight mile trip to town.

In an hour he had the horses saddled and waiting nervously while he checked to make sure all the doors and shutters of the cabin were securely bolted. He would be gone five days and he wanted no surprises in the form of furry mischief makers when he returned. With one last glance around, he mounted the Paint and headed her south. Eager for the trail, Whiskey bounded ahead.

It was a sobering thought that the people of the small village were his closest neighbors, and Jed thought wryly that only one of them, if he were still alive, would miss him if he did not show up for his fall visit. Jed had not had any human visitors at his clearing for almost six months and he was lonely for conversation. He talked with the animals that visited the clearing unashamedly, but they could only respond with curious looks. And it was true that he talked to himself more than occasionally, but, in view of the interminable stretches of silence and the isolation, that could not be considered unusual.

Jed rode in silence now, listening to the forest sounds, watching the birds fly ahead of him. Whiskey would show surprising energy in chasing an occasional rabbit, only to return a short time later empty jawed. Jed knew the simple reason for his dog's bloodless return, Whiskey wasn't hungry. The dog possessed a native instinct for hunting and was expert as a predator when necessary. The dog had been bred for the rigors of the north. He stood two feet six inches at the shoulder and weighed ninety pounds. Though he was three quarters Husky, his amber eyes belied the timber wolf heritage of his sire. He had proven himself in the stalk, the pursuit, and the kill many times. He could be an awesome beast in a fight, a fact that was well concealed as he trotted complacently ahead of the mare.

Without losing an unthinking consciousness of the trail and the forest about him, Jed's mind drifted to another time. The day had been very like this one, the setting similar.

ANOTHER TIME, ANOTHER PLACE: "This is the only time that a guy oughtta ride . . . this an' the early mornin'. Oughtta hole up in the middle of the day when it's so damn hot."

"It's a nice time to ride all right," Jed replied absent mindedly.

"Damn right it is," the other rider said as he spat to the side and reached into the top pocket of his open shirt. "Wanna chew?"

"Naw Mark, think I'll pass."

"Copenhagen, an' it's fresh. See . . . lookit the date," Mark proffered the can.

"I think I'll just have a smoke." Jed pulled the old broken stemmed cob pipe from his shirt pocket and struck a match with his thumbnail. When the pipe was lit, he blew out the match and wet the coal at its end with saliva soaked fingers, then crushed the tip and threw it aside. "Timber's tinder dry," he said, giving Mark a sideways glance. "Can't be too careful."

"Damn hot weather an' no rain . . . do it every time. Still think ya oughtta take up chewin'. Yup," he grunted and spat again as he hooked his right knee over the saddle horn and settled into the saddle, "hellish dry weather."

"How much further?" Jed asked, drawing deeply on the pipe.

"Shit, them old cows gotta be about five miles up ahead yet . . . just set back an' take 'er easy."

Jed followed Mark's example and swung his leg over the horse's neck, easing into the gentle rocking rhythm of his mount's lazy walk.

"Yup, ain't no reason to rush a fine evenin' like this . . . Hell, it ain't gonna get dark till nearly ten thirty anyhow." Mark's young face sometimes came up with the damnedest expressions. Right now it bore a rather exaggerated boyish smile that was almost a caricature of his normal pleasant countenance.

"What's on your mind?" Jed asked with a bemused smile of his own.

"Aw nothin' outta the ordinary. Just thinkin' that you an' me oughtta take a run over to Wallace sometime an' see if that pay-pussy is any good."

Jed could not refrain from laughing outright. "What in hell makes you think it's any different than the local stuff?"

"Aw nothin', 'ceptin' maybe that I heard they'd do damn near anything for a extra buck."

Jed laughed a retort. "Probably get crabs or a good dose of the clap."

"I dunno . . . a fellah oughtta try it once . . . else how's he gonna know how it stacks up against the hometown stuff?"

The pair eyed each other knowingly, and rode in silence for quite a spell. The air was choked with the dry hot smell of a parched forest, but it was a good smell. Most of the normal chatter of the wild birds had dwindled and the day had grown thoughtfully silent except for the clip-clop of the horseshoes on the rocky trail and the occasional angry buzz of a blowfly. Mark finally broke the silence.

"Gotta helluva view when we top this next rise . . . can look at a pretty good piece of Idaho an' Montana both . . . There's a couple of them ol' bitches now! You ride low an' I'll head for the ridge after we get to the top. That way we can cover more territory an' maybe pick up most of 'em."

"Sounds all right to me. You want to link up somewhere down the line or just have each of us take what we can get and push them down to the lower meadow?"

"Why don't I meet ya back by that salt lick we passed . . . you know, that there second block. I'll give ya whatever I pick up an' you can push them down while I pick up any strays that are on the rest of the ridge an' whatever else happens along."

"Good enough," Jed replied, accepting the instructions of this younger, but more experienced cowhand.

"Jesus! Ain't this a view?! I don't never get tired of it."

"Sure is," Jed said, taking in the views of miles and miles of territory. "If it was water, I'd try and drink it all."

"When I die, I hope I get buried right here. God, wouldn't that be a nice place to spend eternity?" Mark said with an uncommon philosophical depth.

The sun had reached its zenith when Jed reined in the mare and took a break for lunch. The creek that followed this part of the trail provided the horses with cool water and its banks with feed in the form of lush, still-green grass. A large muskrat made his way nervously along the edge of the creek and quickly dove into the icy water when one of the horses pawed the ground and snorted. Whiskey was oblivious to the entire world as he snoozed peacefully on the ground next to his master. Jed gazed over at a tree that had an old blaze on it and chuckled. He had put the blaze there on his first passing of this trail. It hadn't been necessary, the path had been indelibly etched on his memory with that first trip. Jed squinted an eye at the sun. To any ordinary person the change in the sun's position would

have been imperceptible, but in fact it had shifted just
enough to tell Jed that a half an hour had passed. He rose,
stretched, yawned widely, caught up the reins of the Paint,
and mounted to resume his journey.

That evening Jed made camp in the usual place. At the
edge of a small grassy meadow a large rock overhang made
a shelter. Blowdowns on either side of the rock completed
a natural three sided enclosure. At the mouth of the shelter
was a stone reflector fireplace that Jed had built the first
time he had used this place for a night's rest. A couple of
stones had been knocked loose, but it was still recognizable
as a fireplace. Jed looked after his horses before looking to
his own comfort. He picked up his saddle and carried it
into the rock shelter and set it well inside. Swiftly he undid
the tie strings that held his down sleeping bag and unrolled
it, fluffing it to insure a warm night. He spent a short time
collecting firewood.

Once the preparations for the night were complete, Jed
went to the limp panniers and reached in to get his pack
rod and reel. He carefully assembled the rod, seated the
reel, and ran the line through the ferrules. He then tied
one of his favorite flies, a bulky, rather ugly affair known
as a "muddler" in the west, to the end of a long leader and
tested the spring of the rod, bending it almost double, with
loving familiarity.

Whiskey rose to follow at his master's heels as he
headed for the deep pools of the creek. For a while the dog
cavorted in the tumbling water and lapped at its cool
sweetness, then he returned to the bank, shook himself,
and watched with fascination the long looping arc of fly-
line as it arched forward and backward in the calm evening
air. With each of the first three casts the muddler would
light only for an instant, then careen backwards as more
line was stripped from the reel. On the fourth cast it would
rest lightly atop the swirling water as the tip of the tapered
rod traced its movement downstream. Slowly Jed worked
his way downstream, wading in sock feet, fishing each
pocket of calm water. Suddenly it happened, the muddler

was engulfed, the rod bending heavily under its burden. Jed let the line run free for a moment, then moved his thumb to press against the free-wheeling reel. Instantly the fish turned about and the line was briefly slack before Jed could begin reeling frantically. He felt the line tighten once again and watched as it sliced feverishly from side to side as his finned adversary tried to free itself of the tiny barbed hook that had been hidden in the body of the insect imposter. Down to its last bag of tricks, the trout leapt high in the air, shaking its body side to side, flashing silver red in the evening sun. Soon it was over and the trout lay listlessly on the grassy bank, glistening droplets running down its length. Jed made two more catches from the pool, then returned to the bank, put on dry socks and his boots. He filled and lit his pipe, its pungent fragrance filling the crisp autumn air, making Whiskey's nose twitch. Jed smiled at the dog and squatted to clean the fish.

During the short walk back to camp, Jed stopped to watch a golden eagle as it soared majestically through the air on its way home. The great bird lived up to its name as its iridescent feathers reflected the setting sun, a truly beautiful sight. Back at camp, Jed kindled a small fire and set about weaving a green stick grill. The fire was going well, a bed of glowing coals emitting a steady heat beneath the pop and sputter of newly added dry twigs, by the time he had finished the grill. He laid the grill on two flat stones, suspending it above the fire, and arranged the trout on the simple structure. He squatted on his heels, savoring the mixed aroma of frying trout and pine smoke. Whiskey was sniffing too, and drooling a bit, as the dancing fire reflected in his eyes. It was not long before the two travelers were enjoying the trout, devouring them ravenously.

Yawning widely, Jed prepared for the night's rest, laying his pistol belt by the saddle and leaning the rifle next to it. He hung his clothes on a piece of wood that was jammed into a crevice in the rock wall and slipped into the bag, shivering as the cold nylon met his skin. Whiskey curled up at his feet and sighed deeply. The two were soon asleep, each with his own dreams.

It was sometime in the middle of the night when the fiendish scream split the darkness, bringing Jed instantly awake, his eyes struggling to adjust themselves. Whiskey was at the shelter's edge, neck hackles bristling and ears laid back. A deep growl rumbled in his chest. "Puma!" Jed swore silently. His first concern was for his horses and he peered out to see them standing nervously nearby. Reassured, he swiftly built up the dying embers of the fire, knocking down the reflector stones. He picked up his rifle, strode quickly to the horses, and led them nearer the camp, tying their picket lines to the blowdown adjacent to the rock. He squatted by the fire and stared into the black night. He moved his eyes methodically from left to right. Abruptly he froze, feeling the hair on his own neck stand. Two iridescent orbs were reflecting from the darkness. Back and forth they moved as the great cat paced impatiently. For a few moments Jed watched, fascinated, then the crash of his rifle sent the animal fleeing into the night. The damp air held the smell of burnt cordite close to the little camp, like a protective blanket. No predators would visit the rest of the night. Jed returned to his bed.

The icy chill of the morning breeze wedged Jed from the dreamless slumber. Opening his eyes slowly, he blinked as smoke, held low by the cold, wafted into them. Sitting up in his sleeping bag, he rubbed the sleep and smoke from his eyes. "Whiskey," he called, "come over here." Obligingly, Whiskey romped onto the sleeping bag, mocking ferocity as he tussled happily with his master. For a few moments, dog and master tugged, laughed, and wrestled, oblivious to the world around them. Squirrels stopped chattering to watch this strange "life and death" struggle, and brave little chickadees hopped closer to get a better look at the contestants. It was a good beginning for a day.

Jed brewed a small pot of coffee and munched a handful of pemmican for breakfast before saddling the horses. Whiskey picked up the scent of the puma and pursued it for a while, but was back just as Jed was mounting the

Paint. "What's the matter, she give you the slip Whiskey?" Whiskey's answer was a soft gaze and a lolling tongue. Jed laughed and set the horses at a fast walk. Town was not far now, and he meant to be there in as short a time as possible.

Jed topped the final rise in the trail that led to town and looked down on the sleepy village. It lay in a small hollow of an oval shaped valley. A single white steeple of the only church poked out above the smudge of smoke that hovered above the cluster of buildings and tailed out over the southern end of the valley. From this vantage point, Jed could make out the square corrals and hodge-podge of buildings that comprised the Diamond Bar outfit. It was owned by Bob Price and did a meager business during the hunting season as compared with Jim Raudsep's outfit on the north edge of town. For the past two years Jed had found lodging for himself and stables for his horses with Price whenever he came to town and he guided the mare in the direction of the half-breed's outfit.

Jed was half way up the road to Price's house when Bob noticed the rider, horses, and dog. It was the dog he recognized first. "I'll be," he muttered and dropped the horse's hoof he'd just finished shoeing. "Go on, girl," he said as he unsnapped the lead that held her to the corral fence. "Louise! We got comp'ny," he hollered at the open door of the house. He clambered stiffly over the fence and walked out to meet Jed.

Jed removed his dusty Stetson and banged it against his thigh. "Hello Bob," he said amiably, "got room to put me up for a couple of nights?"

"I think I can manage. Only got three hunters in yet, four more comin' tomorrow or the next day. How's things goin'?"

"Not too bad, I guess," Jed replied as he swung down from the saddle. "I'll be needing another horse and some pack rigging. You got any to spare?"

"Got the horse, but you'll have to get the riggin' in town."

"That'll do."

Bob walked with Jed to the bunk house where three hunters sat drinking beer on the porch. The men eyed Jed curiously as he unsaddled the horses and stored his gear at the foot of an empty bed. Jed greeted them with a nod and followed Bob as he led the horses to a corral. Jed told him that he would rest the horses the remainder of the day and go to town tomorrow to get his stores. He'd stay one more night and then head back at dawn the next day. They settled on a price for the lodging and the horse Jed would need for the return trip. Bob commented on the mare, one he'd sold Jed on his spring trip. Jed's pleasure with the purchase was evident as he recounted the steps in her breaking. It was the easy, friendly talk of two men who, although they knew each other slightly, shared an understanding of each others world.

"Louise'll have supper in a couple a hours," Bob said as Jed turned toward the bunkhouse. "Beef stew an' pan biscuits. Oh hey, one of my guides said that he run into one of Raudsep's hands an' he told him that MacKelvy got a shot off at a big griz. Guess he wounded him an' blood trailed him somewhere to the north of your place."

"Great," Jed spat disgustedly. "That sonofabitch never could shoot straight. It sure as hell won't make that bear easy to get along with."

"Maybe he gutshot him an' he crawled up somewheres an' died. If he didn't, God help the poor bastard that crosses trails with him."

"Yeah," Jed replied. "I'm gonna go get a shower and catch a nap . . . been riding since dawn."

"All right, the bell ul get ya up fer supper."

Jed showered and changed clothes, dusting off his trail clothes and stowing them in his saddlebags. As he rolled out the mattress, one of the hunters sauntered in, hitching up his pants a notch. "Hullo," the man said, sticking out a hand, "I'm Bill Cunningham out of Dallas. You going to be our guide?"

Jed took the man's hand in firm grip and smiled wryly.

"Not likely. Name's Jed Marsh. I'll just be bunking here for a couple of nights."

"Oh," Cunningham said with obvious disappointment, "I was hoping that we'd get ourselves a real guide instead of that old breed or one of his wet behind the ears kids."

Jed shot the man a cold look. "That old breed and his kids are probably the best guides in the territory. If it was big talk and lots of liquor you wanted, you should have gone to Raudsep's."

"No offense, okay?" Cunningham laughed nervously. "I was just making conversation." He paused briefly. "Did hear, though, that Raudsep's head guide got a crack at a dandy grizzly. Sounds like those boys are having a hell of a hunt."

"MacKelvy gets a lot of cracks at things, he just has trouble delivering. Bob will deliver, you can take my word for that." Jed stretched out on the bed and closed his eyes, leaving the man from Dallas standing there, not knowing what to do. He finally walked off, giving wide berth to the giant dog that walked over and casually laid down at the foot of Jed's bed.

CHAPTER 4

BOB HAD Jed's horses saddled and ready to go early the next morning. Jed stayed for the breakfast of sausage, eggs, and hashbrowns. He told Louise not to expect him for lunch and then rode to town. He reined in his horses in front of Milligan's Mercantile and Emporium. The building had been built around the turn of the century and the soft red brick of its walls was pitted and worn from years of enduring the harsh northern weather. The sign on the false front of the building had been recently repainted in bright red letters. Jed hoped that it did not signify a change in ownership. He tethered the horses to the old fashioned hitching post and walked through the door.

He saw with satisfaction that the old wood stove still occupied the center of the room and the shelves had not been rearranged since his last visit. A young man with short hair and a full beard peered out from behind the main service counter, returned the spectacles to his nose and walked to offer his assistance to the customer. "Can I help you?"

Jed did not know this young man and asked tentatively, "Is Pete still around?"

"Oh sure, he's in the back sorting through the shipment." When Jed did not reply immediately he asked, "Do you want me to get him?"

"Please." The man disappeared through the back door that led to the office and storeroom as Jed let his gaze drift around the shelves. He walked to a stack of bright plaid wool shirts that were heaped high on one counter and was sorting through them when the two men returned.

Pete did not have to see Jed's face to recognize him.

23

He'd followed that broad-shouldered, narrow-hipped torso over many trails while he had taught Jed the tricks of the trapping trade. He'd sold Jed his trapline rights and staked him to his first two years here. Pete hadn't worried that Jed had been a complete stranger, there was something about him that inspired confidence. And he hadn't been disappointed. It had taken Jed two years to repay Pete, but he'd made the grade in a difficult way of life. Pete's only disappointment had come when Jed had decided to make his permanent home in the wilderness, disdaining the line shack and a home in town for the sturdy hand built cabin. He'd worried about Jed that first cold winter and his joy at seeing him after the spring breakup, despite the spare catch, was unmasked. Now the yellow teeth formed a broad grin beneath the drooping white moustache that made the old man resemble a bull walrus. He called out gruffly, "Jed, you damned old coyote, when did you blow in?"

Jed wheeled with a smile on his face and a twinkle in his eyes. "With the last cold gust, Pete. Winter's comin' on old man."

"Yes indeedy, it sure as hell is. Your ready for winter this time?"

"Hell no, that's why I'm here. I've got my list all made up."

"Give it to John," he jerked a thumb at the young man. "You an' me got some cathcin' up to do." Pete led Jed to the office in the back of the store, where he pulled the bottle of twelve year old, plus, Scotch from a bottom drawer. "You know where the glasses are," he said.

"Sure do." Jed reached up to the shelf and retrieved two glasses and set them down on Pete's cluttered desk. "How much of that do we have left?" Pete held the bottle aloft, showing a third of a bottle of the amber fluid. "About two more years' worth I'd say," Jed laughed.

It was an old custom between the two friends. Each year, whenever Jed came to town, they would share a drink from the bottle and then carefully cap it and return it to its storage place. They each had a wager that rode with the contents of the bottle. Pete bet that Jed would move to town, at least part time, out of loneliness before the bottle was empty, and Jed bet that the old man would outlive the bottle. Pete raised his glass, "Here's to ya." He drained the contents while Jed sipped at the fiery liquid, rolling it in his mouth.

While the two men talked in the back room, John filled Jed's order, stacking the items in a growing pile at the far end of the counter and itemizing the costs. It took an hour for him to complete the list. When he'd finished, he took the order form into Pete. Pete glanced at the bottom tally and looked up at John. "Now take off fifteen percent," he said flatly and returned the form to John. John stared at Pete, shrugged his shoulders, and left the room. The form was tagged to a canvas pannier that was atop the pile of goods when Jed and Pete finally came out from back.

Pete busied himself about the store while Jed packed the panniers with meticulous care, testing the balance weights expertly. When he had finished, he joined Pete and they walked across the street to balance their account at the bank. Jed withdrew the money from a savings account, noting the remaining balance in the small bank book. The last three years had been good. After all expenses he found that he had sixty three hundred dollars left. "I'll buy you lunch, Pete," he said magnanimously.

"I'll take ya up on it," Pete replied.

Jed and Pete parted company after lunch. Jed walked along the prim sidewalk with a contented, peaceful feeling until he passed the young woman. For a moment, he almost thought it was her, but that was impossible. Cassie was dead. The realization reopened the wound that had lain dormant in his heart for so long. He turned to look after her. She did not have Cassie's walk, the swing in her hips was wrong and her step lacked the lightness Cassie's had. He attempted to shake off the feeling, tried to recapture the contented mantle that had left him, and paid his quarterly visit to the barber.

In the early afternoon Jed wandered aimlessly around
the town, unable to shake the dark eyed, auburn haired
ghost of his lost love. He quit trying and abruptly turned
on his heel to return to Milligan's Mercantile and Emporium. He stopped briefly out front to check his horses and
acknowledge Whiskey's faithful sense of duty in watching
them. Jed took little time in saddling and loading the panniers on the pack horses, securing them with a practiced
hand.

Before Jed left for the Diamond Bar, he reached into
his saddlebags and withdrew a poorly wrapped package.
He returned to the store's interior and drew up an aging
chair next to Pete's. He held the package out to the old
man. "Well, Pete, I guess it's time. Merry Christmas."

Pete smiled and held out a slim box tied with bright red
ribbon to Jed. "I reckon so, merry Christmas to you too,
Jed." He opened the package with gnarled hands and exposed its contents. There was the deer jerky that had become a standard gift over the past three years and a tiny,
intricately carved replica of a bear trap. "Thank you Jed,"
he said softly as he wadded up the wrapping. "I'll add the
carvin' to the others on the shelf."

Jed smiled to himself and opened his package. It contained a hand carved cherrywood pipe. Pete had remembered Jed's comment about the expensive pipes from last
spring. "Pete! What can I say? You remembered. Thanks
Pete, thanks a lot. I'll think of you every time your special
blend is glowing in its bowl."

"You take care out there, lad, you've become like a son
to me. I wouldn't want anything happenin' to ya." The old
man's face showed a smile of gladness, but the mist in his
eyes countered with the sadness of parting.

"I will Pete, don't worry. John," Jed said, turning toward the door, "you take care of this old scoundrel. He's an
endangered species you know, and I want to see him in
good shape come spring."

"Yeah, I'll do that," John replied.

Jed shook hands with Pete and walked to the door.

"Maybe I'll see you next spring," he said warmly to John. John gave a nod and took Jed's hand. Jed returned the nod, gave a last tentative wave to Pete, and walked out the door. There was nothing left to be said, and no point in prolonging the goodbyes.

As Pete and John watched Jed ride out of town, John said wistfully, "Boy, I'd give anything to be able to live like that man does."

Pete looked at the young man solemnly and quietly replied, "No you wouldn't, son. It takes a special kind of man to live like Jed does. Behind that quick smile and easy manner there's a whole lot of hurt ridin' with him, an' a whole lot of hate. It's a heavy burden to carry. It's been four years now, he seems to have mellowed out some, but I ain't sure. A couple of more years mebbe . . . Damn that breeze is cold on these old bones, let's get inside."

Jed got back to the Diamond Bar well before supper time and stowed his gear in the barn. He'd spend the night out there, not wanting to be delayed in the morning when he planned to be gone before sunup. After supper he settled up with Bob and turned in. He slept fitfully that night and passed it off as anxiety to return home to the snug little cabin in the woods, but his subconscious kept invading his dreams with the truth. He was running once again, fleeing the memories that still refused to fade.

ANOTHER TIME, ANOTHER PLACE: Cassie stood bent over, her delicate hands resting lightly on her knees, the light from the battery lantern hanging behind her casting a halo around her pretty head. Jed smiled at the look of consternation on her face as she brushed a wisp of auburn hair from her eyes. "It won't be long now," he reassured her. Heidi, the oldest doe goat in the small herd, was taking her time giving birth, as usual. Jed had been through this with the small tan goat a half a dozen times, but this was Cassie's first experience. When Jed had been gone for half an hour she had donned her plaid mackinaw, and pulled on her boots. Jed had heard the door slam and looked up to see her running, arms folded and hands tucked under her armpits, toward him. He liked to watch her, for she was as beautiful a creature as God had ever made. The moon glinted off her swinging hair and her breath came in short little silvery puffs.

"There we come," Jed said quietly as the kid's feet began to show, "come on baby, we'll have you out into the world in no time." Jed worked with the goat, he could tell that this was going to be a large one. Its forelegs slipped out and a tiny nose poked into the cold February night. Heidi gave a momentous push and the nose slipped out a couple of inches and no more. Jed allowed her two more tries to dislodge her kid before he gently, but firmly grasped the two wet and slippery forelegs and gave steady pulls whenever the doe bore down. Cassie danced in agitation, repeating over and over, "Can I help? Can I help?" Jed calmed her momentarily with a soothing reply, but she was soon back at it, like a little girl.

Finally the shoulders cleared the birth canal and the rest of the body shot out with a loud slurping sound. It lay there, shining wetly in the lantern light. "Ohmagosh," Cassie wheezed, "it's dead." Jed shook his head, chuckled to himself, picked up a piece of straw, and tickled the inside of the kid's nose with it. The kid convulsed once, sneezed, gurgled, raised its head weakly, and shook it, its little ears slapping noisily. The moment the kid gave a little high pitched baa, Heidi was up and at him, cleaning his coat with her tongue. Jed wiped the slime from his hands on the straw, finished on his pant legs, stood up, and slipped an arm around Cassie's waist. "Well, what do you think?" he asked her.

"Oh, she's beautiful!"

"I think it's a he."

"Are you sure?" she asked. "It looks too pretty to be a he."

"Yeah, but it's too damn big to be a her." Jed brushed Cassie's forehead with his lips and said, "I'll check." He took two short steps and lifted the hind leg of the newborn animal. "Yep, I thought so, a fine young billy, unless they are inventing new equipment for girls."

Cassie wrinkled her nose at him and stood marveling at the process. "Isn't it wonderful," she said. "Isn't it just absolutely wonderful?!" She grabbed both of Jed's hands and looked at him with shining, mischievous eyes. "Come on, let's go make one of our own."

"Don't be ridiculous," he replied teasingly as he gave her backside an affectionate pat, "I can't sire a goat."

"Don't be so sure," she shot back immediately, "you've always been full of the devil around me, and isn't he part goat?"

Jed laughed, picked up the newborn kid, and deposited him beneath a heat lamp in the nearby shed. "Take good care of him, Heidi," he said and then to his wife, "Come on, let's go see what we can do about that goat you want."

Jed awoke in a cold sweat, whispering Cassie's name. He sat up, rubbed his eyes, and then tried to go back to sleep. It was no use. He had the horses packed and was waiting impatiently for the sun to brighten the sky behind the ridge when Bob walked in.

"Coulda used the bunkhouse," he said, "then ya mighta gotten a little better sleep. Or were ya that anxious to hit the trail?"

"Sorry, Bob, I didn't mean to wake you."

"Ya did that at three. I seen the light come on in the barn just after the horses got restless, they're who woke me."

"Guess I've gotten used to not having anyone around to disturb," Jed said sheepishly.

"Well, it don't matter none. I hadda be up early anyhow. We're headin' out for the first hunt today, them other guys got in last night. Louise thought ya might wanna take this with ya. Says ya probably miss a woman's cookin'."

"Tell her thanks for me." Jed looked out as the eastern sky turned from black to gray. Bob helped him lead the horses from the barn and tie the leads to the saddle eyes, forming a single file string. "I'll be going now," Jed said. "Hope I see you next spring."

"I'll be here," Bob replied. "Have a good season."

"Yeah," Jed answered and the toe of his boot found the stirrup. He swung aboard easily, clucked to the mare, and headed the string north.

CHAPTER 5

J̲ENNIFER RACHELLE PETERS turned twenty on the sixteenth of September. It should have been a happy occasion. She sat looking out the front window at the leaves that fell from the giant maple in the front yard, dabbing at her eyes. She felt abandoned, alone, and depressed. Her father had been angry with her this morning, growling about the dishes that lay stacked and unwashed on the kitchen counter, the dust that had accumulated on the furniture, the paper that lay scattered on the livingroom floor. Martha would never allowed her house to fall to such a degrading state. What the hell was the matter with her, her father had wanted to know, didn't she care what people thought? Hell no, she didn't care. A clean house wouldn't bring back his wife and Jennifer's mother. That was the real rub, the bone of contention that continually threatened to tear what remained of a once happy family apart.

Phillip had left home a short six months after her mother's death, leaving Jennifer alone to cope with those dark moods that had descended on their father. Her half-brother had no intention of "being swallowed up" in his father's grief over that "other woman," besides, he'd been through this all once before. At twenty four, he was fully able to strike out on his own and he figured that he should have done so a lot earlier, but he had shared his father's passion for hunting. He had stuck around for those paid trips to Montana and Canada, where he and Dad could compete against one another without fighting like they did at home.

Jennifer guessed that she had always been a little resentful that she had to call her father "Father," and Phillip could call him "Dad." But she had always forgiven her father his faults and adored him. He, in turn, had showered her with gifts when she had repeatedly made honor society, and had called her his "talented kitten." She had, in fact, been a happy child growing up in the traditional midwest home in Rockford, Illinois. She had been pretty and bright, and knew it. She used it to get her own way more than once, but she was a "good girl" in every midwest sense of the word. She didn't drink, get involved with drugs, or fool around. The only thing her conservative father could even remotely consider rebellious in the girl was her passionate involvement with the environmental movement. If she had merely concentrated on air and water pollution, it would have been okay by him, but when she had "heard the call," as she put it, it had been to save the poor, endangered animals. That, to Jennifer, included the whole of the animal world, not those limited species on the national list. That attitude conflicted with John Peters' "rights" as a sportsman, and he let her know in no uncertain terms that discussion on the subject was a closed matter at home. Still, he did not try to prevent her involvement in school related subjects on that topic. All in all, he was a fairly tolerant man. At least he had been until Martha had died.

When Jennifer had complained to her current boyfriend, seeking comfort last night, he had replied abruptly that not only her father, but she as well, was suffering from a coping crisis. Having abandoned pre-med, psychology was his current passion and he expounded at length on how Jennifer and her father should handle their problems, quoting copiously from current thought in the field he did not fully understand. That had led to a bitter argument between himself and Jennifer. She had called him an insensitive clod and invited him to leave. He informed her that she was an unhappy, spoiled child, and, mustering that impassive, enigmatic countenance he thought apropos for a psychologist, he had left, expecting her to call when she came to her senses.

It was in that frame of mind, cradling her hurt and a touch of self-pity in a chasm of loneliness, that Jennifer spent her birthday. The card and small package left on the dining room table by her father, moments before he left without even saying happy birthday, remained unopened. She did not hear the mail slide through the slot in the door as she sat with her knees drawn up under her chin, trying to grasp the fragments of her shattered life.

John Peters had felt badly as soon as he opened the door of the Lincoln. He almost returned to the house that morning, but thought it was better to let it lie, let her get it out of her system. It was better for him as well, better to get to the office and cleanse his spirit in the rigors of business. He was good at what he did, and proud of it. When he had taken over his father-in-law's small fastener manufacturing plant, it had been deeply in debt. He had done what his father-in-law had been unable to do, lay off several employees, cajole loans from the banks, and seek new markets aggressively. His long hours, ambition, and ruthlessness had paid off. The company had come back from the brink of bankruptcy and had worked itself into black ink. At the critical moment, John had made a decision to switch from the old equipment to new machines, once again cutting labor costs. He had removed the "dead wood," those older employees that couldn't or wouldn't adapt to the sophisticated machines. When the machinists' union had started to give him trouble he went against convention and declared his shop open, refusing to negotiate with the local. That had been a dangerous move, it almost cost him his business, but he weathered it and when the other small shops began closing down there was a hungry labor force eager for jobs at a "reasonable" wage. In those few short years he had made himself financially comfortable, if not wealthy.

He felt better at noon and tried to call Jennifer. If she was at home, she didn't answer. No matter. He'd make it up to her tonight. He called and made reservations at the Clock Tower for dinner, then went to Cherryvale to pick up

a little something extra for her birthday. She'd been dropping hints about a camera before Martha had fallen ill, and
he remembered them now. A simple thirty five millimeter
would have filled her wishes, but he was a man of excesses
and he bought an entire system. If he couldn't talk his way
out of a bad situation, he's always been able to buy his way
out. It would work again, he thought.

That night he drove home in a happy mood. His happiness was twofold; one, he was sure the gifts and his own
happiness would wedge Jennifer from her depression, and
two, a call in the afternoon had confirmed his reservations
for his annual fall hunt. The bookings had been made a
year in advance, as usual, and now that Phillip had left,
he'd decided that he'd take Jennifer. Raudsep had said that
he could provide her with a photography guide. That
should make her happy, he thought.

To a certain degree his strategy worked, for Jennifer
did seem to lose that morose cloud that had been hanging
over her. While jewelry had always been one of her weak
spots, she had been more excited with the camera system
than with the expensive Black Hills gold ring that her father had cajoled her into opening upon his arrival home.
She began to feel better as she dressed for dinner, turning
to admire her own figure in the full length mirror on the
closet door. It was striking in the simple, slinky cocktail
dress she had chosen, and her light application of makeup
had put a glow in her cheeks where there had been none
earlier. She began to feel better about herself and her relationship with her father. Maybe things would work out,
she desperately hoped so.

The proposed trip had left her with mixed feelings. In a
way she looked forward to it with anticipation, in another
with dread. It might serve to more closely bind her relationship with her father, but there was also that faint fear
that, in view of their opposition on the subject of wildlife,
it might widen the gap between them. She mentioned
nothing of her misgivings to him that night, choosing instead to try to recapture the happiness and love that once

went unquestioned.

It was two weeks before they were to catch the flight to the northwest and every time she thought about broaching the subject of her misgivings, her father's obvious mood of glad anticipation made her find excuses not to do it. Finally, there was no more time, they stood waiting in line to board the aircraft, her father looking out of place in his newly purchased woolen hunting costume (he always wore it on the plane as if to signify his intentions to the world). Jennifer wore her best wool traveling suit, not wanting to be singled out as a backwoods moron in cosmopolitan Chicago. Her father had had one too many bourbons at the lounge, and her uneasiness with the trip increased with each boastful statement that tumbled from his lips. When he turned to a fellow traveler and began to recount past hunts with obvious relish to the tolerant listener, she wanted to leave, to go home. Too late, the plane was beginning to taxi. The uneasiness in her stomach rose with the plane as she contemplated the specter of the wilderness that had been such an easy topic of glib conversation.

CHAPTER 6

Jed WALKED AWAY from the steaming iron kettle where the last set of steel traps were undergoing their final cleansing before being put to use. He stripped off the heavy rubber gloves and dropped them on the ground next to the rucksack before walking to the far side of the compound. Squatting down, he lifted the small trap door that concealed the two foot by three foot cellar that held his homemade scents. Commercial "lures" were available, of course, but Jed preferred the tried recipes that Pete had passed on to him when he had taken over the trapline. He carefully unscrewed the lid on a mason jar marked "Weasel," held it at arm's length, and lifted the lid a fraction of an inch. The powerful odor exploded in the sun-warmed air, making his eyes smart and his nose revolt. Quickly he replaced the lid. "Whew! Hot damn, that's potent!" he exclaimed with satisfaction. The working and ripening over the summer months had turned the milky mixture of finely chopped musk glands, selected parts of the entrails, and spring water into the thick, brown-black liquor of its finished product.

Jed returned to check the progress of the boiling traps, and, satisfied that the water level was high enough, retired to his cabin to wash the residual taste of the weasel lure out of his mouth with a fresh cup of coffee. He looked over his shelves with satisfaction as they were now filled with neatly arranged rows of canned goods and packages. He'd been back at the cabin for three days now, and already the pace of his life had settled into a familiar routine. There were only three and a half weeks left in which to prepare for the trapping season, less if you counted beaver. He'd set his river traps within the week. The rich aroma of the coffee reached him. He poured a mug and wandered into the main room of the cabin that served as livingroom, bedroom, and study. It was a lazy sort of day and Jed felt no guilt in sinking into the willow and hide chair by the fireplace. He viewed with obvious pleasure the opposite wall of bookshelves filled with all his old friends and five new ones. That was Jed's one extravagance, he had a voracious appetite for reading. His books had held no interest for the officials at the bank sale five years ago, and he had had them shipped up to Pete's house when he'd decided to make his move. It had taken four trips with the pack horses to bring his library to the cabin, but it had been well worth it. Those volumes, more than anything else, had helped Jed maintain a mental balance during those first two crucial years. The five new books included three on United States, Canadian, and European history and two works on recent developments in the natural sciences. He used to read a lot of novels, but they had begun to lose their significance during the last couple of years as his appetite for knowledge had increased once again. Now the bulk of his library was factual, comprising some six hundred volumes.

Jed stretched and groaned, then rose and walked to the large footlocker that rested at the foot of his bed. He opened the lid and reached in to retrieve the buckskins that he'd finished making only a month ago. He ran his hands down their smooth, supple structure. They were unadorned, unless the long fringe could be considered adornment. He had made them to fit snugly, allowing a flair in the pants from the knee down to accommodate his heavy western boots. The shirt was a long sleeved, pullover type, with long tails and lace eyelets that ran from the throat to mid-chest. He laid them on top of the footlocker and picked up the new boots he's bought in town. He spent the rest of the afternoon rubbing mink oil into every inch of the boots, and attending the traps. Tomorrow he would begin retracing the familiar trails that were his trapline, setting the steel traps and wiring them open so they would be familiar and not frightening to the furbearers he sought during the season. There were deadfalls and snares that had to be checked and rebuilt. There was much to do.

The next day's mid-morning sun found Jed astride the Paint mare, leading his two pack horses up a rocky trail, with Whiskey trotting patiently ahead. He made his sets as he went, stopping the horses along the trail, selecting a trap from the panniers, and disappearing to one side of the trail or the other. His movements were swift and sure, the purpose and conservation of motion bespeaking experience. He would work silently for a time, only to break out in song or a whistling tune out of simple joy. He did not try to sneak or in any way conceal his presence, he was the supreme predator in the forest. The long barreled forty four that rested comfortably in its holster on his hip and the thirty-thirty in the saddle scabbard more than compensated for any deficiency he had in size or swiftness.

He made camp in the open that night, at the edge of a small meadow where his horses could graze until morning, when he would complete the first stretch of his trapline. It took an average of three weeks of hard work to finish laying out the entire line, but once done, it was a simple matter to maintain and harvest its catch. When the winter weather was agreeable, he could run the line and returned to the cabin in a two day period. More often than not, however, he was forced to run the trails on successive days when winter's fury precluded a night's stay in the wilderness. For that reason, the main line ran in a wide loop that started a mile from the cabin on the east, swung north to its furthest point of eight miles, then gradually returned to its end a mile from the cabin on the west. That way he could run either the west half of the loop or the east, and then return on a trail that ran from the center of the trapline directly to the cabin.

Two days later Jed pulled the patched, old canoe from its shelter by the river near his cabin. It was time to begin the river harvest. He would take only thirty beaver this year. Doubtless, he could take more, but by limiting his catch each year he remained reasonably sure of an equally good catch the next. The key was to leave enough breeding stock to maintain the population. That meant knowing which lodges held animals in their breeding prime, avoiding them, and concentrating on the older lodges and a portion of the newer ones. Jed was more than a trapper, he was a manager. Part of that was his natural inclination, part his education, and part, as Pete had often said, just plain common sense. No longer was it possible to trap out an area and move on, those days were long since past. The cost of trapline rights these days made old methods dependent on unlimited catches obsolete, and the men who still pursued them doomed to failure in the final analysis. Jed's method was more like farming the area and, barring a natural disaster, it would last generations.

His canoe slipped up the east side of the river, blending in with the tangle of brush on the bank. He'd traveled almost four miles, setting his traps with care, when he spotted the Mackenzie boat floating downriver in midstream. He paddled hard on the left side of the canoe and slipped silently behind a curtain of river willows. There he remained hidden as the approaching boat drifted with the current. Manning the stern paddle was MacKelvy, the coppery glint of his hair and beard was unmistakable. Jed's eyes caught the movement of the moose in the waters of the west edge of the river just as the animal raised its head above the water. MacKelvy had also spotted it. The point of the prow of the boat turned swiftly in the animal's direction. Jed watched the scramble of the two men in the boat as they raised their rifles and vied for a position at the bow. Jed saw the flash and smoke first, the heavy thump of the magnum reaching his ears with almost comic slowness. The moose cleared the water with amazing rapidity, and gained the flats before the first round ripped into him. Jed watched with disgust as the moose's rear quarters collapsed underneath him. He tried to regain them, dragging himself along with powerful forelegs, as a dark stain grew on his right flank. There was a moment of silence before the barrage opened up. The magnum must have been a semiautomatic, judging by the rapid spacing of the shots. Every time a bullet scored, a spray would fly from the point of impact. The hunter was walking up the animal as if he were using a mortar instead of a finely balanced and sighted weapon. Finally, the animal collapsed and MacKelvy put into the shore. He jumped out and ran towards the fallen beast. Jed heard the report of the pistol as MacKelvy delivered the coup de grace.

Whiskey whined from the blankets in the bow of the canoe. Jed looked at him and held a finger to his lips. The dog instantly became quiet. There was little chance that the dog's whine would carry across to the far side of the river, but Jed wanted to avoid a confrontation with Raudsep's head guide. There was no reason for a conflict, but MacKelvy had a way of making chance meetings between himself and Jed combative. Despite the inept shooting of the moose, and Jed's quick anger at the poor marksmanship when a clean kill was possible, there was nothing illegal in the act. Jed understood and even sympathized with the excitement that often threw an inexperienced hunter's aim off. The animal was a trophy, something to be mounted and talked about in some man's far off study or trophy room, recalling, perhaps, a once in a lifetime experience. Jed did not begrudge the man his moose. He did begrudge the killing, it should have been swift.

Jed waited until MacKelvy and his party had gutted, quartered, and loaded the animal. He listened as the small outboard motor sputtered and caught, propelling the happy hunters back upriver. For a moment Jed considered abandoning the remainder of the river trapline for the rest of the year. MacKelvy would probably hunt this part of the river intensively for the rest of the season. Jed knew that once that man had scored, he tended to return again and again, until it was obvious that he'd gone one too many times to the well. For MacKelvy, a kill insured the high pitch of excitement for his hunters, often causing them to shoot into the brush along the river, swearing that they had seen game. Often he knew that it was only buck fever, but he went along with them, for in those years when game was hard to come by, it meant customers would return, certain that it was them and not the guide that had failed. As he sat turning those facts over in his mind, Jed came to a decision. He would not give up his rights as a trapper. He was not a man to run and, if push came to shove, he could stand his ground with the best of them. He knew it and MacKelvy knew it.

ANOTHER TIME, ANOTHER PLACE: Jed had been walking the street for half an hour, not quite sure of what he wanted to do. He had some time to kill before Pete was due back and the small room in the back of the store was confining. He needed air. Just ahead of him the door to the Blue Angel opened and a bear of a man staggered out, cursing at the bar owner, making lewd suggestions about the man's maternal heritage. Jed stopped momentarily to relight his pipe, hearing MacKelvy's name shouted for the first time. MacKelvy stumbled in Jed's direction. Jed tried to step out of his way, but MacKelvy wouldn't allow it, he was spoiling for a fight.

"Wassa matter puppy?" he leered, whiskey on his breath and an evil gleam in his eye. "I ain't gonna hurt ya . . . much."

"You're drunk," Jed replied evenly, "why don't you go home and sleep it off?"

Jed took his eyes off the man for a slight second. It was a mistake. MacKelvy reached out and snatched the pipe from Jed's mouth. Jed heard the stem break from the bowl with a sharp crack. It had been the pipe that Cassie had given him just before . . . His right hand shot out, catching MacKelvy by the beard as he brought his left up, smacking with a satisfying thud on the big man's nose. Blood gushed and covered the beard as MacKelvy struck out with both hands, furious that he'd been hit first. Jed retreated before the onslaught, dodging the heaviest blows, taking the lighter. It took only a few moments in the chill night air for

MacKelvy to sober up enough to know that he was up against a quality opponent. His left eye was starting to close, and his lip beginning to swell. He withdrew, circling and studying the man in front of him. MacKelvy had the edge on weight and height, but Jed was well muscled, quick on his feet, and cold in anger. MacKelvy grinned in satisfaction and got down to the serious business of fighting. While he was normally a brawler, he was schooled in the fundamentals and he knew that he could not bully his way through this one.

For the first five minutes the contestants tested one another, feinting and striking, oblivious to the small crowd that grew outside the bar. Jed assessed his opponent's ability, finding that the man was surprisingly agile despite his bulk. MacKelvy could take a punch, even on his heavy square jaw. Jed was beginning to show signs of the battle, a cut opened up above his right eye, the blood slightly obscured his vision. Still, he fought with tight-lipped determination. MacKelvy had broken something that linked Jed with Cassie, he'd pay for that.

Jed landed a solid blow to MacKelvy's midsection, and when MacKelvy dropped his guard in surprise, he was on him like a cat. MacKelvy didn't recover from the temporary lapse, he fell back as Jed pressed the advantage. MacKelvy felt his arms grow sluggish and his mind clouded, and a savage grin twisted across his face with incredulity. He was against the wall as Jed pummeled him. In a last desperate try, MacKelvy brought his knee up sharply. Jed felt it coming and twisted away, catching it in the left thigh and stumbling sideways as the tired muscles charley-horsed. MacKelvy cleared his head a little, spun around, and aimed a blow at Jed's head. Unable to move away quickly, Jed jerked his head to the side. The fist grazed his forehead and smashed into the wall with a sickening crunch. MacKelvy dropped to the ground, cradling the hand. Jed stood up slowly, looked at the figure at his feet, dropped his fists, and turned. In that instant MacKelvy made a move for the knife at his belt. It was a mistake. Jed had turned his head for one last look and the blade caught the moonlight as it slipped its sheath. Jed spun on one foot and delivered a devastating kick under MacKelvy's jaw, snapping the man up and laying him on his back. This time MacKelvy did not move.

For a moment, Jed reached out with a bloody knuckled hand to steady himself against the wall. He saw the silver band of the broken pipe with his good eye. He walked over to it, knelt, and picked it up almost reverently, searching through the street dust with his fingers for the bowl portion. He found it and stood up, holding each of the pieces in a hand like a broken toy. Pete appeared from the edge of the crowd, having returned in time to catch the last moments of the fight. "C'mon, Jed, let's get ya home and cleaned up."

"It was a gift," Jed said haltingly, "from Cassie. . . . a gift."

"I know," Pete replied, knowing there was nothing he could say that would take the pain from Jed's voice.

Jim Raudsep watched as Pete shepherded Jed away from the scene. His face showed a grudging admiration for the man. He had never known any man to beat MacKelvy, even when he was drunk, but bit by bit this newcomer had done it. Raudsep had watched as Jed had methodically picked apart the town champion. MacKelvy fought for the fun of it, delighting in the vicious batterings, but this man had fought in cold anger, Raudsep had seen that cold smoke in his eyes. It was a look that neither he nor MacKelvy would forget. Raudsep wondered what had started the fight and guessed that he would never know the real reason. MacKelvy always had a good excuse for his fights, but they were rarely truthful.

Raudsep motioned to the two men beside him and they were emerging from the crowd to cart the red-haired giant off the field of battle. The outfitter decided that it would be a prudent idea to make some inquiries about the man, what had Pete called him, Jed wasn't it? Yes, that was it. He'd see what the talk was in the morning. There were usually a lot of stories around a morning after a fight.

With a strong stroke of the paddle, Jed propelled the canoe out of the willows and into the main current of the river. There was enough daylight left to complete the sets upstream.

CHAPTER 7

JENNIFER SAT cross-legged on her bunk, sorting the lens filters and deciding which film would be appropriate for the day's excursion. In the all male camp she felt out of place, but generally happy about having made the trip. Oh sure, she had to contend with the off-color remarks and the rough humor of the men, but her guide was quiet and unassuming. She supposed that it was the reason he'd been relegated to her. She noticed that the loudest and most boastful of the guides had drawn the big money hunters. She had noticed as well that a sort of caste system existed in camp that placed the hunters ostensibly at the top, the better guides next, followed by the mediocre guides, the cook, and finally her guide. It bothered her that he was the target of the worst jibes and the crudest jokes. The others resented her presence and they took it out on her guide. It amazed her that he shook it all off with a quiet nonchalance as if it didn't concern him at all.

Jeff Warner stuck his head inside Jennifer's tent. "You about ready?" he asked. "We'll miss the good sun if we wait much longer."

"Just a minute longer," Jennifer replied cheerily, "I've got to finish loading the camera."

"Okay." Jeff stepped back from the tent. It was almost eight o'clock and he'd wanted to be off earlier, as usual, but he'd come to expect a late start from the girl. The other guides and hunters had left before dawn and were well afield by daybreak. Still, he didn't really mind, the girl was good company and trusted his judgement, which was more than he could say for anyone else in the camp. She wasn't bad on the eyes either, he reflected.

"Where to today?" she chimed as she emerged into the

sunlight.

Jeff flashed an easy smile. "I thought we'd follow the river to the north for a few miles, then swing to the west and circle back to camp. We should get a chance at the river birds and, if we don't run into a hunting party, maybe a deer or two. Something bigger if we get lucky."

"That sounds good," Jennifer agreed.

Jeff shouldered the pack and set off on a trail that would take them to the river about a mile from camp. Jennifer followed his easy pace, shifting the weight of her gadget bag whenever the strap started to dig into her shoulder. They gained the river by nine and stopped for an hour while Jennifer took countless shots of the rafts of wild fowl floating in the quiet stretches of water. Jeff looked at the sun and silently motioned to the girl that it was time to move on. As they moved upriver they had two opportunities to see moose, but each time Jennifer was unable to be quiet enough in her movements to get into position to capture them on film. They were spooky and the slightest snap of a twig would send them into flight among the tangle of brush at the river's edge.

"Damn!" Jennifer exclaimed after missing the second moose. "How can anybody be quiet enough to sneak up on them?"

"Takes practice," Jeff grinned. "You're getting better though. At the beginning of the week you would have sounded like a tank coming through that brush. Today it was more like a medium sized bear," he teased.

"The hell with you. Lead on MacDuff." Jennifer was really beginning to take a liking to the young man. Nothing serious, but she didn't see any harm in a little suggestive teasing and a light infatuation.

Jeff grinned back at her and began the turn towards the interior away from the river. It was high noon and yet the sun was so filtered as it came through the spruce and fir that it reminded Jennifer of a cathedral where only shafts of light penetrated the interior through slim windows. She took some photos of the scene and vowed to call them "Forest Cathedral" if they turned out. She still was not confident in her ability to select the correct shutter speeds and f-stops and depended on the camera's light meter for most of the settings. However, her creative instincts told her that she must experiment a bit now and then. As she focused on a particularly intriguing piece of dead wood, she noticed a large pine with long barkless spots that oozed sap. She asked Jeff about it.

"Probably a rub tree," he replied, glancing at it. "Deer and elk rub their itchy antlers on trees when they're in the velvet."

He walked casually over to the tree to confirm his conjecture. As he approached it he realized immediately that he'd been wrong. What he saw were ugly gashes about two feet long with splinters hanging out of the trunk. He stopped four feet from the tree to inspect them. The base of the tree showed disturbed earth and he could almost make out a print. It was not new sign, but neither was it extremely old. He knelt beside the tree and laid his palm across the faint print. It was almost twice the size of his hand. There was still a faint odor of urine clinging to the damp earth. It was a marker tree. His hand went immediately to the holstered pistol that hung beneath his left armpit. The feeling of cold steel against his hand reassured him. He slid the weapon part way out to make sure that it still came away smoothly. He stole a glance at Jennifer. She was approaching with a curious look on her face. He stood to face her.

"Are you in your period?" he asked unceremoniously and abruptly.

Jennifer was shocked at the question. Her eyes snapped and her nostrils flared slightly as she flushed a deep red. "How dare you . . ."

"Damn it, answer my question!" Jeff cut her off.

Jennifer noticed the perspiration that beaded up on his clean shaven upper lip. She hesitated for a moment while she studied his earnest face. "No," she answered flatly.

"Thank God," he said with relief, his face relaxing.

Then, before she could voice any question, he added, "This is a marker tree. It belongs to a bear and we're in his territory. I think we'd better be moving on directly."

"Maybe we'll get a shot of him," Jennifer said brightly, overcompensating for what she thought was an awkward situation.

"Let's hope not," Jeff said grimly. "I'm sorry if I embarrassed you with that question, I didn't mean to get personal. It had to be asked."

Jennifer flushed again. "Why?" she asked naively.

Jeff looked at her and then at the ground. It was his turn to be embarrassed. "Well, uh, the sm . . . uh odor will drive a bear crazy. There's no tellin' what they'll do, but there's plenty of evidence that they'll go after it." He didn't want to tell her the real truth, that menstrual odor had been the reason that more than just a few women had fallen victim to an enraged bear. He guessed, correctly, that she had not paid attention to the several news reports that had covered the grisly deaths.

"Oh," Jennifer said quietly. "I guess I'd better remember that."

"It would be a good idea," Jeff agreed. "Come on, we'd better get back, it'll take us two and a half hours. I don't think it's a good idea to stay in this area for very long."

Jeff took the lead, setting a rapid pace. He wasn't positive, but his instincts told him that they were well inside the bear's home territory. He didn't want to get caught out here with a girl in tow and only a short range weapon to protect them. He knew from experience that even a fatally wounded bear could travel over two hundred yards after it had been hit. He would take no chances. When it became evident that Jennifer was having trouble keeping up, he paused to rest and relieved her of her equipment.

When they gained the ridge top, Jeff paused to look back. He searched the forest below for any signs of movement. He wasn't entirely satisfied. He had feelings once in a while, feelings that something was not quite what it should be. He never shrugged off those feelings. Some

called it a sixth sense, he called it a gut feeling. Whatever
it was, he went with it. He looked at Jennifer where she
sat with her head down, tired from the unaccustomed
pace. He reached into the camera bag, selected a long lens,
and fitted it to the camera. Slowly he covered the territory
once more with the aid of the telephoto lens. He swung the
snout of the camera past the open glade, then stopped
suddenly, retracing the arc. Somewhere near that big
spruce . . . He stopped the swing, staring intently. There it
was, half hidden by the shadows. It was a grizzly, no doubt
about it. The massive hump of the shoulders told him that.
The bear was parallel to their trail about seven hundred
yards away and, although Jeff could see him testing the
air, he had not yet scented the intruders. Automatically,
Jeff checked the slight breeze. It brushed lightly against his
face, it was in their favor. He checked the bear once more.
It was almost fully in the sunlight now, working over a
large rotten stump for grubs. He pushed the shutter release. It would make a nice picture for Jennifer if it turned
out.

Jeff squinted at the sun. If his calculations weren't off
by too much, they could follow the ridge back to camp
most of the way and cut back to the east to pick up the final approach. That way they could avoid attracting the
bear's attention unless the wind shifted radically in the
next few minutes. He walked back to Jennifer, touched her
on the arm, and signaled her to be silent. The ridge ran
almost straight for three miles, and its sparse covering
made it easy to travel. As he led Jennifer down the east
side, the smell of smoke from the camp reached him. He
breathed a sigh of relief.

"Not far now," he said, speaking for the first time in
two hours. "Do you smell the smoke?"

"Yes, I do," Jennifer said tiredly.

"We can slow down now. Matter of fact, let's take a
rest. Smoke 'em if you've got 'em," he said, pulling a pack
of Ovals from his pocket. He lit one of the strong cigarettes
and inhaled deeply.

"I don't smoke," Jennifer said.

"Well, how about a cup of coffee? I think there's some left in the thermos." He reached into the pack and withdrew the small plastic insulated jug and unscrewed the cap. "I think it's gotten a little cool . . . here," he offered the cup to her.

Jennifer took the cup, raised it to her lips for a sip, and set it on the ground. Her hair was falling into her eyes and she reached up to rearrange it. Jeff watched the movement of her breasts as the cloth of her shirt tightened on them as she raised her arms. His eyes drifted down past her waist to where the creases in her jeans formed a neat delta, then thought of his wife, cursed himself a little jovially, and crushed the life from his smoke. His sidelong appraisal had not gone unnoticed and Jennifer appreciated it in the manner it had been conducted. There was no lewdness in his eyes, only an approval of beauty, she thought with mild conceit. She knew she was pretty and she enjoyed the complimentary glances accorded her by the opposite sex.

"Come on," Jeff sighed, "we'd better get going."

The last mile of trail melted away quickly and they broke into the camp clearing just as MacKelvy had returned with his victorious hunting party. The guides, with blood spattered sleeves, were hanging three large mule deer from a heavy pole near the cook tent. Jennifer looked at the glaze in the eyes of the beautiful animals and froze. She had avoided looking at the other animals that had come into camp, but this time it was impossible. Her father was approaching with his deer rifle in his hand and a grin on his face.

"Take my picture, honey," he called to her. "I got him with just two shots!"

Jeff held out the camera bag to her. She felt ill. For a moment she stared at the scene, then broke and ran for her tent as fast as she could go.

"What in hell is wrong with her?" MacKelvy growled, an ugly scowl forming on his face.

"Oh hell," Peters replied, "she's in another one of her

damned moods. Save the animals, save the animals . . . it's all I've listened to for the last four years. Hey! How about you, Jeff? Know how to work a camera?"

"Sure."

"Well, take a couple of shots of me with my buck."

Jeff nodded and fumbled with the bag. He ignored MacKelvy's caustic remark that at least he was "good for something." He took the photos and walked to Jennifer's tent. He returned the bag to her, but she wouldn't talk. He shrugged his shoulders, told her he'd see her for dinner, and left.

Jennifer didn't show up for dinner that night and the cook took a couple of sandwiches to her tent at her father's request. She accepted them silently, and he could tell that she'd been crying. He reported this to her father and Jennifer could hear his angry retort, his voice bolstered by too much bourbon.

"Aw the hell with her. She'll have to get over it. By God, maybe if we take her on a real hunt she'll see what sport it is. Damn sight more exciting than a damn picture safari. Whadda ya think MacKelvy?"

"Sure, why not?" He'd had his eye on the girl ever since Peters and his daughter had hit camp. Maybe he'd get a chance to get in a little touch here and there. Besides, it struck a responsive chord in his sadistic nature. "Probably do her a world of good."

Jennifer felt the sting of the words and made a resolve in the darkness. When MacKelvy hollered into the tent in the morning, there was no answer. The tent was empty. An hour before the first stirrings of the camp, Jennifer had packed a few things into a small day pack, pulled on her heavy coat and boots, and was gone.

CHAPTER 8

For THE BETTER part of two weeks Jed had concentrated on completing his preparations for the winter trapping season and harvesting the catch from his river sets. Already there were eighteen prime pelts on the stretching frames. So far his catch had been good and he had been lucky. He'd been able to avoid MacKelvy and his hunting parties. He was sure that two more runs upriver would satisfy his quota and he could pull those traps in. Today he concentrated on rebuilding and repairing the numerous deadfalls and snares that augmented the steel traps on the furthest stretch of his main trapline.

Near mid-day he came upon the bear pen that he'd built in the fall just prior to his second year of trapping. As he gazed at the pill box of logs that rested atop a shallow pit, he laughed mentally. He had never quite figured out why he had built it in the first place, but he kept it in good repair anyway. Hell, you never knew when it might come in handy. He checked the heavy posts that propped the structure open and peered inside the pit. From the collection of small bones, he deduced that some small predator had used it for its den during the past few months. He left the litter undisturbed, it lent authenticity to the den it was supposed to imitate. The trigger mechanism, an uncomplicated affair consisting of four interlocking pieces of carved birch, had been scattered about the roof of the trap. He retrieved the pieces and checked them. The long piece that held the ends together had been broken . . . a small chore to fix that. With his small Hudson's Bay axe, he cut a small sapling near the pen and made a new one. He had just finished setting the trigger to verify its proper functioning when Whiskey began raising a commotion in the distance.

Jed looked up and whistled. The dog did not return and Jed could hear the continuation of the sharp, piercing yips. Listening carefully, Jed sorted the source from the rebounding echoes. Finally he pinpointed the direction and, leaving the Paint tied to the bear pen, he proceeded up the trail on foot, rifle in hand. He reached a rocky outcrop and stopped to listen once more. Whiskey's sharp yip bounded up the hill to greet him. Jed looked down the steep incline to see Whiskey guarding a nondescript lump, half hidden by brush, near the edge of a small creek. About halfway down the slope lay a small, fluorescent knapsack. It took only a moment for Jed to digest the scene.

Jed started down the steep slope, half sliding on the decayed granite surface where the rock had been turned into a sort of gravely soil. Occasionally he grabbed for one of the scrubby bushes that held tenaciously to the surface. He could tell by the erratic skid marks that played out before him as he descended that whoever had come to rest at the bottom had come down in an uncontrolled tumble. As he passed the pack he could see that both straps had torn free from the main body and its contents were visible through the tears in the nylon.

When Jed reached the bottom, Whiskey bounded up to him, whining, and then raced back to the motionless lump. Jed called to the dog, commanding him to lie down, and approached the victim tentatively. When he squatted and moved the brush away, he could see the fine boned structure of the face. He had a sinking feeling when he saw the wound that still oozed blood from the girl's forehead, sticking her fine, brunette hair to the side of her face. He touched her neck with two fingers, searching for the carotid pulse. It was there, but was weak and slow. She was very pale and there were dirty rivulets from the perspiration that beaded up on her forehead. Classic shock. Jed suspected a concussion as a result of the blow that had caused the wound on her forehead, but he was no doctor and, damn it, there wasn't any for miles. He was ill prepared to deal with the situation, but he instinctively knew that he was the girl's only chance.

Jed worked quickly. With hands that were experienced only in lay veterinary work, he probed for broken bones that might prevent him from moving the girl. He found none, and there didn't appear to be any swelling or other abnormalities in the neck region. Gently he moved her from her resting place to a flatter area on the fallen needles beneath the tamaracks near the creek. Perspiration ran into his eyes as his mind searched for the details of the treatment. Gradually they came to him. He elevated the girl's feet about a foot, stripped off his wool jacket and covered her with it. He had no idea of how long the girl had rested at the bottom of the hill, but he did know that the night and the early morning had been very cold, and that the girl's skin was very cool. He gathered firewood, cleared an area near the girl, and started a small fire. When it eventually warmed into a thick, fiery glow, he gathered some stones from the creek bottom and built a reflector so none of the heat would be wasted. Still the girl did not move.

The whinny of the Paint drifted from the distance. Jed knew he couldn't leave the horse tied to the pen unattended and unprotected for long, and yet he was reluctant to leave the girl. For a few moments his mind wrestled with itself. Finally he decided that he would leave Whiskey to guard the girl while he went for the horse. He could not afford to lose the Paint. There were easier ways to go, but straight up the hill was the fastest. Jed's breath came in short bursts as he crawled up the last fifteen yards. He rested only long enough to regain his wind before setting off down the trail at a lope. As he ran, he reviewed the rough terrain of the area in his mind. There was only one place nearby where he might get the Paint down the slope and to the creek's bottom.

Jed reached the mare, patted her neck to reassure her, then tugged on the cinch latigo to tighten the saddle, and mounted the horse. The Paint pranced lightly as he turned her homeward and he had difficulty turning her when they reached the rough, but negotiable, incline he remembered. The mare fought the bit and danced sideways as Jed urged her to begin the descent. The mare reared, but in so doing, committed herself and Jed to the downward slope. Unable to fight anymore, she stumbled, then caught her balance and started the fast controlled slide to the bottom, practically sitting on her haunches. Jed leaned well back in the saddle, acting as a counterbalance to gravity, talking constantly to the nervous horse. Then they were at the bottom. Jed dismounted. There were hidden holes near the creek, holes that generations of spring waters had carved beneath the giant trees that lined the banks. He tied the mare to a tree and tested the ground, stomping savagely at the ground with his feet. When he was satisfied that he'd found a path that would support the weight of the mare, he retraced his steps and led her slowly to the water's edge.

Whiskey heard them coming, the distant slosh punctuated by steel shoes on the horse hitting rocks, and the lighter swish of water as Jed led her upstream in icy knee deep water. When they reached the makeshift camp, Jed unsaddled the mare and tethered her with a long rope. The horse's nostrils flared a little at the new scent before she lay down and rolled the itch of the saddle from her back in the soft earth of decomposing needles. Jed walked to the fire, dumped the saddle near it, and sat down. He built the fire back up before pulling off his wet socks and wringing them out. When the socks were hung on a stick to dry, he brushed the dirt and needles from his feet, pulled on his boots, and knelt to check the condition of the girl.

She was still unconscious, but she seemed warmer and the ooze from her forehead had stopped. Jed reached into his saddlebags and found a clean bandanna. He soaked it in the waters of the creek and returned to gently wash the blood from the girl's face. Now the wait began. If she was going to come out of it, he'd know in the next critical hours.

It was near dark when the girl first stirred. Whiskey sensed it first, rising with a soft whine and nuzzling the girl with his nose. Jed immediately became attentive. He could see her mouth working, she'd be thirsty of course. He rummaged through his saddlebags and found the dented mess kit cup and filled it with the sweet water of the creek. He returned to the girl's side to find that she's turned her head away from the fire. Jed touched her cheek with a finger. It was hot, and not just from the fire. He swore silently and dipped two fingers into the cup, allowing the water to drip onto the girl's lips. Her tongue moved thickly between her teeth as the first drops reached it. She took the water a few droplets at a time, still not responding in a conscious manner. Before the cup was a third empty, she took no more and her breathing returned to the deep rhythm of sleep. Jed rocked back on his heels studying the girl as he wet the bandanna and laid it on her feverish forehead.

He watched as her body became restless, little muscles twitching at the corners of her eyes, the jerking of her fingers, and he wondered how she came to be in this far corner of his territory. By her hands he knew that she could not have been working with any of the outfitters, for they were uncallused, fine, and delicate. She shivered in the chill air as darkness closed about them. Jed reached for one of the saddle blankets, opened it, and covered the girl with it. The shivering diminished.

When the girl's restlessness increased, her head rolling from side to side, and her arms moving beneath the blanket, Jed knew that it would not be long before she was fully conscious. He put the old cup on a hot stone near the fire and gathered a few juniper berries from a nearby bush, dropping them into the warming water to brew into Injun tea as Pete had taught him. It gave the water a bitter, but tangy flavor that would prevent the girl from choking on it if she drank. With the girl already feverish, Jed did not want to complicate the situation by introducing a foreign substance into the lungs that might cause a pneumonia.

Jed heard the quiet groans that signaled the girl's return to the conscious world. He fished the berries from the cup and walked towards her. With the fire behind him, he seemed to imitate the hulk that had come at her before, her blurred vision unable to discern the differences. As he squatted beside her, she lashed out with her right arm, her fingers curled into a claw as they sought the man's face. Jed recoiled at the scream as much as at the movement. The hot liquid spilling down his front, he dropped the cup, recovered his balance, and moved quickly to subdue the terrified girl. He had her arms pinned to her sides, her legs lashing harmlessly as they became tangled in the blankets. Finally the quiet quality of his voice began to penetrate the fear in her mind and she realized that this was not the same man. Her movements slowed and the tension in her arms relaxed. Jed was aware the instant it occurred and relaxed his own grip on the girl's wrists, continuing to assure her that he was not going to harm her. When he realized that he had gotten through to her, he took his hands away and gently stroked her forehead. Her eyes lost their wild look of terror only to have it replaced with the dull glow of pain before she squeezed them shut against the throbbing in her head. Jed saw the tears that came from the corners of her eyes and rolled down her cheeks as her chest heaved in silent sobbing. With slow and deliberate movements, he returned the blankets to their protective position on the girl and retrieved the cup to brew the tea once more. When it was ready, he gently raise her and made her drink the entire cup slowly.

Jed did not sleep that night and, in that total silence that precedes the dawn, he wondered once more what had driven this young woman so far into the depths of the forest. He shifted from his uncomfortable position near the fire and thought about God for the first time in many months. If He existed, then He must surely have looked after this girl, for all odds declared that she must surely have died. He rubbed his eyes, mumbled to himself that he must be getting tired and sentimental, and dismissed the thoughts. It was just plain dumb luck. He checked the girl for the hundredth time and then allowed himself to doze for a short time. If the girl became restless again Whiskey would alert him.

The chill of the morning turned the dampness of the creek bottom air into tiny spikes of frost that clung to the earth, trees, and any surface not generating enough heat to destroy them. It was the sparkle of these tiny bits of ice in the filtered light of early morning sun that Jennifer first saw when she opened her eyes. She was aware of the large body of heat that warmed her and shifted her head just enough to look into the great amber eyes of the huge dog that lay close beside her. She slipped a hand from beneath the blanket and stroked his nose. The eyes blinked at her and the dog snuggled closer. Shifting her head once more, blinking back the shooting pain behind her eyes, she studied the figure across from her. The man reclined against the hollow formed by the roots of a large tree. His eyes were closed, but there was a tenseness that could be seen in the powerful muscles that bulged beneath the buckskin clothing. One hand rested on the buttstock of a lever action rifle that lay across his lap, its forefinger extended against the smooth metal of the trigger guard. If the man was asleep, it must be a very light sort of sleep. Jennifer made no sound or movement that might arouse him. She had to have time to collect her thoughts.

She tried to think back over the events of the past few hours. She remembered the beginning of the fall, but very little after that. Memories came in bits and pieces, and even then she could not be sure which was fact and which might be fancy. She vaguely remembered some sort of struggle, but the images that flashed within her mind did not have any coherent structure and she wondered if it was a dream. She did recall with clarity the way the man had helped her with the warm drink, the bitter taste of the unfamiliar liquid was still with her. For reasons she could not explain to herself, Jennifer felt safe at this moment. It was a far different feeling than that which she had felt two days ago; two days was right wasn't it?

Jennifer had risen early, determined to quit the camp well before the guides had risen. It hadn't been difficult, her sleep had been light and infrequent that night. She had no intention of being forced to go on a hunt she wanted no part of. She figured that if she disappeared for the day, avoiding a violent confrontation with her father, that the thoughts her father had would have faded by the time he returned from the hunt. She would return in the evening and smooth her father's ruffled feathers and things would return to normal. She tried to follow the river trail Jeff had taken her on and had traveled for two hours, illuminating the rough path with a small flashlight, before the eastern sky had begun to turn gray with dawn.

Jennifer had been naive in her thinking, for no sooner had MacKelvy discovered her missing than he had informed her father. Peters had become agitated, at first angry that his daughter would dare to defy him so openly, and then fearful of what might happen to her in the wilds without her guide. When MacKelvy asserted that he could track her down and bring her back, Peters agreed readily. He offered to go with the guide, but MacKelvy turned the request aside, saying that it would be easier and quicker if he were not burdened with someone less experienced. Again Peters agreed, consenting to wait in camp until MacKelvy returned with his daughter.

MacKelvy checked with Jeff regarding their past itineraries on the photographic tour. After a few minutes of conversation, MacKelvy concluded that Jennifer would stick close to the river, assuming that it would be easier for her to follow without becoming lost. MacKelvy was by no means an expert tracker, but neither was Jennifer good at hiding her trail. He picked up the first sign less than a hundred yards from camp. From there on it was a simple matter to follow the obvious signs. As the signs became fresher, a newly broken branch here, a candy wrapper there, MacKelvy's attitude underwent a sinister change. He was no longer trailing the girl, he was stalking her.

He was little more than three miles from camp when he

spotted the girl. She was walking slowly up a small hill about two hundred yards ahead of him. His eyes picked over the hilly terrain, searching for a trail that would allow him to circle around the and get ahead of the girl. It did not take him long to find it, he was familiar with the area. He set off at a fast pace, sure that the river would mask the sound of his movement. It took him forty five minutes to make the circle, and he peered over the edge of a blow-down to make sure that the girl had not outdistanced him. For a moment he did not see her, then he spotted the bright plaid of her woolen shirt. He watched silently as she approached. Suddenly she stopped in a little clearing. He became apprehensive. Had she seen him? No, he thought not, she was not looking in his direction. From cover, he watched her every movement.

Jennifer was tired, she had been stumbling along this trail for some time now, she wasn't exactly sure how long. Her feet hurt and she was getting hot as the sun beat down on her. She decided that she would make this peaceful meadow by the placid river her resting place for the remainder of the day. She took off the small day pack and rested it against a stump, then sat down to remove her boots. It would sure feel good to soak her feet in the cool river. She shaded her eyes with her hand and squinted at the sun. It was much warmer than it had been yesterday. Maybe she could get a tan.

MacKelvy watched with growing tension as Jennifer unbuttoned the heavy wool shirt. He was disappointed when he saw that she wore a bright blue T-shirt underneath, but he was patient. Jennifer stretched, raising her arms skyward, outlining her figure against the green-brown forest background. MacKelvy convinced himself that she knew someone was watching and was teasing. She probably thinks that damn Jeff followed her, he thought. When she pulled off the T-shirt and stood in her jeans and halter top, MacKelvy could no longer restrain himself.

Jennifer caught her breath and froze when she sat the huge bearded man hurtling at her. At the last moment she tried to dodge aside, but a burly arm reached out and snared her around the waist. She screamed until the breath was knocked out of her when he slammed her to the ground. She fought and squirmed to free herself, but he was too strong. She felt his knee bear down on her belly and a rough hand grab at her breast before it grasped at the fabric and ripped it roughly apart. Her hands were free. With one she clawed at his face, the other searched the ground above her head. She felt the cold hard surface of the stone, it fit perfectly in the palm of her right hand. When MacKelvy had secured her left arm, the pressure of his grip uncurling her fingers, he lowered his head toward Jennifer. The moment Jennifer smelled his foul breath her right hand shot up. The rock struck MacKelvy between the eyes. His grip loosened as a look of surprise crossed his face. Jennifer struck again, harder this time. The pulpy bruise exploded bloodily. MacKelvy's hands went to his head weakly and he rolled to the side and lay still.

Jennifer sat up, breathing hard and covering herself. She was sure she had killed the man, blood flowed freely from the hole in his forehead and he did not move. She dressed as quickly as her trembling hands would let her. She was crying now, heavy uncontrolled sobs wracking her body, tears flowing copiously. She grabbed the pack and ran in panic. She paid no attention to direction and every sound was frightening. She looked back for a pursuer that did not exist. when she came to the channels that held little water, she could not have known that they were part of the same river she had followed earlier. She crossed them without thinking and ran along a game trail until dark. She survived the night huddled in the hollow of an ancient burnt spruce. In the morning she had heard the sound of hoofbeats, steel shod against the rock, and she had taken flight once more. The appearance of the large gray animal on the trail just ahead of her had so frightened her that she had stepped mindlessly off the edge of the slope, lost her balance, and begun rolling towards the bottom. There had been a flash of bright lights, a sudden stab of pain, and then blissful darkness where no one could hurt her.

That same animal that had met her on the trail now warmed her with its own body. She saw the man stir and quickly closed her eyes. He would want to know how she came to be here, if he did not already know, and he gave no indication that he did. Her injury would be her excuse, she would pretend to remember nothing. That way he would have to take her to the authorities in town and not back to the hunting camp.

CHAPTER 9

THE SMOKE of the dying fire wafted in Jed's direction. His eyes opened and he reached to scratch his beard as he yawned. He glanced in the girl's direction and saw that Whiskey was still beside her. She seemed to be asleep yet. He rose and moved silently across the deep carpet of soft earth, stopping to rummage through the contents of the leather saddlebags before proceeding to the edge of the creek. When the girl awoke, he was sure that she'd be hungry and he'd noticed a few deep pools just up the creek. There would be trout lurking there. When he reached the pools, he uncoiled the length of fishline that he always carried and attached a small silver spinner to one end. He used his heavy sheath knife to cut a willow pole from a nearby bush and secured the other end of the line to that. He tossed the lure into the swirling waters just above the first pool and guided the line with the end of the pole. He was not surprised when a fish struck the lure on the first cast. These waters were rarely fished and the trout were hungry this time of year. It took less than a half hour to catch six fine fish. He gutted them at the creek's edge and returned to the camp with the fish in one hand and a bundle of green willow sticks in the other.

Jed laid the fish on a flat stone near the fire and turned to check the girl. Her eyes were open now, and Jed smiled at her. Whiskey raised his head and looked at his master, sniffing at the odor that drifted from the stone. Jed knelt beside the girl and felt the bruise on her forehead. The swelling had subsided somewhat. "Are you hungry?" he asked quietly. The girl answered with a barely perceptible nod in the affirmative. "All right, I'll have something ready shortly." He swiftly wove the green sticks into a grill and

63

placed the trout on it to cook. He was keenly aware that the girl was watching his every move. It didn't make him uncomfortable, but he averted his eyes, not wishing to stir up old memories. Cassie had often watched him work in the same manner.

While the trout sizzled on the grill, Jed brought the saddle to the girl's side and propped her up on it, making sure that she was comfortable. "What's your name?" he asked softly. She answered him with a blank stare and hoped that it was convincing. Jed looked at her intently, studying her face for any change, then dropped his gaze to the dog who lay at the girl's feet. "Whiskey," he said and the dog's head snapped up, his eyes focusing on his master, "go fetch." Jed pointed in the direction of the pack that gleamed bright orange in the sunlight on the side of the hill. He hoped that the bag would hold some clue of the girl's identity. Whiskey paused for a moment, then bounded toward the distant object. Jennifer watched as the dog picked up the tattered pack in his teeth and returned to his master. He dropped the pack at Jed's feet.

Jed reached out to scratch the dog's ears and picked up the pack. He turned the object over and read Jennifer's name and home address that was plainly printed on the leather patch on the back. He looked at the girl and handed the knapsack to her. "Does that ring any bells?" he asked.

Jennifer replied dully, "No."

"Well, at least you speak the language," he grinned. It had been the first word she had spoken since he had found her. "Maybe it will come back to you. I hope so," he said sincerely.

It had been all Jennifer could do to keep her composure when Jed had read the name on the back of the pack. She knew that Raudsep employed a lot of guides, some she had never met. It was possible that this man was one of them. If he was, he hadn't tipped his hand yet. For now she had to continue to play the game. "Who are you?" she asked tentatively.

"Me? Name's Jed Marsh," he replied flatly. "Better see to those trout."

Jennifer watched him as he finished preparing the breakfast. The pain in her head came and went in intensity, but it never completely left her. For the first time she began to realize just how lucky she had been. If it weren't for this quiet man, she very likely would have died. The thought made her shudder as Jed returned to her side with the fish stacked on a slab of freshly cut birch bark. Jed mistook her shudder for a shiver and set the makeshift platter on the ground. He rearranged the wool jacket about her shoulders and checked her forehead once more. She was still feverish.

"Here, eat some. It'll make you feel better," he said, offering her the fish. "Sorry about the dishes, but I didn't exactly plan to overnight out here."

Jennifer picked up a piece of fish with her fingers and tasted it. It was delicious. She hadn't eaten anything substantial in almost forty eight hours and she wolfed down two fish ravenously. They were good going down, but once there they seemed to sit like a rock. She felt a sudden urge to be sick, but choked it back. Jed noticed the look in her eyes and realized what it meant. Damn, he should have made her eat more slowly. It just hadn't occurred to him.

"Are you all right?" he asked.

Jennifer nodded. The feeling passed, but it was replaced by another, more urgent one. "I have to go to the bathroom," she blurted.

That presented a problem that Jed hadn't reckoned on. He knew that she would be unsteady and would need help to some extent. "Hold on just a minute," he said, swallowing hard. He rifled through the saddlebags once more and came up with an abbreviated roll of toilet paper which he handed to the girl. "Let me fix something up behind those bushes." He made a makeshift seat out of some pieces of broken trees, laying the semi-flat slabs across the narrow space between two fallen aspens. He tested the structure for sturdiness and returned to the girl.

Jennifer struggled to rise, allowing Jed to help her and leaning heavily on his arm. Jed walked her to the "toilet" and left her, listening for any noise that might signal that the girl was in trouble. After a few minutes, Jed heard her take a few steps toward him and stumble. He reached out to keep her from falling as she rounded the bush where he was waiting. She was very pale and perspiring heavily once more. Jed could feel her shivers as he put an arm around her to walk her back to camp. He knew that he had to get her to his cabin before nightfall. Another night in the cold, damp air would be more than she could take. He was also aware that transporting her on the horse might aggravate any injuries she might have that he'd missed. He weighed the alternatives before coming to a decision. He stuck with his original conclusion, accepting the fact that something could go wrong, but knowing that pneumonia was inevitable if he did not get the girl to a controlled environment.

Jed made the girl as comfortable as possible near the fire and explained his decision to her. Jennifer was feeling weak and could not have summoned an argument if she had had one. She would have to lean on his strength and trust in his judgement. She realized as soon as he mentioned his cabin that he could not be associated with Raudsep, and felt a sense of relief just before the pain drifted her back into a state of semiconsciousness. Jed worked quickly to break camp, watching the girl furtively all the while. He would have to move fast.

Jed became aware of the pain in the small of his back as he sat uncomfortably on the back of the saddle, holding the girl with one arm and guiding the horse with the other. They had been on the trail over an hour. The cutoff from the center of the trapline should be just up ahead. With the girl slipping in and out of consciousness, it had been difficult for Jed to keep his eye on the landmarks. The old bay would have known the trail and would not have needed Jed's rein to point the way, but Jed had preferred the lively step of the mare to the placid one of the bay. That prefer-

ence became a liability now. Every time the mare started to
dance, Jed drew sharply in on the reins, causing the bit to
bind on the Paint's tongue. He didn't like to do that, it
could make a horse hard mouthed. And yet he knew that
the sharp jostling could complicate the girl's condition. Jed
firmed his grip on the reins, looked ahead at Whiskey, and
mentally silenced the pain in his back.

It was shortly after noon when Jed sensed the change
in the weather. He glanced over his shoulder to see the
darkening clouds gathering in the northwest. It was too
warm for snow, but the rain that would come would be
cold and driving. He could see the wind that whipped the
tops of the towering thunderheads, driving them ever
closer. He reined the horse in and slid off the mare's rump.
Steadying the girl with one hand, he freed the poncho
from the tie strings at the back of the saddle. With some
difficulty, he pried the girl from her stupor and got her to
cooperate in putting on the heavy rubberized rain gear. He
had survived rain before, he'd endure the discomfort once
again. He remounted and continued the journey.

The storm hit savagely, the wind tugging at the poncho
and whipping the fringe of Jed's buckskins. When the rain
came it was in great heavy sheets. Jed was drenched in less
than a minute. They were little more than a half hour from
the cabin and Jed swore at the storm, his bellows barely
carrying to the mare's ears. She began to trot and jerked at
the bit when Jed applied pressure once again. It was still
early afternoon and the sky was as black as night. Jed usually looked forward to these late fall rainstorms, often
falling asleep to the rhythmic drum of the large drops on
the roof of his snug cabin. This one he cursed with a ve-
hemence he'd not felt in a long time.

The last few minutes on the trail seemed to last an
eternity, but finally they were at the porch of the small
cabin, its bulk just visible through the sheets of rain. Jed
dismounted and caught the girl as she slipped from the
saddle. He carried her to the door, reached with the hand
that extended around her waist, and unlatched the bolt. He

booted open the door and stumbled into the dark interior. He caught himself as his cold-stiffened joints threatened to fail him and tottered to the bed where he laid down the girl. He looked out the front door and could not see the mare, she'd probably wandered off to the corral where she knew she would find hay to eat. He'd attend the horse later.

Jed walked to the stove in the kitchen, reached above it for a match, and returned to light the oil lamp on the table. The well soaked wick caught immediately, flickered as he replaced the glass chimney, and brought a warm glow to the cabin. He brought another match to the fireplace and touched off the tinder that he'd left there before he'd set out to work on his trapline. With the fire going, he turned his attention once more to the girl. He stripped off the poncho and saw at once that it had not done its job in the high winds. Her jeans and shirt were soaked. She was burning with fever and not coherent. He covered her with a blanket and stripped off her wet clothing, using the blanket to dry her. The hell with propriety, if he didn't get her dry and warm, she wouldn't live to reproach him anyway.

When he was satisfied that the girl was totally dry, he slipped her naked body under the heavy wool blankets, checking her breathing for any telltale signs of roughness. When he found none, he went out to tend the mare. He'd change his own wet clothes when he returned. After he'd unsaddled the mare, he considered what he could do to prevent the girl's illness from worsening. He'd used the oxytetracycline he kept for his horses on himself a couple of times without any serious side effects and decided that it was worth the risk. He retrieved the large bottle from the tiny cellar in the far corner of the kitchen. He lit the wood in the firebox of the stove, placed the veterinary syringe and a needle in a small pan of water, and set the pan on the stove.

He changed his clothes while he waited for the water to boil. When the syringe had been sterilized, he carefully drew the oily liquid into the barrel and checked it for air.

He walked to the bedside with it and tried to rouse the girl. She mumbled a response and drew the blankets closer. Jed moved the blankets aside to expose the girl's thigh. With deliberation he poised the needle above it and then plunged it home rapidly, withdrew the plunger to be sure he was not in a vein, and then pushed the plunger down. When the contents of the syringe were expelled, he pulled out the needle and held a small piece of sterile gauze from his first aid kit against the tiny puncture. The girl barely moved during the entire procedure. He returned the blankets to their protective position and stepped away from the bedside.

For two days he administered the antibiotic, fed her warm soup during her periods of wakefulness, listened to her murmurings as she slept quietly, comforted her when the nightmares came, and watched over her while he went sleepless. He was on his fifth cup of strong, bitter coffee on the third morning when she came around. He heard her stirrings and walked quickly to her from the window where the light was streaming in. When her eyes fluttered open, he was by her side. She looked at the large squared beams that supported the roof above her head and then at Jed. "Where am I?" she asked.

Jed could have leapt in joy. Her voice was strong and lucid. He touched her forehead, the fever had broken. The crisis was over and she was fully conscious for the first time since they had arrived. "You're at my cabin," he replied softly. "I wasn't sure you'd stick around to see it."

Jed recounted the story of the last few days to her and her eyes grew wide in astonishment. She started to sit up, but instantly felt weak and dizzy. Jed gently pushed her back against the feather pillow and made her lie still. "You are out of the woods, but you're not ready to get too active yet," he cautioned.

Jennifer reached to touch the lump on her forehead, it itched terribly. Jed had applied an antiseptic and a dressing to the small cut in the center of the swollen area. He'd discovered that it was not as serious as the bleeding had seemed to indicate. He was glad that he had not had to stitch it up, he wasn't very good at that. He remembered the jagged Frankensteinian scar that ran half the length of his lower left leg. A girl would not take kindly to such a mark, particularly if it were on her face. Jed had not thought that the wound would leave any more than a fine white line and that, in time, it would probably disappear completely. The girl could not fault him, he had done his best.

"Listen," he said, "I'm going to have to call you something. I think that pack is yours, so why don't I call you Jenny, at least until you remember?"

Jennifer was careful not to betray her secret. She needed to know more about this man before she allowed her memory to return. She answered with an emotionless, "All right." She could not have known what had surfaced in the nightmares when she was just below the threshold of consciousness. She hid her fear and uneasiness behind the deceitful mask of ignorance, using all the will power she could muster to keep from letting the veil fall. Jed knew that he was being fooled, but he let it pass. She would tell him if and when she decided that she wanted to, there was absolutely no sense in pressing the issue.

Jed watched the growing restlessness that Jennifer had displayed throughout the late morning hours. He had waited, wanting to be sure that she was fully in touch with reality. He had noticed the flush that had come to her face when she had realized that she was naked beneath the blankets, but had said nothing. Now that he was sure, he picked up his hat, tugged it onto his head, and walked to the door. "I'll be going out to look after the horses," he said. "I'll be back in a half hour or so."

When the door had closed, and she heard the fading scuff of Jed's boots, Jennifer sat up painfully, every joint and muscle in her body stiff and sore from the ordeal. She saw her clothes were neatly folded and lay beside the shredded pack on the chest next to the bed and recalled the embarrassed look in Jed's eyes as he had left. Thoughts crowded into her mind and she grimly closed them out. She let the blankets fall away and inspected the bruise MacKelvy had left on her left shoulder. It had turned a strange purplish-green. She dressed slowly, every movement causing a little pain in a different part of her body, and felt better once she was fully clothed. She thought bitterly of MacKelvy's attempted violation, and then of Jed's compassion, failing to reconcile the conflicting concepts of men that rattled around in her brain. On the one hand she felt so vulnerable, so helpless, on the other, safe and trusting. Her reflections were interrupted by the soft knock on the door. "It's all right."

Jed entered and moved silently around the cabin's interior. Jennifer could tell that he was nervous by the little muscle that twitched at the corner of his left eye. Jed was, in fact, more than nervous. All the things that had not entered his mind when the girl had required his undivided attention now had to be faced. He figured that it would be at least five days before Jenny would be in shape to travel. He needed that time to pull in the river sets and finish the work on the far stretch of the trapline, but he felt burdened with a responsibility that he thought he's left far behind him. He recalled the nightmares, trying to fit the pieces together. He wasn't sure that the snatches of words were fact or delirium, but he was sure of one thing, MacKelvy's name had been screamed in every dream. He was certain that the amnesia was feigned, but even that left a lot of unanswered questions. Another thing, why hadn't Raudsep's search parties checked his place? Three days was more than ample time to have done so. There was only one possible explanation, MacKelvy had to have been involved in some way with the girl and for some reason was deliberately leading the search parties astray. That would be easy since the downpour would have erased any scent that Raudsep's dogs might have followed. Jed guessed that MacKelvy had assaulted the girl, that would be reason enough not to find her. If Jed hadn't found Jenny, MacKelvy would have been home free.

"Damn his soul to hell!" Jed spit.

Jennifer looked up, startled. "What?"

The feminine voice surprised Jed. He looked at Jenny with a sheepish grin. "Sorry, I guess I'm so used to being alone that I don't even notice it when I think out loud."

"Damn who to hell?" Jenny persisted. She had to know what had slipped out during her illness.

Jed sideslipped the question neatly. "The squirrel that chewed up my saddle strings."

Jenny let it drop. The two would engage in this delicate form of verbal fencing for the next few days, each trying to find out what the other was hiding. It was to prove a difficult time for them both.

CHAPTER 10

MACKELVY had finally come to. He rubbed the knot on the front of his thick skull, looked at the blood that came away on his hand, and grunted. He looked at the sun, trying to focus his eyes. It was late afternoon. Damn, he thought with satisfaction, that little wildcat had really clobbered him. He stumbled to his feet and followed the trail that Jennifer had left. It led north, away from camp. He was sure that she would not double back and head for camp, uncertain of the reason why he felt so. For a moment he considered following the trail before dismissing it. If he went after her now, with the head start she had, he would have to spend the night alone without the comfort of his powerful rifle. That fact stole his courage, he was a lousy shot with a pistol. He washed the blood from his face in the river and sat down on the bank to think. He would have to come up with a believable story before he returned to camp. He would make it simple so he could not be tripped up in the telling. No problem, he was an excellent liar.

The story was down pat as MacKelvy neared the clearing where the tents stood. Peters and the others listened attentively as MacKelvy unfolded the story. They swallowed the whole line, even the part about his fall where his face showed just the proper amount of chagrin. They didn't even ask any questions. Peters reacted as expected, with a proper mixture of worried anger and fatherly remorse. MacKelvy knew he was home free . . . well, almost. He'd seen the narrowing of Jeff's eyes and realized that he'd not swallowed the entire story. MacKelvy shrugged it off, he'd deal with Warner later.

Jeff, in fact, wasn't buying any of it. He knew the big,

red haired man too well. He remembered coming home to find MacKelvy trying to force his attentions on his own wife and then trying to pass it off as a drunken flirtation when he'd been caught. Jeff resolved to go out on his own the next day. He'd find Jennifer if she was out there, and if she was still alive. He wondered how she was making it, knowing that she'd be cold and hungry and scared. He didn't sleep very well that night and was up before dawn.

When MacKelvy found out that Jeff had gone that morning, he swore. Jeff was a better tracker than he was, though he would never admit that to anyone else. If he got on the girl's trail, MacKelvy knew that Jeff would eventually find her. He was like a bulldog, once he was on to something he never gave up. And he trusted his instincts, MacKelvy knew that and knew why Warner had left before a formal search party could be organized. Damn him anyway. Still, there was a chance that he'd believed part of MacKelvy's story and would head towards the interior and away from the true path. MacKelvy didn't really believe that, but he let himself think it.

MacKelvy stuck to his story and organized the hunting party into groups of guides and hunters, splitting them up and sending them in a spread pattern to the northwest. He refused help, saying that he would make a swing to the southeast before turning northward, just in case the girl had lost her way and had tried to make it back to camp. He followed that course until the others had enough time to get well out of sight and then he turned about and began the pursuit. He knew the path whereas Jeff would have to take the time to track it. MacKelvy would use that time differential to catch Warner and deal with him.

Jeff was still well ahead of MacKelvy when the storm struck. The sheets of rain cut his visibility and began erasing the obvious sign. All he could go by now were little broken branches on the brush that marked the passing, and there was no way to distinguish between those of yesterday and those of two days ago. Half a mile before he reached the little meadow, he turned towards the interior, following the same trail he'd led Jennifer on before.

When MacKelvy came upon the prints in the mud, already beginning to wash down to the river, he grinned to himself. Warner had bought part of the story. The severe storm would obliterate any telltale sign, there was no need to pursue the trail. MacKelvy was sure that Jennifer would not survive the rain and the freezing temperatures that would inevitably follow in the night. Sure of his own safety now, he abandoned the girl to her fate and began the journey back to the warmth of the camp. He knew the others would have returned before he got there.

Jeff kept to the trail doggedly, enduring the weather. Jennifer was out here somewhere and he knew deep down that she was alive. Maybe he just wasn't willing to admit that there were other possibilities, but he wasn't going to accept defeat before he'd given it his best. It must have been at least two hours since he had turned when he came upon the fresh breaks in the brush. The path led to the north through heavy cover. Jeff thought for a moment. The girl was smart, and it made good sense that she'd try to find protection for the night and from the storm. He followed the trail, unable to see through the rain the marker tree that stood a mere thirty feet away.

When the trail terminated at the edge of the heavy thicket, Jeff moved along its edge, peering through the storm, looking for a break in the brush. There it was, almost tunnel-like, an opening that would provide cover from the storm and warmth for the night. Eagerly, he entered, crawling on his hands and knees, his nose stuffed by the drainage of his sinuses. He'd always been prone to catching cold in this kind of weather, but he never let it bother him. The odor that clung to the brushy walls never reached the nerves that would have put him on guard.

At the end of the seven yard tunnel Maureen Warner was widowed. The grizzly had known the instant Jeff had entered his private sanctuary. He summoned the reserve in his still sore muscles and waited. When Jeff's head had appeared, he had waited until the man had stood. The look of surprise on Jeff's face would have been frozen for eternity when the huge paw slammed into his chest with crushing force but for the savage jaws that closed on his skull and popped it like an overripe melon.

The bear had worried the broken body for a few moments, sniffing the pistol that still lay in its protective holster. The hated smell of cordite was on the steel and the bear tore at it angrily. Gradually, the pain in the bear's left hip manifested itself in its mind. He grew tired of the senseless thing at his feet. Purposefully, he abandoned the den, heading for a secondary one and taking with him the certain knowledge that this strange creature was not invincible, that he was, in fact, easily dispatched.

Jeff's widow would not have to endure viewing the torn remains of her husband, so cruelly rendered by blind animal rage, for they would remain with other untold secrets locked in the vastness of the wilderness, commingling with the earth and returning to nature the way it was meant to be. That knowledge would not have displeased Jeff.

CHAPTER 11

RAUDSEP was in the camp when MacKelvy returned, having flown in just before the storm had hit. The other parties had already returned, wet, dismal, and discouraged. Peters sat alone in his tent, drinking from the bottle of Scotch in gulps. He was well on his way to being drunk when he stumbled from the tent's entrance toward MacKelvy with a hopeful look in his eyes. When MacKelvy shook his head, the man broke down and cried. MacKelvy turned away, unable to disguise the look of disgust on his face. A man didn't bawl like that.

Raudsep motioned to MacKelvy and they conferred in the privacy of the cook tent. Raudsep knew very well MacKelvy's proclivity for lying, but even he was unable to shake MacKelvy from his story and decided that it must be true after all. He studied the lines in MacKelvy's face one last time, then stood, turning his back on the man.

"Well, I suppose we'd better call it in then. Let the authorities take responsibility. At least we can't be sued, the girl left on her own accord and there's nothing we can do about that."

"I reckon not," MacKelvy muttered.

"Where the hell is Warner? You don't suppose he found her, do you?"

MacKelvy's head shot up and his eyes narrowed. "Ain't he in yet?"

"No. Maybe we'd better wait a while and then call it in."

"Probably be a good idea," MacKelvy agreed. Where the hell was Warner anyway? Raudsep was right, he should have been back by now. Damn that bastard, suppose he'd back-tracked and picked up Jennifer's trail? MacKelvy was

77

uncertain once again. He did his best to hide it. When morning broke, and with it the storm, MacKelvy was up prowling the camp. Jeff was still not back. He consulted Raudsep once more. They would go ahead with the call. In less than an hour there would be four small aircraft aloft, each with an experienced pilot and observer. The authorities would lift the burden from Raudsep's shoulders and coordinate the search. At best, Raudsep figured, they would pursue an intensive search for two weeks, tying up his guides and losing him money. Well, by God, he'd make the best of it. He would make good use of the situation to get as much print and television coverage as possible from the rag-tag group of reporters that invariably followed these stories. He sat down, marshalling his thoughts.

"MacKelvy!" he bellowed. "Break out those extra tents. Let's get set up for this circus. Tom, I want you to fly back and get more provisions. You've got carte blanche. I don't want these people that will be coming in to think that we're a second rate outfit. If there's anyone that needs transportation, see that they get it. No charge." He looked around the camp and saw Peters lying in his bunk, the half- empty bottle laying on its side beside him on the ground. "Get Peters up and get some coffee down him. I want him sober. He's no damn good to his daughter, or us, in that condition."

The search lasted for a week before bad weather closed in again and grounded the planes. Everyone was pleased with the way Raudsep handled things. Everyone except MacKelvy. Raudsep was stealing his show. He should have had the limelight. Hell, the only time Raudsep ran the camp was when there was an extra benefit in it. The rest of the time he shunned the "great out of doors" for the comfort of his lavish home and young wife. MacKelvy was seething, but turned his anger and envy inward, appearing morose, and avoided the rest of the people in the camp, especially the reporters. When it became apparent that Warner was not coming back, MacKelvy watched with awe Raudsep's cold blooded use of it for personal publicity. He was good, MacKelvy had to admit that. Damn the bastard, he was good. He didn't even have to resort to the lies that MacKelvy thought so necessary, he used the truth like a flexible tool, making it suit his own needs and purposes.

Finally the search wound down. the conferences had come down to a boring set of exercises in map reading. The reports of the bush pilots had dwindled to fewer and fewer possible sightings. At the end of sixteen days the consensus was unanimous. Jeff and the girl were lost, there was no chance that they could have lived through the storms and cold temperatures that had marked the past few days. The agreed to abandon the search, except for the routine flights made by the bush pilots. They alone would keep the vigil, flying low to investigate any signs that might come to their attention.

The track of the grizzly had been erased almost as soon as it had been made, and, but for the old marker tree, the search parties had not found his sign. He had watched them from the protection of cover, or rather he had sensed them with ears and nose. As they pressed closer, he re-treated further into his territory. He was not yet willing to test his power against more than one of these creatures at a time. He would content himself to gain knowledge.

Peters had given up hope at the end of a week, but had felt it his duty to remain throughout the search. Now that it was ended, he was almost glad that it was over. He certainly felt relieved. On the return flight he sat alone with his thoughts. The ceremony would be simple, a remembrance rather than a funeral. He had nothing to bury but his attacks of guilt. He'd bury those in work as he'd always done, there wasn't a grave deep enough to hold them. He'd always acted on impulse and it seemed to him that it had always been a plus in business and a detriment in his personal relationships. It had been impulse that had brought Jennifer along on this trip. Now she would never come home. He accepted the drink from the tray held by the flight attendant and swallowed it bitterly in a single gulp.

Maureen Warner was on the same flight, sitting with

one child beside her and one in her womb, the last vestiges of her bitter-sweet relationship with Jeff. She was going home to her parents in Ohio, back to the security of the rolling farmland she had grown up with, away from this rugged, frightening land Jeff had loved. Well, it was his now, his forever, she thought bitterly. And yet, she had loved it at first, maybe because she had loved Jeff and his wild, crazy approach to life. It had been all right before the job with Raudsep, but things had not gone well since then. Jeff had not made excuses, he'd just pointed out the simple fact that since the mills had closed he couldn't get another logging job and this was better than starving. She wondered if he still thought so and looked at her young son before laying her hand on the child that was yet to be.

Raudsep had ordered the camp to be struck and moved to be joined with one further west. Business went on as usual. The excitement had died down and he had gone home to his sprawling log home and his warm, soft, young wife. MacKelvy hunted with a vengeance. Jeff slept with eternity, and the object of his search, Jennifer, was warm and safe in the cabin of a stranger to the east, and no one knew.

CHAPTER 12

J ED PLOWED the water firmly with the wide blade of the paddle. He was thinking of the past few days with Jenny. They hadn't been easy, the girl seemed bent on making his way of life an issue. At first he'd excused it, but now it was beginning to grate on his nerves. He recalled the words, and the mood.

He had returned from the trapline that night, having put the finishing touches on it. He was eager to see if Jenny had recovered from the dark mood that seemed to dominate her. She still maintained that she had no memory, but her unwillingness to talk and the depression seemed to say otherwise. He had left her sitting in the willow and hide chair beside a cheery fire, hoping that a prolonged absence on his part would induce her to activity. He had been wrong, she still sat in that same chair, having not even bothered to keep up the fire. The cabin was dark and the chill from without had penetrated deep inside the solid log walls. Had Jed not known something of depression, he would have been angry. But Jed was slow to anger now and he was, in many ways, an easier man than he had once been.

Jennifer's eyes had dully followed him as he had returned the Winchester to its place above the mantle, then fixed on the pistol that rode easily on his hip. She had stared at him as he had rebuilt the fire. The words came back at him as if the had just been uttered.

"You're one of *them*, aren't you?" she asked unemotionally.

Jed stiffened momentarily, then continued to lay the fire. It was perhaps a minute and a half before the flames began to sputter. Only then did he pivot, still squatting on

heel and toe, to face her. "One of them?" he asked quietly.
"The killers . . . the men who thrive on the blood of innocent animals."

It was the first time she'd really showed any sign of emotion. Jed thought for a minute before replying evenly, "That's your way of looking at it, not mine."

Jenny looked away, her arms resting listlessly on the arms of the chair. "My father's one . . . that . . ." she had difficulty saying the name, " . . . MacKelvy too."

Jed's eyes narrowed, the girl's memory was back, if it had ever been gone. He understood part of it now, at least he knew for certain how Jennifer had come to be in his domain. "About your father, I don't know. MacKelvy, well that's a whole other story."

"Hah! I suppose you're different?!"

"Do you find it so easy to judge everyone?" Jed asked, unruffled by her sarcasm. When she looked away without replying, he added, "At least you're showing some fight. That's a good sign."

Jenny sniffed loudly and ran a hand under her nose, refusing to look at Jed. She had made up her mind to dislike this man, needing no other reason than the fresh beaver pelts that were drying on the willow stretchers beneath the eaves.

Whiskey barked at the door and Jed rose, crossing the room to let him in. "I take it," he said as he stroked the dog's head, "that you ran from MacKelvy's camp. That explains how you wound up in the draw." Jed reflected for a moment, realizing full well that even the carnage of the fall hunt would not have sent the girl fleeing into the wilderness aimlessly. No, it was something deeper that made this girl seek escape. Maybe it lay in the secrets of the nightmares, maybe in something like he'd felt when he'd lost Cassie. The girl maintained her silence and it irritated him. "I'll put dinner on."

Jennifer continued to remain quiet throughout the meal, picking at the rich stew that Jed placed in front of her. Jed's mood gradually returned to normal. Lack of conversation was something that he'd grown used to over the past few years. Without thinking, he talked aloud to himself once again. "I better get the snowshoes ready, won't be too long now. Come on Whiskey."

His back was already turned when Jenny looked up. she realized then that he had not been talking to her. Her shoulders shook a little as she stifled a sob. In him she saw only those bad qualities that she identified with her father. Like Jed, he had voiced his thoughts to no one in particular, ignoring her mother's soft replies. It had always been so, ever since Jenny had been a child. She had never understood how her mother could simply smile to herself as she cast a loving glance at her husband, and went about her household chores.

Jennifer remembered how proud her mother had been when they had moved to the big house in Rockford. She remembered how little they had seen of her father after that. She had felt somehow at fault that he seemed to have less and less time for her and her mother. Her father had seemed to grow cold over the years, showing his affection for the family by buying things. Things, only things. The thoughts twisted about in her mind, bent by the pent up rage that turned sour and inward for lack of trust.

Jed leaned against the far wall, working leather snowshoe straps with mink oil to soften them, and watching the procession of expressions that crossed Jenny's face. There was no joy in any of them and Jed wondered what lay behind. "You want to talk about it?" he asked.

Jenny looked up sharply, feeling that he had intruded on her private thoughts, as if he had some mystical powers of divination. "You wouldn't understand, you're one of them."

"Ah yes," Jed said knowingly, "one of them."

"Who in hell are you to mock me?!"

"The one who pulled you out of the bottom of that draw, cleaned you up, and made damn sure that you didn't catch pneumonia by nursemaiding you for three days and nights."

"And God knows what else while I was out!"

Jed shot her a disgusted look. "Right. You really believe that, don't you?"

Jennifer looked down at the table. "No . . . no I don't."

"All right then," Jed said, dropping his voice a bit, "whatever it is that's bothering you is your business. I won't ask. You'll have to work it out for yourself. I will tell you this, if you keep it bottled up it will tear you apart."

"How could you know?" Her reply had been meant as a retort, but somewhere the fire had gone out of it.

"I've been there . . . it's a lonely place."

Jennifer studied his face, searching the weather-hardened lines for a chink. There was none, but somehow there was a compassion that flickered in the glint of his steel gray eyes. She guessed that somewhere, hidden behind that implacable iron face, an ocean of emotion rose and fell as it lashed against that impenetrable barrier of self-control. Here stood a man who showed none of the frivolities of her former boyfriends, none of the crudeness of some of her father's business associates, and none of the outward signs of worry that showed so readily on most faces. He seemed as formidable as the mountains he lived in and as emotionally barren as a snow swept hill. It almost frightened her that he was so much in control, and yet there was a peace about him that bespoke inner conflicts were absent.

Jed walked slowly to the fireplace and picked up the small can of lacquer warming on the hearth. He heard the scuff of Jennifer's chair, and her shoes on the floor, but he did not turn to acknowledge her presence. Instead he concentrated on relacquering the webbing of his snowshoes. He had tried to go to her and it had not worked. Now, she would have to come to him, or live with it. To Jed it really did not matter. Jennifer would be ready to travel in another couple of days and Jed would return her to the town and her father.

That had not settled the issue, for even this morning Jennifer had persisted in asking bothersome questions

about his trapping. Here was this little slip of a girl questioning everything Jed did. By what right? She made silly
assumptions about the wild world that must have come
from some book or pamphlet written by somebody who
didn't know what he was talking about. Jed dug harder
with the paddle, his jaw muscles working. He overshot a
set and had to return with the current. At that moment,
Jed made the decision. He relaxed and nosed the canoe
into the ice skim near the shore, listening to the brittle
sound of its breaking as it gave way under the weight of
the bow.

The trap was gone from its position four inches below
the water. Jed knew that it held a beaver. He reached to
the bottom of the canoe for the long stick with the hook.
He carefully slid the stick down the slide wire of the set,
feeling for the trap in the dark waters. Finally the hook
grabbed and he brought the trap to the surface. The beaver
it held was not huge, but his practiced eye told him that
the skin would make a medium. The pelt was thick, rich
dark brown. Prime and worth the catching even though the
price had been down for the past couple of years. This was
the last set. He pulled it and added it to the pile of traps in
the bottom of the canoe. It was still early, he would skin
the beaver here and then head back to the cabin.

The air was cool and there was the smell of a distant
storm that carried to Jed. He reflected on the light odor
here and the one he remembered from the past, one that
was not nearly so pleasant.

ANOTHER TIME, ANOTHER PLACE: The darkened sky
hung heavy over the dank Illinois farmland. Jed trudged in
manure-caked boots across the feedlot. The stink of pig
and cattle mixed thickly and lodged in his nose. From the
south the stench of the half-rotted sow drifted to him and
sank to the pit of his gut, killing his appetite for the lunch
he was headed to the farmhouse for. The damn thing had
lain there for over a week, decaying progressively in the
mild weather of late fall until it had begun to turn to jelly

and run down the slight graveled slope. Jed had wanted to get rid of it quickly, but old Bill had refused to let him, saying that there might be others shortly. He always said that, sometimes with justification, sometimes without.

Jed spat to the side in disgust, kicked the crap off his boots near the pump, and hosed off the soles. Out of habit he checked the sky before walking to the house. It had turned white under the dark clouds. Snow on the way. It was overdue. He wondered where Bill had been all morning, he usually showed up to check on him sometime in the morning. It was something that Jed had never gotten used to. Back on the ranch in Montana, Jed had almost always worked alone, trusted to get the job done without supervision. He resented this fool who thought it necessary to show him "how to do" even the most menial task. This job sure as hell wasn't what his cousin had said it would be. Manager hell, it was a hired man's job, and Jed had told Frank that he had wanted no part of such a job. The things that had swayed Jed had been the big salary, the promise of bonuses, and the repeated reassurances from his cousin. Damn him anyway.

Still, Jed was determined to see the job through the contract time of one year. After that he would make his decision, probably to return to Montana, despite the low wages paid in that area. At least they didn't try to strip a man of his pride out there. He was a westerner through and through, no doubt about it. He didn't, and wouldn't try, to fit into the circumscribed customs of midwest farm life. He'd be damned if he'd walk two steps behind the boss and "yes sir" the man every time he spoke, even when he was wrong. That was against Jed's grain. His attitude would cost him, it already had. He was making the best of a bad situation, learning all that he could that might help him and avoiding Bill's wrath by avoiding Bill.

After he had finished lunch, Jed thought about the dead sow once more. He picked up the phone and called the rendering works and told them to pick up what was left of the animal. He heard the cough of the old diesel tractor that announced Bill's arrival just as he hung up the phone. He tugged on his coveralls, pulled on the rubber boots, and let the door slam behind him as he went out. Bill's face was sour, as usual, screwed up in its own special way beneath the little eyes, making him closely resemble the pigs that he kept. Jed suspected that it was that face, and the poor conditions in which the animals were kept that lent to his present feelings about pigs. He hated them.

"I don't s'pose ya got them crates cleaned, did ya?" Bill shot as he clambered down from the oil stained seat of the tractor.

"Long time ago," Jed replied tersely. He kept the far-rowing sows clean in the barn. He knew what was coming, Bill didn't like to clean crates, he let them go and then dumped the dirty job on Jed. He'd probably done that to every man that had worked for him.

"Well then, ya can go over to my place an' clean up those ones over there too," he said triumphantly. "An' while yer at it, get Bobby's too."

Jed looked at the small, round man coldly. "Isn't that supposed to be his 4-H project?"

"So?"

"I always thought they were supposed to take care of all aspects of their own projects. So far I've done the far-rowing, the feeding, and the record keeping. Seems like I ought to get the award if he wins."

"Don't get smart-mouthed with me. Ya do like I say, I'm the boss in case ya forgot again. Now get goin'. I'm goin' up to check on that bunker."

Jed spat on the ground in Bill's direction. They both knew the defiance that was intended, and they both knew that it was a standoff. Jed didn't have enough saved to quit, and Bill couldn't find a way out of the contract with-out paying Jed in full for the term. Bill pushed it as far as he had courage to, stopping just short of Jed's full anger. He was more than a little afraid of that explosive temper. He'd seen it just once so far and it scared the hell out of him. But he couldn't let it lie and try to get along, it was more fun to play the stupid game.

Jed passed the dead sow on his way to the pickup and cursed the bastard and his filthy operation, knowing that Bill would twiddle away the afternoon talking with the tenant farmer just up the way. Tenant farmers, that was what most of these prideful, arrogant men were for the most part. Few of them owned their own farms. They cash rented and share cropped, and kidded themselves that they were the final holdouts in family farming. Corporations in Chicago held the real power over the land that they farmed. Doctors, dentists, lawyers with an interest in making a buck without working for it, or in need of a tax write-off.

Jed grunted a coarse laugh and picked up the glistening carcass of the beaver, flinging it into the brush for the scavengers that would strip it to the bone and leave that for the mice to chew on. At least it wouldn't sit around and decay slowly, he thought, and turned his back on the carcass and the thoughts running through his mind.

He had regained his good humor as soon as the canoe began slicing through the water on its return trip. The current carried him swiftly downstream, there was little need for the paddle except in steering. He looked out on the placid stretches of water that reflected the remaining fall leaves that still clung to the branches of trees, falling with every breeze. Soon the trees would be bare, waiting to be clothed in ice and snow, waiting for the heavy stillness of winter to silence the rustling of paper thin leaves and the quiet gurgle of the river. Jed was waiting as well. Of all the seasons, he loved fall best, but it was time for the winter, time to feel the sting of cold snow, the rawness of the air, and the awesome silence of the north country in sleep.

As the canoe slipped in towards shore, Jed made mental preparations. He would tell Jenny upon his return, she had no say in the matter. He pulled the canoe ashore, emptied it, and carried it to its shelter on the high ground. He put it to rest, sealing it in a sarcophagus of branches and brush until resurrection time next summer. He returned to the water's edge, picked up his paddle, pelts, and gear, and turned towards the path that led to the cabin. There was a spring in his firm step. It was always so when he had resolved a problem or come to an important decision, the mantle of deliberation having been lifted.

CHAPTER 13

IT WAS A CHILL Wednesday morning when Jed boosted Jenny aboard the big bay. He'd been up well before sunrise preparing for this unanticipated trip to town. The frost had lain heavy on the ground and clung to every projection from the earth's surface. The fog had been thick and still hung close, opening to show patches of blue sky above only occasionally.

Jed checked the shutters and barred the door before mounting the Paint and beckoning the sullen girl to follow. Despite her quarrelsome questions, Jennifer had begun to see a part of Jed's position and had even begun to trust him in certain respects. She had almost been ready to open up a bit to him. His announcement the previous night that he would be taking her to the authorities in town had slammed the door on those feelings and had plunged her back into an angry depression.

Even if Jenny had shared her secrets, it would not have altered Jed's decision. It was obvious to him that Jenny was not experienced in the kind of life he led, its hardships and dangers, and he doubted that she could adapt to such a life readily. People like Jenny and her father could enjoy short outings that imitated his lifestyle, but the day in day out strain and tedium were another thing. There was little room for the kind of mistakes that might be made over the long haul.

Jenny resented his arbitrary decision, but realized that it was irrevocable. She was idealistic and somewhat romantic about life. She constructed situations in her mind, situations that sounded good but were rarely grounded in common sense. It never crossed her mind that she might be intruding where she was not really wanted or that she

90

might present an added burden to an already tenuous situation. She could not be expected to understand that Jed's calm self-assurance was often hiding doubts in his constant struggle in life. She seethed as she perched atop the tall horse uncomfortably, already wording her farewell address to the impregnable fortress of a man that rode ahead of her. She'd show him, she'd reduce that fortress to rubble.

Toward mid-morning a wind sprang from the north and shattered the calm with a frigid blast. Jed stubbornly ignored the warning and set a faster pace. By noon angry clouds were boiling over the mountains and spilling into the troughs of the valleys. The freezing air turned the carpet of forest litter brittle, and twigs snapped like firecrackers beneath the horses' hooves. Jed reined in and turned to face the storm. All the signs of the past few days flooded into his mind, signs he'd chosen to ignore in his resolve to return the girl safely to the world in which she belonged. Even the scent of the previous night's air had been unmistakable. He'd known the storm was on its way.

Now, as he sat judging the intensity and the course of the storm, he realized that he had made a serious mistake. It would be impossible to reach even the trail camp. They had to turn back now, and he had serious doubts that they would even be able to reach the cabin before the storm's fury caught them. He looked at Jennifer as she huddled in her coat, shivering from the cold as the temperature continued to plummet. He looked again to the north where the arctic storm continued its relentless march. Such a storm held no mercy for an innocent girl, or a stubborn man, and Jed knew it.

Jed swung down from the Paint's back and untied the saddle strings that held his heavy sheepskin coat. He held it out to Jenny. "Put this on," he said quietly and without alarm, "we'll have to turn back."

Jenny's anger came to the surface, the words she spit into the rising wind were fire tempered and brittle edged. "No! Damn you to hell! Get out of my way . . . I can make it to town!"

The bay jumped, startled by the hard kick Jenny's heels delivered to his ribs. Jed's hand shot out to grab the rein and jerked the bit hard against the horse's tongue. The bay lashed out viciously with a rear hoof that missed Jed by inches. For the first time Jenny's impudent, spoiled behavior elicited an emotional response from Jed and she felt the frightening fury of his anger that matched the impending storm in cold intensity.

"Now you listen, and you listen carefully," he ground out ominously. "This storm is going to be a heller. We'd freeze to death before we could make it to town, we damn well might anyway. Our only chance is to turn back now and make tracks, but if you want to choose death, I'll not stand in your way, but I'll be damned if I'll sacrifice my horses without a fight. You've got thirty seconds to make up your mind. Turn that animal around or get the hell off and start walking. It's your choice . . . make it!"

Jennifer stared down at the coat he thrust at her, stunned by the torrent of words that still stung her ears. Without really thinking, she took the coat, struggled into it, and turned the bay. Jed whistled to Whiskey and caught up the reins of the Paint.

The storm worsened steadily, the wind gusting with near gale force, followed by the sting of ice crystals driven hard against the riders. Slowly the flakes became larger, but the unabating wind still hammered them, turning the landscape into the blank terror of a blizzard white-out when Jed and Jenny were little more than a mile from the clearing that held the safety of the cabin. Jenny hunkered down in the heavy sheepskin and held blindly to the saddlehorn with mittened hands. The shiver that continued to course through her body was more from the concentrated fear she felt than from the cold. Riding behind her, with Whiskey's warm body next to his belly where the dog lay across the saddle, Jed strained his squinted eyes against the blinding whiteness of the storm. Occasionally a sudden shift in the wind would part the blank curtain and confirm that the girl remained on the bay ahead of him.

Whiskey's impatient yip and sudden struggle to be set
free told Jed that the trusted old bay had led them
unerringly back to the compound. He released his hold on
the dog and let him slip to the deep snow that would have
exhausted the dog had he been forced to make his own
way through it these past few miles. Suddenly the bay
stopped, causing the mare to bump into his rump. She
shied backwards and to the side before Jed placed a reas-
suring hand on her neck, calming her. Jed dismounted and
gave the mare's reins a gentle tug, moving her to the bay's
side. He could hear the nervous pawing and whinny of the
pack horse in the shed and groped blindly along the corral
rails for a moment before his hand struck the hard, cold
iron hasp of the gate, It was only minutes before he had
led the horses and Jenny to the safety of the horse shed.
Whiskey tumbled in through the half open door behind
them. Jed lit the hurricane lamp that hung just inside the
door as Jenny dismounted and collapsed, a lump of bulky
sheepskin and snow, onto the earth next to a stall. In the
sudden flare of the light, she saw Jed's ill-defined image,
eyebrows and beard heavily encrusted with ice, snow
mantling his hat and shoulders. He turned toward her and
smiled with relief. His smile caused his chapped lower lip
to split, sending a rivulet of blood down the crust on his
beard, staining it red. He reached absently to touch the lip,
examined the tip of his finger, and turned to attend the
horses.

Only when the horses were rubbed dry and in their
stalls munching contentedly on their hay, did he return to
Jenny's side. Whiskey lay curled next to her. Without
speaking, Jed knelt and secured a short length of rope to
the dog's collar. He rose, stretching a hand to Jenny. For a
moment she hesitated, but then reached for it, half expecting it to be cold and clammy like her father's. It wasn't.
It was rough and callused, but warm, and once she was on
her feet it gave her small, delicate hand a gentle squeeze.
Her eyes rose to search his face once more, but he's already turned toward the door.

Jed put out the burning wick of the oil lamp, wetting his fingers in his mouth and crushing the life out of the ragged edge of the wick. Once again he extended his hand. This time Jenny took it eagerly. His light grip could not mask the power of work hardened muscle that Jenny could feel beneath the roughened skin. Jed tied the loose end of the rope from Whiskey's collar around his other hand and, when the shed door was latched securely, called to the dog, "Find home, son, go on, find home!"

The trio stumbled and slipped toward the snug little cabin, unable to see the tiny bastion from the storm that waited for them a mere twenty yards away. Jennifer clung desperately, with both hands, to the strong arm that pulled her along. It seemed an eternity to her, but suddenly they were behind the door, safe inside the cabin. Still holding onto Jed's arm, Jenny's eyes sought his and stared at him with a soft gaze. Jed felt the shudder run through her and saw her eyes begin to cloud as her mind began to grasp the stark reality of all that had passed during the last three weeks. Jed's reaction was involuntary, a throwback to some earlier time. She felt him pull her close and envelop her with those strong arms. She buried her face in his chest and clung to him as tenaciously as life. Twice he had stolen her back from the clutches of the Dark Angel to whom her own foolishness had threatened to carry her. Twice she was grateful and, as the realization of it penetrated her mind, she released herself in a flood of tears.

It was well that Jenny did not see Jed's face, for an expression of confusion crossed it as his perplexed mind sought to sort out the conflicting memories. It had been a long time since he had held a woman and felt the feelings that hovered within him now. Yet, he was unwilling to allow those feelings just now, afraid to release his hold on the memories, afraid to chance the reopening of old wounds, most of all afraid that history repeated itself. He would have to keep Jenny at arm's length to avoid commitment, but that was impossible now as he rocked her gently, seeking to quiet the sobs that racked her. He raised

a hand to touch the soft hair that hung below the collar of
the coat, touching its fine silkiness. He thought of Cassie
and his hand shot away from the hair as if it had touched
fire.

Jenny felt his muscles tense and sensed the change.
There was nothing she could do, the moment had passed.
She disengaged herself and sat in the chair, turning her
head away from Jed. Jed busied himself at the fireplace,
building a roaring fire to drive the cold from the cabin.
There was an unnatural silence in the room, even Whiskey
lay quietly beside the hearth, shifting his eyes from the girl
to the man. Of all the inhabitants, only he knew what he
felt, loyalty and respect for the man and affection for the
girl. As Jed looked at the dog he thought that it must surely
be easier to be an animal than a human, and then he
laughed at himself. Man was just another animal. He just
happened to be possessed of a mind that could make
problems where none existed.

Jenny's mind had another, more practical side and, as
she looked through the little window in the door at the
raging storm outside, it manifested itself. She knew instinctively that she was trapped here and that learning to get
along with this man was necessary for survival. That meant
learning to trust and depend on him, and he on her. So far,
she knew, she hadn't given him any reason for trust. She
knew that he must have viewed her as a capricious and
foolish girl. She was more than that, but she would have to
prove it to him. There was another thing, Jenny had never
felt so drawn to any other man. It wasn't just the assurance
with which he moved, nor the rugged good looks. There
was something else, something that had fire to it, something that wasn't tangible. If there was to be an understanding between them, if nothing else, then Jenny would
have to begin. She sighed softly, shucked the coat, and began telling her story to Jed's back.

Jed did not interrupt, and, at first, he did not even turn
to face her. When he did he could see the intensity in her
face. She had never lost her memory, she had just not

trusted him. When she got to the part about MacKelvy, he understood why. Jennifer was succinct and to the point. The tale was not long in the telling. At its end, Jenny searched his face for a reaction. His face was stony, but he dropped his gaze when her eyes sought his and turned to add wood to the fire. Jenny watched his fluid movements, the economy of motion, wasting no effort. In relief she laughed. It was the first time she had done so in weeks and the first time Jed had seen her do it. It floated lightly to him and touched him with velvet softness. She rose from the chair and walked toward him.

"I'm glad that's over, aren't you?" she asked.

Before he had a chance to reply, she had raised on her tip toes and brushed his lips lightly with hers. He felt the color rising in his cheeks and sat down heavily on the hearth.

"That was just a thank you," she said simply as she sat, folding her legs beneath her in a way only women seem to be able to do. "I didn't mean to embarrass you."

"It's all right," Jed said irritably, making no effort to move away from her hand that rested lightly on the back of his neck. "Jenny, I don't think you have any idea of what you've let yourself in for. Life out here is a total commitment, it has to be just to survive." He'd noticed the look in her eyes. "My life is a total commitment."

"There's no room for a woman?"

"No," he said flatly.

"I don't believe that, and neither do you," she said with calm assurance.

"How long do you think it will be before you feel the resentment you've already showed me? If it were just because of MacKelvy I would understand, but it runs deeper than that. No, I think you were right to start with, you are just feeling grateful. It'll pass."

"You told me not to judge so easily once. Can it be that you are judging now?"

"No. I'm asking you to look inside yourself."

"I did. On the way back today."

"That was a stress situation," Jed replied. "Try it when that kind of pressure isn't on."

Jenny grew silent. Maybe there was something in what he said. Maybe she was reacting out of gratitude. How much did she know about Jed? Very little. If he were different from MacKelvy, as he claimed, perhaps she should ask for an explanation. "Tell me about yourself, maybe it will help me decide."

"It's a dull story," Jed replied, looking around slowly, and added, "I don't see how it's going to help you."

"Now you're making my decisions," she chided. "Besides, you say you're different from MacKelvy and the others. I want to know how."

"All right," Jed acquiesced, "but you might not see the distinction. It's not black and white."

"I have to know."

"Okay," Jed sighed in resignation. "I'll try to be as direct as possible. I differ from MacKelvy in that I don't kill for pleasure. I'm not saying that there is no pleasure in the kill, only that pleasure is not the purpose. MacKelvy is the kind that would kill a songbird just to see the feathers fly."

"And you wouldn't?" Jenny interjected.

"No, and don't interrupt. This is hard enough. I see myself as nothing more than a sophisticated predator, with many advantages over other predators and many failings unknown to them. I trap because I have to have something to trade for the things I need. Despite what you may think or what you may have read, it is no more cruel than what animals do to each other in the wilds." Jenny opened her mouth, but Jed cut her off with a wave of his hand. "One of the things I need is some sense of financial independence, but I trap according to populations. If something reduces a species, I trap accordingly. I figure that if I manage it properly, these woods will have changed very little by the time I am dead. There, I'm done. I'll leave it to you to make sense of it."

Jenny thought for a moment and then spoke. "I guess that I can accept that as a logical explanation, but it doesn't tell me why you do it."

"I never said I'd explain my reasons."

"But you don't live up here all the time, do you?"

"Yes. That is except for short trips to town."

"But why? It's not normal to live like a hermit. Something had to make you come here."

Jed smiled wryly. He'd never thought of himself as a hermit, but he had to admit that the term had merit. He did not answer.

"I mean, it's so isolated here."

"You've just answered your own question," he said cryptically.

"I don't understand."

"I didn't think you would."

"Are you hung up on the man against the wilderness thing or something?"

Jed chuckled. "Man against the wilderness? That kind of attitude would have earned me an early grave. There's no way to go against the wilderness, only with it . . . if you've got the skill and adaptability. And only for so long as the wilderness will tolerate you. I'm here because I want to be and I'll make no excuses for it."

"I'm not asking you to. I'd like to stay for awhile at least. If you'll let me that is."

Jed jerked at thumb at the storm beyond the window. "I don't think I have much choice in the matter. I will tell you this, there's a possibility that someone will come through here to check on my operation. If that happens I suspect that you will be more than ready to return to the comfort and security of the civilized world. Until then, we'll have to make the best of it."

That ended the discussion. Jed sank into the familiar silence, retreating quickly from conversation. It made him uncomfortable to have to explain to anyone his life, and particularly to an idealistic young woman with whom he was now forced to share his small cabin. He saw tensions ahead that could only lead to problems. Jennifer contented herself to bide her time and plan her strategy. The man was not made of stone and he was hiding something. Of that she was sure. Whatever it was, it wasn't anything sinister, rather it was like a warm ember that he kept within him, perhaps afraid to let go. She settled for the calm feeling that time would work for her.

CHAPTER 14

URSUS HORRIBILIS, the horrible bear, the unafraid giant, the undisputed master of the forest. Grizzly to most, so named because of the white-tipped hairs of his coat which make him appear frosted or "grizzled." Once a great predator of the high plains and mountains, the insurgence of human population has driven him into the remote areas of the Rocky Mountain regions. Now a rare and awesome sight, he is protected by law and can be taken as a game animal only by special permit in special areas. The bear knows not of laws, other than those of his own making, and is still known to come into conflict with man.

There are reasons for these conflicts. The bear is a wide-ranging but territorial animal creating, therefore, conflicts within its own population whenever there is a growth in its numbers. The new, or territorially defeated animals must move on. If they establish territories within that claimed by man, conflict is inevitable. If man establishes himself within the bear's territory conflict is not necessarily inevitable, but it is still very possible. A grizzly's very nature is to protect his territory against all comers. If he is reluctant to leave when man has intruded, one or the other will eventually be driven out . . . or perish.

The grizzly padded around the clearing where MacKelvy's camp had stood. It was deserted now. It had been for several days now. He sniffed at the traces of odor that still lay on the ground, sorting them one from the other. When the odor of the man, the pursuer, sprang from the earth, the hackles on his mighty shoulders stood. His great shaggy head wagged side to side as his eyes grew red at the memory. A massive paw reached out and slapped an upright log to which the odor clung. It careered across the clearing, coming to rest forty feet away in a slight hollow, its bark ripped away by four inch long, deadly claws.

The icy breeze that drifted from the north ruffled the bear's shaggy coat. He stood and pointed his nose toward it. The smell of a storm carried to him. He dropped to the ground and turned reluctantly homeward. Reluctantly because he still had no fat for protection against the long winter. Even had MacKelvy's bullet not bitten into his hip, he would have still been unready for sleep. The year had been dry and the berries few, grubs sparse, and prey scattered.

He moved deliberately, gauging the movement of the storm, hunting as he went. He pried mice and ground squirrels from their burrows, leaving monumental excavations for a single morsel. Half rotted stumps exploded at his touch and he greedily wolfed the tidbits that resided within. He grazed on dried grass, slapped a stupid grouse and ate it, feathers and all. Still he was ravenous, knowing that somehow his inner clock had not coincided with nature's, knowing that he would have to return to the hunt once the storm had passed.

The first flakes were flying in the stiff wind when the bear reached the foot of the hill where he had dug the earth from between the roots of a giant spruce for his den. He entered the warm, dark, leaf-lined confines with the knowledge that the long sleep of winter would not be his and he shifted in restlessness throughout the long storm.

When the winds abated and the final flurries faded, the grizzly clawed his way through the snow-blocked entrance and made his way out into the whitened brilliance of the wintry forest. Two days of forced confinement and intermittent sleep had revitalized him and left him with a gnawing hunger. He began his hunt.

The storm had forced the deer to yard up, the snow lay belly deep on the grandest buck. After two hours of wandering, the concentrated odor of the herd floated to the bear. He changed directions quickly, working his way toward the yard. On his final approach he could hear the milling stamp of their tiny feet. It was a good sound. Saliva flowed from his mouth and his tongue flicked at his nose.

He began his charge just forty yards from the herd and they scattered the instant they understood the danger. One fat young buck was knocked down in the confusion, he would never know the freedom of the forest again. A mighty blow crushed the bones in his neck with a loud snap and his last perception was the blur of the brown-silver monster whose charge carried him past the dying eyes. The long dark knives at the end of the bear's paws bloodied themselves as he ripped open the belly of the deer and gorged on the warm soft contents. He stayed with the carcass two days, driving the wolves from it whenever they came.

On the morning of the third day he chanced upon a doe and, not hungry for the moment, chased her for the sheer pleasure of it, savoring the scent of fear that rolled from her fleeing body. He stopped abruptly at the top of the hill, sending a small avalanche down the steep slope, his profile magnificent against the brilliant blue of the winter sky, and bellowed victoriously.

Because of his appetite he would extend his range to almost seventy five miles. Because of his leanness he would not sleep, but be consumed with the hunt this winter. And because of his unnatural behavior he would become one of the most feared and hunted animals of the north.

CHAPTER 15

A FULL DAY had passed since the end of the storm. In the gray light of early morning, Jed swallowed a final cup of coffee and looked at Jenny, her face illuminated in the glow of the oil lamp, as she cleared away the few dishes left from the breakfast. The time had come, the snows and bitter cold temperatures would make prime the fur of the animals he sought. He had four months to make a year's wages. There was no time for idleness from here on and, despite the reservations he had about leaving Jenny alone, there was work to be done. He pulled on a heavy coat, strapped on his snowshoes, and shouldered his pack. He whistled to Whiskey and the pair headed for the first leg of the trapline.

He stopped at the top of the first hill and looked back over the silent, white landscape. It was familiar territory, his domain. To the south and west he could see the gray-white plume of smoke from the cabin as it rose straight into the blue sky above the snow mantled trees. He thought momentarily of Jenny, her weak smile as she stood in the doorway of the cabin. He'd noticed the way she brushed her hair from her eyes and the little shrug she had given as she had closed the door against the cold. He had not wanted the responsibility, but he was saddled with it and he accepted that as fact, without rancor. He had started her education the second day of the storm. She now knew how to use the big double barreled twelve gauge. He hoped that she wouldn't have occasion to use it, but the knowledge that she was competent in its handling gave him a certain measure of confidence. He had to force her from his thoughts, the tortuous trail and the dangers that might lurk required his total concentration.

He reached the first set and jammed the butt of the small semi-automatic .22 caliber rifle into the snow where it stood like a sentinel while he worked. With painstaking care, he retrieved the trap from beneath the quilt of snow. He unfastened the small piece of wire that held its jaws open and placed it to the side. Using an old spatula, his hands clothed in cumbersome rubber gloves, he refilled the cavity with snow until it was an inch from the top, and replaced the trap. He reached into his pack, pulled out a small sack of dried leaves, and scattered a few over the trap. Using the spatula once again, he deftly covered the trap with a final, light layer of powder dry snow. The leaves and the residue of beeswax from the boiling process would keep the trap from icing up and failing when an animal stepped on the pan. He made sure that none of the chain that was wired to a drag, in this case a small bundle of brush, was exposed and visible. He used drags for the most part because they prevented an animal from getting anxious and chewing off a foot by giving him a sense of mobility. Most times the smaller animal, ermine, marten, and such, went into shock and froze to death quickly. Sometimes not, and the lead-weighted baton Jed carried was needed. The final act of brushing the snow to erase the sign as he left completed the process.

The day would become an exercise in redundancy, a continuation of the process. Leave the trail, find the set, make it catch-worthy, clean away the sign on the return to the trail, and move on. Most of the sets were trail sets, marked by the passing of animals, such as the first. Bait sets presented their own peculiar problems, but Jed was familiar with all the intricacies. The deadfalls would be set, their sensitive multipiece triggers of carved wood baited and ready, waiting to be filled. Jed worked with swift precision, breaking only for a short mid-day snack which he shared with Whiskey.

The moon had just risen above the eastern horizon when the pair broke the clearing. Whiskey, who had been on alert at the point all day, relaxed and broke into a trot, gaining the porch where filtered light spilled out from a window of the cabin. Jed's face broke into a smile, cracking the accumulation of brittle ice on his beard. It was nice to come back to a home with a cheery glow reaching out to greet him. He was more used to returning to a dark, empty cabin with the chill just beginning to creep in as the last embers of a banked fire were dying. He quickened his pace.

When she had closed the door, Jenny watched Jed disappear into the snow laden forest with that strange shuffling gait that was half run, half skate peculiar to snowshoeing. When she could see the man and dog no more, she suddenly felt the silence close in on her. Used to the busy sounds of city traffic, and more recently the bustling sounds of animals preparing for the winter in the forest, the wind in the trees, the lack of sound was eerie and alien. There is a fear that sometimes comes with utter silence, and it crept in on Jenny as she suddenly realized how totally alone she was. She ran to the fireplace, clinging to its warmth, holding to each sputter and pop of sap, seeking protection from the world without and the fears within. It was a primeval urge, very little changed from that felt by the earliest of men seeking the protection of the Promethean gift.

For what seemed a long time to the girl, Jenny sat by the fire feeding it splintered morsels, watching the embers drop to the floor of the chamber and die. The heat generated by her attention finally drove her back. Away from the roar of the fire, she could hear the squabble of jays and chickadees as they fought over the balls of suet that Jed kept hanging from the boughs of trees near the cabin. There was the muffled, but steady, stomp of the horses' hooves in the corral. All came with the brilliance of the sun as it cleared the ridge to the east. The sounds reassured Jenny and she shook off the visions that had been forming in her mind. In that instant she regained control of her mind, firmed her grasp on reality. If Jed had been there to watch, unseen, he would have uttered a satisfied chuckle. He had known many such moments, would know many more, as would Jenny. He would have been pleased at the girl's resiliency and her resourcefulness.

After spending a few moments at the frost decorated window gazing at the splendor of the winter world beyond, she busied herself within the log walls. For the first time she took stock of the cabin's interior. Jed was not the best of housekeepers, dust accumulated almost everywhere, there was a sort of carelessness about the way the two rooms were kept. Jenny searched the sole closet in the kitchen for rags and, finding none, turned to the spacious livingroom-bedroom. Under the bed she found a box that contained old pants, shirts, and assorted other articles of clothing that Jed had planned on mending or making use of when there was time. Somehow he never seemed to find that time and the torn garments always made do until he could buy new on his trips to town. Jenny made use of two shirts that were beyond repair.

She cleaned with a vengeance, drawing water from the well over which the cabin had been built, remembering Jed's instructions on priming the pump in the kitchen. When she came to the wall of books, she wondered if she dared remove them. She looked in wonder at the diversity in titles, pausing to scrutinize the collection of texts with their well worn covers. These were the heart of Jed's love of books, they had been read again and again. Checking the careful arrangement of the volumes on the shelves, Jenny decided that she had better wait and ask Jed's permission before disturbing them. When she was finished, it was early afternoon and Jed's small cabin had not shone like this since the final stages of its construction.

Jenny normally ate little for lunch and the small bowl of sugared oatmeal was more than enough to satisfy her appetite. She knew, however, that Jed's appetite was monstrous after a day of hard work, and she was determined to show him that she had some skills in the kitchen. She had seen him go to the cold house for meat and knew its location. She bundled herself against the cold and took the shotgun from its rack above the fireplace. Jed had told her never to leave the cabin without the gun and she had promised. She considered the weight of the gun an encumbrance where Jed considered it a comfort, but she did as she had been told. She paused to pat the horses in the corral and watch the birds that still bickered over the suet balls before going to the cold house. Once there, she unbarred the door, went inside, and selected a hefty roast hanging from the bent spike that served as a meat hook. There were several other pieces of meat that hung from the hooks, some had been smoked and the fragrance hung heavy in the small enclosure.

The firebox in the kitchen stove still held embers from this morning and Jenny built them up with new wood from the storage box against the far wall. She found a large pan and a few spices, combined the ingredients, and placed the roast in the oven. She laid the dried vegetables, flour, and sugar on the small cupboard. She would finish the preparations for the rest of the meal later.

She whiled away the remainder of the early afternoon by sorting through the box of discarded clothes. Some were piled for rags, some to be repaired or made over for her own use. She would ask Jed for the necessary tools this evening. Such tasks, she hoped, would occupy her time during his absences and prevent the recurrence of the thoughts that had plagued her in the early morning. As the sun dipped low, Jenny lit the oil lamp on the table and the hurricane lamp that hung by the stove in the kitchen. She finished the preparations for dinner.

When Jenny heard Whiskey's paws on the porch she knew that Jed had returned. She ran to the window like an expectant child, nervous and excited. Jed was crossing the open space between the forest edge and the cabin, the frost of his own breath lying heavy on his beard and shining in the light of the moon. She opened the door to greet him. He answered her and bent over to take the snowshoes from his feet. She was a little disappointed at the brevity of his reply, but tried not to show it.

Jed entered the cabin, rubbing the cold from his hands vigorously. He did not notice the change in the cabin immediately, nor the smell of the roast, for the cold was so strong upon him that all else was beyond his concern. It had been that last mile that had done it. It didn't concern him, it would work itself out by the fire. His mind was already at work on the final leg of the trapline and in his preoccupation he did not see the discouragement in Jenny's face. He walked to the fire, working the stiffness from his fingers. Only when he had completed the warming ritual did he turn away from the fire. The smell of the roast finally made it through the thawing passages of his nose. He ran his eyes around the interior of the cabin, shaking his head. The logs hadn't shone like this since before he'd put the finishing touches on the home.

Jenny took Jed's silence as a sign of disapproval and sank back into a minor depression. They ate dinner with only a modicum of conversation. Jenny still avoided asking questions about his work, she had no desire to reopen the arguments. After so long a time as a bachelor, with only that brief time that had been spent with Cassie, Jed was at a loss to express what he felt. He still wanted to keep the distance between himself and the girl. For four years he had avoided any deep personal relationships, it was the only way he knew how to protect himself. He was aware that Jenny was withdrawing into her shell once more, but what was he supposed to do?

Jenny finally broke the silence as Jed was filling the cherrywood pipe that Pete had given to him. "I'm sorry," she said plaintively.

Jed stopped filling the pipe and turned, asking in a puzzled tone, "Sorry for what?"

"For doing things without asking first . . . I thought you would be pleased."

"I am . . ." Jed stammered. "What makes you think I'm not?"

"You have a funny way of showing it," she replied.

"I guess I'm not used to having anyone around. I'm sorry, I guess I should have said something."

"There's still time."

Jed shuffled his feet and looked at the floor. It had been a long time since anybody had reproached him for his manners and he felt uncomfortable. "All right, the place looks great and the dinner was just fine," he said gruffly.

"Yeah, sure." There was dejection in Jenny's voice and an angry, hurt look on her face. This was hardly the kind of compliment she had expected. It had the cold quality of a thanks, but no thanks.

Jed's head snapped up and there was a flash of anger in his eyes. "What in hell do you want from me?!" he demanded.

Jenny looked back defiantly at him, and then, as her illusory fantasy about the way things could have been began to crumble, burst into tears and ran into the kitchen. Jed looked after her in frustration. He guessed what she wanted, but felt unable to deliver. It would open up possibilities that he did not want to consider right now. His anger faded and was replaced by an emptiness.

That night, as he lay in his sleeping bag by the fireplace, he could hear her crying softly in the bed. More than anything he wanted to go to Jenny, to comfort and hold her, to feel the touch of a woman, the pleasures. Cassie's memory kept him from it and, with a great deal of difficulty, he mastered the urge and imposed that iron curtain of self-control. As Jenny had sought the protection of the fire, so Jed sought the strength of mind that sealed the pain of memory inside a cold wall. There it could not hurt him.

For two days Jed returned to the cabin to find it much as he had before Jenny had come abruptly into his life. She did nothing, preferring to sit in the willow and hide chair by the fireplace, not even stirring when the fire began to die. She refused to talk and ate only when Jed's anger made her yield. Even then she did little but pick at the food on her plate. She seemed to have lost hope and, in a way,

she had. She no longer felt confident that she could turn
Jed's feelings around. She was unable to cope with the lack
of attention her looks had always brought her. It became
easy to let depression feed her mind and the fact that her
time of the month was now here did not help matters.

Jed recognized the signs. He decided that it would be
better to ease off for a while, she wasn't responding when
he tried to make her angry, to give her back some fight. He
continued to run his trapline. The catch was exceptionally
good. The early snows and the cumulative years of experience were paying off in a big way. He was happy when he
could forget the problems that clouded the tiny cabin while
he was in the woods, but knew as he returned home that
they would be waiting there for him. He did as he had
done before, he endured, knowing instinctively that something would jolt her out of it. It would happen, but in a
way that neither of them expected.

CHAPTER 16

THE INCESSANT ringing of the phone pried Raudsep from sleep. He groaned, turned over, and looked at the illuminated figures on his digital watch. It read three thirty. "Who in hell can that be?" he growled as he reached for the receiver. "Yeah?"

"Jim?"

"Yeah . . . who is this?"

"Sorry to wake you. O'Malley here. We got a problem in the area I thought you better know about . . ."

"Jesus Christ, O'Malley . . . couldn't it wait 'til morning?"

"I expect it could . . . just thought you might want to get your livestock in," the constable said evenly. "I'm over at Simpson's right now. Seems a grizzly did a job on their dairy herd."

Raudsep sat up and swung his legs over the edge of the bed, scratching the back of his head. Simpson's was just a short mile up the dirt road from his place. "You sure it's a griz?" he asked suspiciously.

O'Malley's answer was irritable. "Of course I'm sure. I was born in this province, eh. I know the sign when I see it."

"All right, all right. Don't get your dander up, just doesn't figure that a grizzly would be about now. Should be denned up." Raudsep thought for a moment. "Well, I guess I'd better roust the boys and bring in the horses and mules. Damn it anyway!"

"Right, well I'll ring off then."

"Okay. Hey! You want me and the boys to come up that way in a little? Maybe the bugger is still hanging around. We could bring the sleds and some artillery."

111

"I suppose it would be okay. Old Simpson got a round off, but he thinks it went wild. Doubt if he's still about, but we could give it a look, eh?"

"Yeah, give me an hour." Raudsep replaced the receiver and looked over at his young wife who stretched languidly. He reached over and fondled her. "Keep that warm, will you? I've got to go out."

Jeanne slapped at his hand playfully. "What'sa matter? Who was that on the phone?"

"Constable O'Malley, R.C.M.P., seems he's got a situation he can't handle," Raudsep exaggerated. "He had to call out the calvary."

"How come you can't say 'cavalry'? Didn't you learn anything in school?" Jeanne teased.

"Aw shaddup . . . I learned enough to keep you in satin sheets and black lace."

"That's all you ever think about." Jeanne turned over and pulled up the covers.

Raudsep patted her soft, well-formed behind and said, "Yeah, and you love every minute of it."

He dressed quickly and hit the switch that turned on the floodlights in the main yard. By the time he had crossed the snowy expanse to the bunkhouse, the adrenalin was flowing. They didn't get much chance to go after game, particularly something like a grizzly, after the season was past. It gave him a feeling of vigor. He stomped up the stairs of the bunkhouse porch, turned the knob, and kicked the door open. "MacKelvy, you sonofabitch! Get your ass outta bed! The rest of you men get with it!" he roared.

Someone threw a boot at him and yelled, "Get off it, eh?! What the hell is goin' on?"

Raudsep caught the boot neatly and returned it. Above the grumbles, he let them know who was boss. "Can it!" And when they grew quiet, "O'Malley just rang me up. Grizzly just hit Simpson's. Fred, you, Bart, and Jimmy get the stock into the corrals. Put as many in the barn as you can fit. MacKelvy!" Raudsep put a boot against the man's rump and pushed him out of bed. "Damn it MacKelvy! How the hell come you always gotta be drunk when something happens?!"

"Jesus! What in Christ's name is yer beef?" MacKelvy swore, scrambling to his feet and unclenching his fists.

"Get a cup of Joe and get sobered up. We gotta get out the sleds and head up to Simpson's place. I know ya didn't hear it the first time, so I'll repeat it. Grizzly hit the herd at his farm. O'Malley wants some troops and we're it. You and the guys that aren't bringing in the stock break out the machines and get them gassed up. I'll meet you out front in a half an hour."

MacKelvy scratched his beard and sat down on the edge of the bunk. He watched as Raudsep walked out the door and hurried back to the main house. "All right," MacKelvy hollered, "Buck, Sam, and John . . . grab yer pants and get out them sleds. Boss'll be rarin' to go when he gets done."

"Gets done what?" one of them yelled.

"Aw shit, Fred, you know every time he gets his blood up he gets horny. He's just goin' back to get good an' warm 'fore we get started."

"I wouldn't mind warmin' up that sweet little piece he keeps," MacKelvy growled. "Bet she'd like it too."

"MacKelvy, you'd go for a bitch in heat if the mood hit you," Sam rejoined.

"Damn right . . . but she's gotta be a purebred, I don't want no mutts." A boot flew through the air once more, hitting MacKelvy on the shoulder. "Dammit Buck! If you don't keep that damn boot to yerself, I'm gonna make you eat it!"

There was raucous laughter that permeated the room and MacKelvy basked in it. This was the way he liked it, the crude humor, the rough laughter of men. He was more than one of them, he was their leader. Raudsep thought he was, but MacKelvy knew better. He knew the jokes traded behind the boss's back and encouraged them, joining in the laughter every time. He rose from the edge of the bunk and imitated Raudsep's walk, exaggerating the strut, hitching up his britches.

"Buck, where's my goddam coffee?" he mimicked.

"Here boss, here boss," Buck groveled.

"That's a good boy, there now, bend over."

Buck did as he was bid and MacKelvy delivered a swift, bit painless kick to his posterior and Buck crawled away, making faces at the men as he went.

"Now then," MacKelvy continued, "I think I'd better run up to the house." He put a hand to the side of his mouth and talked around it. "Gotta see if the old pecker still works, eh?"

The room exploded with laughter. Buck rolled on the floor, holding onto his sides, kicking his feet. MacKelvy stood at the far end of the room, his legs spread far apart, taking it all in. He gave them a few minutes and then cut it off.

"All right!" he roared. "Let's can it and get goin'. We don't want to keep the man waitin'."

When Raudsep came to join them, the snowmobiles were purring quietly in the yard. He walked to the big, empty one up front, got astride it, and waved an arm, signalling the men to follow, as he revved up the engine. O'Malley saw the bobbing lights of Raudsep's party as soon as they turned onto the road. He swallowed from the cup that Marie Simpson had given him. She made the best coffee in these parts, he thought, not like the crap you got at the cafe in town. He hated to leave it, but he didn't want Raudsep and his rowdies running amuck out there either. He would go with them. He was waiting out front when they zoomed into the Simpson's yard.

"Halooo O'Malley!" Raudsep hailed. "Here comes the calvary!"

O'Malley made himself swallow a retort and grimaced. "Come on, I'll show you the way."

"Oh crap, O'Malley," Raudsep said, ignoring the sniggers behind him. "Don't be so stiff, this could be fun."

"Simpson didn't find anything funny or fun about it, I'm

afraid," O'Malley said. "Seems the beast slaughtered six head of good Gurnseys. Let's go have a look, eh?"

O'Malley led the way to the small pasture to the northeast where the remains of the cows lay scattered on the ground. The men lost their sense of humor when they saw what had been done. MacKelvy knelt beside one of the dead animals and studied the track next to her. He measured it with his hand, studied the shape. He wasn't sure, grizzly track looked pretty much the same, and yet there was a nagging feeling in his mind. Raudsep sauntered up and leaned over.

"Well, MacKelvy, what do you think?"

"Dunno. It's a big un, all right. Probably a boar, never seen a sow's print this big. Looks a lot like the track of that one I shot up by camp . . . Naw, it can't be, I know I hit him better than that. He probably just curled up and died somewhere. Gotta be another one." There was a lack of conviction in his voice.

"Hell," Raudsep said, "you know damn well that it was over sixty miles from here that you shot that one. There isn't a bear around that'll travel that far."

MacKelvy looked up at him. There was a malicious smile on his face. "Winter bear will. A winter bear'll do a lot that ain't normal."

"Winter bear?" Raudsep replied ignorantly. "What the hell do you mean, 'winter bear'?"

MacKelvy shook his head and chuckled gruffly. "That's what the old breed calls them down to the Diamond Bar. He run into one once before, back in fifty two or there about. Likes to talk about it when he gets sauced."

"Damn it, MacKelvy, skip the background, just tell me what it means."

"Means a bear that don't sleep away the winter. He stays out and makes a problem out of himself. Does stuff like this," MacKelvy pointed at the carcasses. "Not very common, but they sure as hell get remembered."

"Well then," Raudsep said, "maybe we'd better get on to him right away. We don't need any more damage done."

"There ain't no reporters here now," MacKelvy answered sarcastically. "You don't have to give a speech."

"Damn you MacKelvy! You don't have any call to talk to me that way," Raudsep shot back. "You work for me, remember?!"

"Yeah, I remember. I'll tell ya this, though, it won't do to go after him in the night."

"What's the matter, MacKelvy? You afraid?"

"Only a fool would try to take that animal at night. We get into the woods and he'd have the advantage and I somehow don't see him bein' cooperative."

"Maybe I ought to talk to Price. At least he's dealt with that kind of animal before," Raudsep said, trying to anger MacKelvy into doing something. He did not want to be made a fool of in front of O'Malley. He thought he would be if they didn't go after the bear right now.

"Maybe you should," MacKelvy returned hotly. "He'd tell ya the same thing."

O'Malley walked up. He'd gotten the drift of the conversation and decided that it would be better to put a stop to the altercation before it got started. "Jim, I don't think there's any point in doing anything more tonight. Like I said, Simpson got off a shot. More than likely the bear high-tailed it. Maybe you can get Tom up in the chopper tomorrow morning and scout the area. If he's around, you'll be better able to get a fix on him."

"Yeah, maybe that would be better," Raudsep agreed, glad that there was a graceful way out of the situation. "Maybe he won't be back."

"Maybe, let's hope so," O'Malley said. "Let's call it a night then, eh?"

It was six thirty when they got back to the barn. Raudsep put in a call to Tom Phillips before he crawled into bed. Tom had agreed to take him up, if the weather didn't take a nasty turn, and he'd be ready to go at eleven. That gave Raudsep time for a little sleep. He set the alarm for nine thirty and was snoring loudly within minutes.

When the alarm went off he reached out and fumbled

for the switch, rubbed his eyes, and got stiffly out of bed.
The inside of his mouth tasted like it had been walked
through. When he reappeared from the bathroom, he felt
better. He was fastidious about his appearance and had
taken time to shower and shave. He passed Jeanne on his
way to the spacious kitchen. She was watching television,
one of those early morning soaps they picked up on the
dish that was on the roof. He paused to kiss her on top of
the head and told her he was going out. She didn't ask him
where, he rarely told her anyway. After grabbing a biscuit
and some cold bacon, he filled a steel thermos with coffee
and headed out the door for the new Surburban. It took
only a few minutes to drive to the private airstrip where
Tom and the other two bush pilots kept their planes. Tom
had the chopper warmed up and waiting.

"Let's go see if we can spot him, Tom," Raudsep
shouted above the *whump, whump* of the rotors.

"I'm ready if you are . . . get in."

"He really tore up Simpson's cows," Raudsep said as he
buckled himself in.

"Yeah, so I heard," Tom said. "I talked to O'Malley over
coffee this morning. Guess that really wipes Simpson out.
O'Malley said he was talkin' about quittin' last night."

"Well, you know Simpson. He says he's gonna quit
farming every third week. Never does, probably never will.
Let's swing over his place and see if we can follow the
track for a while. It shouldn't be too hard to spot out in the
open."

"All right, but we'll lose it if he heads into timber, and I
bet he does."

"Wouldn't surprise me. We'll just fly in bigger and bigger circles then, like we did to spot game this fall."

The plowed line through the deep snow that marked
the grizzly's passage did indeed lead into the timber. Tom
and Jim followed their plan, but turned no further sign or
sighting. After spending little over an hour in the air, they
could see the approach of yet another squall line. There
was a storm brewing to the north again. Tom pointed at it.

"See that?" he asked.

"Yeah," Raudsep replied, "I see it."

"We better take the bird home. I don't want to get caught in those winds. If that develops, it'll wipe out any ground sign too. I don't think you'll be tracking him."

"Maybe not this time," Raudsep agreed.

"You think there'll be another?" Tom asked.

"I know there will be," Raudsep growled. He was determined that he'd find a way. He wanted the respect, however grudging, that had been in MacKelvy's voice when he'd talked about Bob Price last night. Yeah, he'd get his winter bear, and MacKelvy was just glory greedy enough to help him do it. He thought about his head guide malevolently. The man was easily used. MacKelvy would do the dirty work and Raudsep would take the credit, as usual.

CHAPTER 17

THE BEAR topped the rise and looked back on the lights that sped into the pasture. Once again he had run from the sound of gunfire, once more he had smelled burning cordite. This time there had been no pain. He had traveled long and hard to find game and he had found the big, stupid animals easy to bring down. There was no particular reason to kill more than one, he had just done it. The lights had stopped moving, but the bear knew that he must get to the protective cover of heavy timber. He gave out a little mewling sound and reluctantly left the rest of his meal to the two legged adversary.

He traveled swiftly, in a northerly direction. He could smell the storm that was brewing far to the north and was moving instinctively toward the den that was at the heart of his territory. The winds and snow came before he reached it. He was forced to den under a collection of blowdowns. He stayed there for two days while the storm raged and blew itself out. The storms became his ally, erasing the sign he left, trapping deer in small yards. Still, the effort required to locate prey and dispatch it consumed large quantities of energy. He maintained himself, little more.

His wanderings carried him gradually to the northwest, eventually bringing him to the river's edge two miles below Jed's clearing. He was hunting the burrows near the banks when he smelled the smoke from the cabin. He stopped and tested the breeze more carefully. Mixed with the smoke was the scent of the stew Jed had put on to cook slowly over the main fire as he worked his trapline. The bear began to slowly work his way toward the clearing. He had learned to be cautious when he approached such odors, they usually spelled the presence of man, his two legged adversary. He circled the clearing twice, stopping often to test the air.

The bear's second circle brought him closer to the outhouse that stood downslope from the cabin. There a strong odor attracted him. Mixed with the stench of decay that weighed heavily on his sensitive nose was a weaker, but more pungent scent, tainted with blood. He approached the small wooden structure tentatively at first, growing bolder with each step as the scent drew him like some powerful, unseen magnetic force.

When the door did not yield to the light touch of his nose, his massive paws tore it off its hinges. There was nothing inside, and his agitation grew. The scent hung suspended, intangible, and irritating in its elusiveness. His shoulder scraped on the tip of an exposed nail that had not been totally clinched and he swatted at it irritably. The front left portion of the building disappeared in an instant, leaving ragged wooden edges and a scattering of splintered planks. The odor persisted.

The bear turned his attention to the cabin, eyeing the structure balefully. Wisps of smoke darted from the chimney and hurtled southward, held low by the pressure cell of weather. He stalked to the western flank of the building, tested the strength of its walls with long, raking claws, and followed around its sides, probing for a weakness. The aroma of stew escaping through the tiny cracks in the door signaled that he had found it. He hesitated at the scraping sound from within. Then that sweet, blood-tinged fragrance floated to him from the interior and he waited no longer.

Jenny had seen him. Right after the sound of breaking wood, she had seen him. He had turned from the broken outhouse and stood, his stance peculiar to those of his kind, almost squatting on his haunches, yet with a perfectly vertical spine, nose pointed skyward sifting the breeze, and forelimbs dangling slightly forward of his sides. Even at a distance, Jenny could see the sunlight playing across the blackness of the long claws.

When he dropped to the ground he swung his head back and forth, emitting a spume of breath that marked a grunt that was barely audible to Jenny at this distance. When the massive head stopped swinging, the grizzly's baleful gaze engaged Jenny's. Jed had told her that bears were notoriously nearsighted, and yet the animal's gaze held hers hypnotically. Only when he began his deliberate advance on the cabin was Jenny able to break the spell, and the fascination turned quickly to horror.

Jeff's warning in the woods that day that seemed so long ago leapt into her mind. She immediately understood the reason for the bear's attack on the outhouse. When she thought of the short time that had passed since she had visited the small structure, terror began to set in. She had not even bothered to carry the shotgun as Jed had instructed her to. What if she had been there when the bear had come? She dared not even consider it. The bear had begun to move along the back of the cabin and Jenny tore her eyes away from the single tiny window. The main window of the cabin was shuttered to keep the cold from the cabin. There was no time to drop the final shutter that would add protection.

Fear does different things to different people. It freezes some, causes others to flee, and makes a small few fighting mad. After the initial shock, Jenny's mind cleared. She rushed to the fireplace and built up the fire before reaching for the double-barreled gun that hung on the iron pins above it. On the mantle she found the box of double ought buckshot and fumbled a couple of shells out. She had an impulse to rush out and confront the beast, but Jed's training kept her riveted to the hearth. If the bear gained entrance she would have a clear field of fire. Her grip tightened on the stock. She waited.

At mid-day Jed had broken his affair with the trapline. The venison in the cold house was dwindling fast, much faster than when only he had drawn upon it. It had been one of the problems he had envisioned when Jenny had come. He had cached his furs and pack in a small rock cave he had constructed for that purpose two years ago. He worked his way along the game trail, following the trench dug by thin legs and dragging bellies of the deer. He moved noiselessly on the surface of deep powder snow, the leather webbing of his snowshoes sinking out of sight just beneath the surface, cradling his beloved thirty-thirty gently. There was an icy grin frozen on his face, partly from squinting into the sun, partly from the joy he felt. Hunting was good for Jed, a sort of renewal, a confirmation that he still was.

He reached a point just below a rise and carefully peeped over the top. There was a small trampled area where deer had been in yard. There were none there now, only the bloodstains and scattered bones of one of their number. Jed levered a shell into the chamber and set the hammer at quarter cock. He searched the surrounding area for the silent, ghosting shapes of wolves. He saw none. At the yard he read the sign as easily as most people read books. The drama played out before him. There had been wolves, track and bone cracked for the marrow told him that. But he had to look beyond the yard for confirmation of the partially obliterated tracks that lay beneath all the rest. When he found the trench leading into the yard, he used extreme care in excavating the new snow that filled it. He brushed the last inch away with a branch cut from a spruce. There it was, and there could be no doubt. It was grizzly track.

Jed rocked back on his heels, considering the situation. He feared not the wolves that ran in great packs, they rarely caused him problems, but a grizzly out in the middle of winter was a serious matter. Like wolverines, they would use a trapline for a dependable food source if they located it. Then too, he had to consider the proximity of his own abode to the location of this kill site. Little more than three miles straight line travel, five if you followed the trail. He doubted if the bear would bother, from the track in, this animal made its own trail. It was obvious that the bear had stayed with his kill for some time, Jed found the silver-tipped hairs in the trammeled area of the yard. The questions was, where had he gone?

Jed followed the exit trail for a short distance, determined its general direction to be southeast, and turned back towards home. He was too aware that his horses would present the bear with an ideal target. Today they would be all right, he had left them locked in the shed, but there would be other days when they would have to be out in the corral for exercise. He couldn't stay with them all the time. Maybe he'd get lucky and the bear would drift off and den up like he was supposed to. He thought for the first time of Jenny, remembering that it was her time. He tested the direction of the wind. If the bear had continued on the same path, he would eventually intercept the scent. Jed swore and made tracks for the cache of furs on the main trail. He'd left Whiskey there to guard them, not wishing to put the dog through the strain of deep snow travel. Speed seemed suddenly necessary.

Jenny's spine arched at the screech of claws being dragged down the wooden planks of the door. It seemed as if all her senses had become more acute, for the rank smell of the boar grizzly permeated the cabin. The odor of urine and the stench of carrion on the animal enveloped her and, in spite of herself, she cried out for Jed. The depression of the last few days was replaced in her mind by fear and anger. She knew what motivated the bear, and she prayed that the door would hold, and vowed that she would not depart without a fight.

Her piercing shriek served only to anger the bear, who now tore at the door. A splinter caught in his pad, sinking deep into the tissues with its ragged edge. He bellowed with rage. Jenny's second scream was punctuated by the shattering of glass as a huge forepaw smashed through the open part of the front window. Jenny thumbed the safety and raised the gun as the bear's face filled the opening. His eye caught the glint of the fire on the barrel and he retreated instantly, but not before the explosion rocked the cabin and a .32 caliber pellet bored under the skin of his left eye. The heavy bone of the orbit stopped it from doing serious damage.

There was a brief moment of silence after the first shot and Jenny thought she might have killed the bear. The grizzly silenced the thought with a thunderous blow to the door. Jenny could see the planks give with every impact, but it held. Calmly, almost as if she was detached from the scene, she opened the breach of the gun, slipped the spent shell from the chamber, and replaced it with a fresh load. At least she'd have two chances.

Jed was a quarter mile from the cabin when he heard the flat report of the shotgun. It was followed by the bellow of an enraged bear. Sound carried clearly in the crisp air. Whiskey broke into a run the instant the sounds carried to him, but Jed's voice checked him. Jed continued his deliberate pace that would carry him to the edge of the clearing within five minutes. The thought of approaching faster did not enter his mind, the expenditure of such energy would leave him winded and probably spoil his aim. In that condition he would be of no use to himself or Jenny. He knew the cabin. The bear could not gain entrance though any of the windows, they were too small. The only possibility was the door and Jed trusted its construction to hold off the animal for some time. He had no doubts that it would eventually yield, and he wondered how long the bear had been trying it as the sound of the blows carried to him.

"Whiskey! Heel . . . that's a good boy," Jed's voice was calm.

Jed approached through the dense stand of trees, skirting to the south of the clearing. He could see the bear now, it was working at the door, prying chunks from the planks. Jed wanted to have the advantage of position without risking a round penetrating the small cabin. The fading of the sun into the chill of the evening horizon turned the wind capriciously and Jed's scent carried to the bear. Whiskey emitted a low growl, inching forward with fangs bared. The advantage was lost. The bear, flanked on two sides, chose flight and his great bounds carried his bulk rapidly from the clearing. Jed didn't waste a shot, for only chance would have carried the bullet to its mark, and Jed had no desire to face a wounded grizzly. He let the rifle butt slide from his shoulder and slowly emerged from the thicket. There would be another day.

When he was half way to the porch, Jed called out in a loud voice, "Hey! Hold your fire, I'm back!" He heard a hoarse reply from within, but couldn't make out the words. He continued to the door and waited for Jenny to slip the bar that held it closed. The door opened a crack and Jed quickly entered with his dog and closed the door behind him. Jenny still gripped the shotgun with her white-knuckled hands, and the strain on her face was obvious. Jed reached for the gun and gave it a gentle tug until she released it.

Jenny looked up at Jed, it seemed incredulous to her, but he was standing there with an enormous, boyish grin on his face. Her reaction was instinctive and she lashed out at him with both hands. "Damn you! Damn you to hell! You think it's funny?! I'll show you funny!" she screamed.

Despite himself, Jed burst into laughter as he picked Jenny's flailing arms from the air near his face and pinned them to her sides. Could this be the same young woman who had done nothing but mope around for the last week? Dodging her feet as Jenny kicked at him, Jed got his laughter under control. "Stop it, I'm not the enemy," he chuckled, "you already chased him off. Come on now, dagnabbit, calm down."

Slowly Jenny regained her composure and quit struggling. Jed released his hold on her and retrieved the shotgun from the bed where he had tossed it at the beginning of the fracas. He returned it to the pins above the fireplace mantle after ejecting the two live rounds. Jenny watched as he put the shells back in the box, shucked his coat, and sniffed the aroma of the stew. "And how was your day?"

she asked sarcastically.

"Obviously not as interesting as yours," he grinned.

"I still don't see anything funny about the situation."

"There isn't, but there is some joy. Look at it this way, you outlasted the bugger. He's gone and you're still here and your hide is intact. When you tell your grandchildren about it, I think you'll probably do it with a sense of humor."

"Grandchildren," she snorted.

"Grandchildren," Jed nodded sagely. He watched the progression of moods cross her face. "You would make a damn poor poker player," he said matter of factly.

Jenny stifled a giggle and then almost as suddenly broke into tears. "Oh God, oh God. It was horrible . . . he . . . he was going to kill me. My God, he was going to kill me!"

Jed had known that it was just a matter of time before this reaction set in and he was ready for it. "If he could have, he probably would have. But you were just as ready to kill him, weren't you? Come here," he said and she came to him. He folded her into his protective arms. "Maybe now you understand a little of what I was trying to tell you." He could feel her head nodding yes on his shoulder. "Well, I hope we can get along a little better now. Having someone here that I can't talk to is worse than having no one here at all. You've been driving me batty. I'll have to thank that bear when I get the chance . . . just kidding."

The tension between them didn't exactly dissolve, but the ice did begin to break a little. It would take more than a single incident to resolve the differences between them. Jenny had thought at one time that she could make Jed see things her way, change him to suit her ideals. She could see now that that would not be possible, for circumstances were dictating to her, not to him. She was the outsider and it was up to her to adapt. She thought about it consciously, but it wasn't really necessary. The mode of existence has a way of forcing change on individuals in a way that often goes unrecognized. Both Jenny and Jed were already victims, or rather subjects, of this process, and neither one of them would have been able to point to specific changes. Time is the ally of change and in the wilderness of the northwest there is an enormity of time.

CHAPTER 18

JED STOOD back to admire his handiwork. Except for the slight difference in the luster of the boards, there was no change in that appearance of the outhouse. The door was completely replaced with a stronger one. He still had to fix the main cabin door and broken windows, but they presented no problems.

The sun was high now and, despite the position of the mercury in the thermometer, it was warm. It was time to give Jenny her lesson. He returned to the cabin, stomping the snow from his boots on the porch. Tomorrow he would have to return to the trapline, and try to shoot a deer. He steeled himself for what must be done now.

Jed walked to the bench under the window and lifted the seat that concealed the storage space below. He moved a few things aside. There it was, still in its fleece-lined case. He lifted it with shaking hands. He had not touched it but to move it since that time almost five years ago. It brought with it many memories, some he'd rather have forgotten. He never really understood why he hadn't gotten rid of it, he just seemed unable to part with it. He laid it on the table and opened the big zipper. It was really a beautiful weapon, but it had no real place out here. Cassie had not thought it had any business in their home either. She had always called it a "people killer," and maybe it was. He touched the smooth grain of the polished walnut grips and ran his finger over the blued steel of the slide.

It was a Browning 9 millimeter automatic. It was perfectly balanced and deadly accurate. At one time Jed had had use for it, before he had known Cassie. He had kept it after because he appreciated the craftsmanship, and the feel of it. He had used to target practice with it and he remembered with a smile the tight little patterns it had made in the paper. Then he remembered the last time he had taken it out. That had not been an occasion to remember fondly.

ANOTHER TIME, ANOTHER PLACE: It had been a hard year and Jed and Cassie were struggling to hold onto their small farm. Still, Jed was optimistic. It had taken two years of hard work just to break even and it looked like they might make a small profit in the coming year. If only the bank would ride with them for a short few months.

Jed was tired, it had been a long day. There were rumors that there would be layoffs at the mill. It was true that the wood products industry had suffered many setbacks during the last six months, but there was still hope for the coming season. Jed hoped that his seniority and attentiveness to his job would keep him on. The headlights of his old battered Chevy pickup picked their way along the icy road and found the unplowed lane that led to his small house. Half bald tires found the ruts and the truck slithered up to the open shed. Jed pulled in and shut off the motor.

Cassie was usually at the door to greet him, but not tonight. Jed noticed that the door was open and wondered why when he did not see Cassie. She was not one to let the cold in and drive up the heat bill without good reason. She, even more than he, watched the budget closely and carefully. He yelled to Cassie before he reached the porch. There was no answer. He felt that cold come over him whenever something was wrong, and it was with him now. He quickened his pace.

Just inside the screened door of the porch he found Red, their big Irish setter. What he saw sickened him. He didn't hesitate over the ruined animal, but hurried past its bloody form. He found Cassie lying in the livingroom, naked and battered, just barely alive. He rushed to her side, unable to suppress the tears that flowed hotly down his cheeks. Her eyes had flicked open for a brief moment

when he had touched her face and the dull glow of pain
and terror that they reflected would stay with him for the
rest of his life.

He would never remember the wild ride to the hospital
in the nearby town, only carrying Cassie wrapped in a
blanket to the emergency room. The doctor came quickly,
took a quick check, and laid his stethoscope aside. He
grasped Jed's elbow firmly and ushered him from the
room, commanding him to sit on the bench in the hallway.
For two hours Jed remained, brushing aside the questions
of the two sheriff's officers, waiting for word from the surgeon who had been called in.

Jed had known the moment he had seen the droop of
the doctor's shoulders, it wasn't even necessary to hear the
words spoken. Something in Jed snapped. The officers had
not seen the look in his eyes and they made the mistake of
turning their backs to question the surgeon. Jed slipped
away, running to the pickup in the parking lot, the hate
foaming up in his soul. Without knowing who he was
looking for or even what might distinguish the criminals
from others, he began prowling the roads. The Browning
that usually lay beneath the seat of the pickup lay in his
lap. They hadn't even allowed him a proper goodbye with
his beloved Cassie. The one thing that he loved more than
anything else in life had been brutally stolen from him. His
thirst for revenge was powerful.

Immediately upon receiving the news that Jed had
slipped away from the protective eyes of the deputies, the
sheriff issued an all points. He knew Jed, and knew that if
Jed chanced upon those he believed to be guilty they were
dead men. He didn't want to be the man that would have
to send Jed to prison. It had taken ten hours, but they had
finally found him. He was slumped over the steering
wheel, eyes red from fatigue, clutching the Browning in his
right hand. For his own safety they had put him in a cell
for two days, hoping that his temper would cool and grief
would set in. Even then, the sheriff wasn't sure Jed would
end the search. If the man or men responsible weren't

caught quickly, it was a certainty that Jed would regain his composure enough to begin a cold, relentless search. Jed had ways of getting information and he was dogged. He would never give up.

The most massive manhunt ever conducted in the three county area was mounted, and the criminals were brought in just after Jed's release. The evidence showed that the crime had been committed under the influence of drugs and alcohol. The trial had been swift and the verdict swifter, the jury deliberated for only twenty minutes. Guilty as charged, all counts. The judge set a sentencing date, but it wasn't over. There were appeals and appeals and appeals.

Time dragged and Jed moved through the haze of a world that had lost all brightness and wonder. He was never quite the same after. He lost interest in the farm, he quarreled at work and was laid off. He would have been fired, but for the understanding nature of his boss. The foreclosure by the bank had come eventually and Jed had run, run to the only true and lasting thing in his life . . . the security and solace of the great depths of the forest.

The events still haunted him at times and he still carried Cassie's memory with him. He picked up the pistol and walked to the door. Jenny watched the pain in his face as he stood there. Finally he turned toward her.

"I'm going to teach you how to shoot this. If the bear comes back when I'm not here, it will give you more than the two shots you get with the shotgun. If we're lucky, he won't be back, but that twelve gauge won't be enough if he does."

"You're not going back to the trapline with that creature out there?" she asked incredulously.

"I have to, it's my life, my only way of surviving." He laughed, and there was a touch of irony to it. "You know," he said, leaning against the jamb of the door, "that bear and I aren't so different. We both prey to survive. It's a pity that we have to come into conflict."

"How can you say such a thing?! You don't know what he is like! That animal was going to kill me! He'd be better off dead . . . I want him dead!"

"Yeah, I know. Funny, isn't it? That's one of the beasts you were so bent on saving. He's rare, you know, rare and doomed. He might get us, but someone will eventually get him . . . and all the rest of his kind."

"What do you mean, 'might get us'? You don't really think . . ." Jenny never ended the sentence. The thought that Jed could make such a statement so matter of factly stunned her.

"Does that surprise you? It shouldn't, it's a fact of life out here. It's something that I live with all the time. It's funny, until you showed up there 's nobody that would even miss me if I died out here. At least not until spring when old Pete would be expecting me. Yeah," Jed mused aloud, "if I didn't show, old Pete would come looking. If he found me, he'd give me a decent burial."

"My God," Jenny gasped.

"It was my choice, freely made. I've never regretted it. I told you once before, you can only go with the wilderness, and only as long as you're tolerated. Maybe this little episode will make it clear to you. Come on, put on a coat and I'll show you how to use this. At least it will give you a fighting chance if the bear comes back."

The lesson was short. Jenny, like most women, proved to be a natural shot with a pistol. Jed was glad, there wasn't much ammunition for the Browning. After today's shooting there were only enough shells to fill two clips. That would be more than adequate, in fact one clip would have to do. If Jenny had to face the animal again, she would probably not have time to reload. Jed knew that, but he didn't tell Jenny. As he worked on the remaining cartridges, filing through the copper jackets to make a cross in the noses of the bullets, he thought about the chances of her using the weapon effectively.

"I know you've never killed a living thing," he said, "but in this case you don't have a choice. It won't do to scare him off, he doesn't seem to have much fear of gunshots. I've seen it before. There was a bear that kept coming to my farm in Montana . . ." he broke it off. Good Lord, what was he doing?

Jenny leaned forward expectantly. "Yes . . . go on."

"Never mind," he said gruffly. "It's not important."

"If it helps me deal with this it is."

"It won't help you. Just remember that you have to hit him in the heart and lungs. It's the best target. If you can't do that, if he's too close, aim right in his mouth. It will blow out the base of his brain and drop him on the spot. Any place else and he will just get enraged."

Jenny reflected. She hadn't been prepared for the harsh lesson in reality, she had been so consumed in self-pity. It frightened her, but at the same time gave her back the will to go on. It made her damn mad. There was no time for the wasted emotions. she had brushed with her own mortality and time suddenly became significant. She couldn't understand how Jed could be so accepting of death. She didn't know that in accepting its inevitability, it gave Jed a zest for life, that each day, each danger overcome was a reaffirmation of himself. It was a dangerous game that few men dared to attempt. It was far easier to accept the comforts of a *normal lifestyle* and relieve the boredom in petty diversions. Easier to live vicariously and watch the men who took the risks. Easier to confine the predator instinct to preying on their fellow citizens. It was more *civilized*.

"I've killed," Jenny said suddenly.

Jed looked up curiously. "What?"

"I've killed," she said flatly. She had glossed over the part about MacKelvy when recounting her story to Jed earlier. "I hit MacKelvy with a rock twice . . . hard. He was bloody in the face and didn't move, I watched him for a while before I ran."

A look of consternation crossed Jed's face, then he thought about it for a moment. "I don't think you did."

"You weren't there, how could you know?"

"They broke off the search too early. They never

checked in my direction. If you had killed him, they would have come here. My guess is that you put him out for a while and then he made his way back when he came to and fed the rest some cock and bull story. I'm afraid you're the one they think is dead. MacKelvy would have misdirected the search to cover his own tracks. He's not the brightest star to ever hit the universe, but he's not stupid either. He knows that if you were found, you would blow the whistle on him. And he knew that with the weather and your inexperience that you didn't stand a chance of surviving. He's probably a big hero now, even if he didn't find you. The bastard!" Jed slammed a fist into the table, rocking the oil lamp violently. He reached out quickly to steady it, getting a handle on his temper. If he ran into MacKelvy, he's settle the score. He'd get his satisfaction out of the burly, red-headed giant. Maybe it would make up for what had been done to Cassie and for what MacKelvy had tried to do to Jenny.

Jenny sighed with relief when Jed sat back down and his face lost the contorted look of hate. The violence in his eyes had scared her more than the fist that had lashed out. More than ever she was curious about his past that he kept locked away. Twice now that chiseled, stony face had shown her glimpses of strong feeling that she had intuitively known existed within. Maybe the box beneath the window held some key. She had seen stacks of paper with writing on them among the contents. Tomorrow Jed would return to the trapline. Tomorrow she would open the box. If it turned out to be Pandora's, then so be it.

CHAPTER 19

THE SKY was an even, deep blue and the morning sun was reflecting off the cold white blanket of winter to stab at Jenny's eyes as she stood looking at the empty trail. It had been almost an hour since Jed had slipped silently from sight down the slight hump that marked the trail's beginning. Jenny had busied herself about the cabin, picking up where she had left off, as if the week of depression had never occurred. She tried to pretend that the bear was a thing of the past, that he wouldn't return. It didn't help much, she was still frightened.

Jenny pulled her gaze from the world without and stepped back from the window that Jed had repaired. There hadn't been enough extra glass, so he had boarded up one of the shuttered windows and robbed the glass from its frame. Jenny sized up the job and as she did so, felt her eyes drawn to the window seat with its hidden compartment. She almost walked away from it, but then a little scrap of paper hanging from one corner beckoned to her with an irresistible force. She lifted the lid and peered into the interior. Near the right side, a portrait of a hawk stared back at her with fierce pride. Its lines were clean and sharp, and the lack of color did not detract from its almost primitive beauty. The eyes were, without a doubt, the portrait's most dominant feature. They stared at Jenny with arrogance, and she could almost feel the wind that ruffled the feathers about the bird's head.

Jenny had indeed opened a Pandora's box, for this was the place where Jed hid his secrets. This was where the stern mantle that masked his true feelings was cast off and his soul laid bare. Very few had been allowed to see past the stoniness and only then by invitation. Jenny was intruding, and she knew it.

Still, she could not stop herself. The portraits fell away one by one, each cast by a loving hand that appreciated not only the natural beauty of the subjects, but also the pride, the foolishness, the elation, and the agony of each subject unto itself. The last of the pen and inks was finally laid aside and a loosely bound sheaf of papers waited. Jenny scooped them up and began to read hungrily the words set to paper in a bold, flowing hand.

Journal — Book 1

Portrait of a Predator

The hunter crouched beside a moss and lichen encrusted rock, clutching his weapon, searching the well-tracked trail for prey. His hair hung, matted and stringy, and the growth of beard held tiny bits of brush and grass in its tangle. On his forehead gathered beads of cold sweat that ran into his eyes, momentarily blurring his vision with a sting. His shoulders and back ached, the tendons of his legs were taut from maintaining a motionless position too long, but he dared not move for fear of betraying his presence to potential quarry.

Three days, and now the fourth was slipping quickly away, had been spent in pursuing prey that existed in abundance, that survived by senses keener than those of the hunter, that continued to elude him, testing his patience and frustrating his perseverance.

Suddenly a noise. Only the eyes dare move. An abdominal growl . . . hunger pains. Silence, frustrating silence. The stomach noise might have frightened off the prey. It could have. Still, he remained motionless. Another noise and the prey was visible, but not fully. Motionless, with sweat now running freely, he waited, anxiously hoping that the capricious breezes would not change direction and once more thwart his effort. The nose of the animal tested the air, the ears were forward, straining for sound. The prey was predator wise and very cautious. Finally, with painfully slow motions, he presented a full lateral view. The hunter seized the opportunity and launched his projectile. The prey bounded at the instant of penetration, blood streaming down its flank, the wound not immediately fatal. The wait had been too long for the hunter, the fluidity of his motion had been stolen and his aim warped. The prey found its legs and disappeared swiftly down the trail. There was a grunt that might have been a curse from the hunter as he, too, found his legs and began a relentless and grueling pursuit.

The trail was well marked with blood and the hunter would ultimately realize his success, but his hunger would gnaw at his gut and his lack of prowess would plague his mind. It would be almost dark when he caught his prey and delivered the final blow. The scent would have carried to the scavengers and marauders of the night. He would not sleep this night, but be consumed in defending his kill with primeval ferocity.

This could be a portrait of some ancient hunter consumed in simple survival, but it is not. Yet, the story would be unchanged except that the projectile was launched by smokeless gunpowder and the necessity for predation was a newly acquired one for survival. Still, the frustration and emotional strain must not have changed much between the ancient hunter and this modern one. The portrait is mine, and the hunt my first for survival. Gone was the sheer thrill of being out for the annual sport hunt, for I had allowed my food supply to dwindle into nothing. For someone who prides himself on his ability as a woodsman, this was a foolish mistake. Perhaps I was still steeped in the myths of the magazines and felt that game was so readily available that all I need do was step out my front door and pick off the animal I wanted. Perhaps I was deluded about a great many other things concerning life in the wilderness.

Contrary to the grandiose narratives, trout do not leap in rabid competition for the lures cast into the clear, sparkling waters (the waters are first of all not always clear and the trout often sulk in the depths without paying the

slightest attention to any offering). Nor do grouse and rab-
bits wait anxiously for their turn to leap into the stewpot.
Since it takes so much time to simply keep oneself from suc-
cumbing to the harsh elements of wilderness living in the
north, too much time would be wasted in pursuing small
game and only that chanced upon is taken. So, the reason
for the hunt has now been ascertained. So also has the fact
that this journal has been delayed until this, my second year.

As Jenny was finishing the first entry in the journal,
Jed was making sure that those circumstances would not
be repeated. He had left the trapline after the first two
hours. For some reason the catch had dropped off. It neither surprised nor troubled Jed. A line would be hot for a
while, then suddenly grow cold. No matter, he'd readjust
the line a bit and the catch would pick up.

Jed worked his way along the ridge slowly, skirting the
open areas, staying always in the shadows. He glided
through the trees, ghosting through the spaces between
them low to the ground. He had seen the steam rising below almost thirty minutes before he saw the small herd of
deer. Easing the barrel of the thirty-thirty across the limb
of the tree that hid him from view, he took aim. The buck
flicked an ear nervously an instant before the bullet took
him down. The rest of the herd scattered into the woods.

It worked out well for Jed, he could easily drag the
deer downslope until he intersected the trail. He smiled to
himself. It was early yet and he could make the trip back
without feeling pressured by time. It took only a short time
for him to gut the animal and attach a length of braided
nylon cord to the antlers. The light powder of snow over-
laying the packed snow made the dragging easy.

Whiskey met Jed at the edge of the trail, eagerly wagging his tail and whining. Jed paused for a short time to
show the dog some affection. He and Whiskey had been
together for five years now, and Jed wondered how well
he would have done without the dog. Whiskey was an
added set of eyes and ears that Jed trusted even more than

his own. He was a predator, willing to lay down his life for
his master. He could be as playful as a puppy and as vicious as a wolf. Jed hugged the dog close to him, digging
his fingers into the dog's thick coat. Yes, Whiskey was
more than just a companion in these lonely northern wilds.

The dog gave his master a soft gaze and shared the
lunch that Jenny had packed for them. Jed thought about
her in wonder. She was so changeable, her moods had already swung to both extremes. Without realizing it, he was
comparing Jenny to his memories of Cassie. Maybe that
wasn't fair. After all, Jenny had been thrust into this
strange, new world without much preparation. Cassie had
never had to face that. She had had Jed to lean on, and,
secure in his love for her and hers for him, learning his
world had come easy. Even then, Cassie had not had to
face the brutality of this sort of isolation. Jed wondered if
she could have borne it without mixed feelings. He
doubted it, but then he would never know.

While Jed sat thinking about Cassie, Jenny returned to
the journal after having poured herself a cup of coffee. She
picked up the papers and a letter slipped from between the
pages. The handwriting that could have only belonged to a
woman intrigued her. She picked up the letter and began
to read.

Dear Jed,

Since I have found some of your essays scattered among
the books and journals that you sent home for storage, I
have taken the liberty of reading them. The act was one of
familiarity since you once shared your written thoughts with
me during those earlier years. I am shocked and even a little
bewildered at the bitterness and despair that has crept into
these recent and most personal expression of your present
attitude.

Jed, I wish I could reach out to you and touch you in a
way I once did. In those many years when I first became ac-
quainted with a fussy, hungry bundle, through those happy

years to the more settled, but surely optimistic years, I felt some reassurance that I was communicating. Now I feel lost and inadequate.

Although you have outgrown much of my place in your life, may I call upon shared memories and ask you to do a few essays for me? Write a full description of a flower you love. Do not make it a study in the manner of Aggasiz. Instead make it a written testimony to God's handiwork. You have done it so often with a camera and captured so much beauty.

For the second, and I know this may be difficult, perhaps you would write of your first feelings about Cassie. Despite what you may think, I know something of what you have gone through. Losses are very hard to take for anyone, but it has been almost two years now, and you must begin to sort the memories and put them into perspective.

Your last assignment may be hardest of all, for you must select it yourself with the only provision being that it be a subject of joy.

Now that I have dropped the gauntlet of challenge, you may choose to ignore, reject, or pick it up. I hope it is the latter, for I know the great powers you have for happiness if you will only allow them to surface once again. As a mother I have cherished all of your years spent with or nearby me. Your great capacity for warmth and depth of feeling, your sense of humor, your quick perception, your very lust for adventure and challenge must be evidenced in your essays as the bleakness you presently feel.

Once I could hold you and assure you of better days to come. Now I come almost as a stranger who feels helpless, for I know neither the playing field nor the rules of the game. I love you so much and pray that you may once again find and embrace the joys of today and tomorrow.

My love and devotion are always yours,

Mom

There were tears in Jenny's eyes as she held the letter to her breast. For a moment she could not continue to read the papers that were attached to the letter. She thought of her own mother and how much she missed her, how very much the sentiments in this letter echoed those of her memories of the way her mother was. This was the first tangible tie to Jed's past that Jenny had come across and the sting of the pain in it was real. Jenny cried for Jenny, she cried for Jed, and she cried for Jed's mother.

When the tears stopped, she returned to the pages, recognizing the bold handwriting that she now knew was Jed's. They were answers to the requests in the letter. Two were half-hearted and incomplete. The third gave Jenny an insight into Jed's makeup, a partial reason for his reluctance toward herself.

CASSIE

The time was spring and the flowers danced whimsically in the sprite breeze that sped through the sun-bathed meadow. Cassie smiled up at me as I ran my fingers through her long auburn hair. I drew her close, feeling the warm softness of her body next to mine, smelling that lingering fragrance of her subtle perfume that blended so well with the setting. For the first time we kissed, and a fire kindled and burned deep within me as my heart pounded uncontrollably. Her soft lips parted from mine, then brushed them again.

A doe and her fawn entered the meadow noiselessly as we stood so close together. A whispered "don't move" prevented the quiet pair from being startled. For a moment Cassie stiffened, then relaxed, conforming her body to mine as we watched the graceful animals depart.

There was nothing said, words had no place in this first moment of love. It is in the first hours of young love that the silent communication between a man and a woman is formed, a communication that can later only be perfected. It is the first bond of an enduring relationship and the reflections deep within the eyes become a key to unlock the inhibitions of acquaintance.

My world became entwined with Cassie's. We were inseparable. With each passing day she became more beautiful to me, not in the physical sense that first attracted my attention, but in an enduring way that far exceeds physical beauty. She was a sensitive girl, and I came to measure her moods by the changes in her deep green eyes. We could speak with each other on many levels, we could disagree without becoming angry and argumentative. In short, she was everything I had ever wished for in a woman. A woman, a girl, a lover, intellectual and frivolous, a mood for every moment, each appropriate for the time.

After two and a half years, I still find myself talking to Cassie, smelling that fragrance, hearing her quiet voice, feeling the softness of her hair as it blows against my cheek in a gentle spring breeze. And though she has gone from me, she seems perpetually near. Her laughter still rings in the forest springtime, her smile reflects the sunlight eternally where the water breaks against the rock, her touch is still felt in the warm nights of summer, her beauty captured in the fall as the trees become her mirror. Only in the deepest part of the winter does she drift from me, and the sadness in my heart begs her to return the joys of spring.

Though Jenny could not have known, when Jed had finished his essay of love that day long ago, he had dropped his pen with trembling hand, rose and walked to look misty eyed at the white world outside. His hand reached out to be bitten by the cold glass and, within these same wall, this man of iron will had cried in anguish for a love lost forever except within his mind.

Jenny laid the essay aside on the table and turned to look out that same window. The scene was the same, the perception different. She understood the depth of feeling that Jed had for this faceless young woman from his past, and she knew that if she ever hoped to fill the void left by her passing she must compete with Cassie's memory. Jenny knew that it would require a lot of effort, a lot of giving, for there is nothing so difficult to compete with as a memory. All too often a memory approaches a kind of perfection that is unparalleled in reality.

Jed paused not two miles from the cabin at the same time Jenny was returning the papers to their resting place. He let the sling slip from his shoulder, releasing the strain on his muscles. The shadows were growing longer and the dragging of the deer slowed his pace. He allowed himself a smoke, the first of the day. The smoke curled back at him and he waved a hand in front of his face to clear the sting of it from his eyes. Whiskey returned to sit at his feet and Jed absently played with the dog's ears, unable to feel the silkiness of the fur through his heavy mittens. He felt an urgency to return to the cabin, his thoughts drifting once again to Jenny who waited for him. It would be so easy to take what she might be willing to give, so easy to reach out and touch her vulnerability. It was too easy, too much danger of falling into the trap and expose himself to pain once more. Angrily he shrugged off the feelings of tenderness, put away his pipe, and pursued the trail.

The glow from the oil lamp lit the windows once more, he could see them from the top of the rise. He got that warm feeling inside, as if he had just drunk a good brandy. He hadn't felt that way in a long, long time. The feelings he had so arbitrarily shrugged off only a short time ago returned. There was a voice that whispered within his mind. Perhaps it was time to let go and try again. Perhaps.

CHAPTER 20

A FULL WEEK had passed since the bear had struck at Jed's clearing. The time had passed quickly for Jenny. Each day Jed had gone out to check his traps, each evening he had returned to the cabin with his catch. Jenny had overcome her reluctance and had begun to learn how to skin and flesh the animals. The conversation had become easier and the tension that had existed between them had begun to dissolve. Jenny had come to understand that Jed held a reverence for the wilderness that could only come from having lived in it. There was a genuineness to it that made all the talk of her environmentalist friends seem false.

She sat at the table, waiting for Jed to return from the day's run, figuring the days that she had spent here, and trying to reconstruct a calendar. Jed didn't keep one, he said it was pointless. To her it was not. A calendar kept her in touch with reality, and the diary she kept with it measured the changes she had undergone. As close as she could figure it, it must be near the fifth of November.

Jenny finished her latest entry and walked to the window to look out. It was beginning to grow dark and there were angry clouds pressing down from the north. Already there were flakes of snow beginning to drift in on the small clearing. She began to feel apprehensive. If Jed was still far out on the trail, the storm would overtake him. She thought about that day that seemed so long ago when they had been caught in a storm that looked much like the one now approaching.

Jed had watched the sky for two hours, knowing what it held. He was well aware that he might not make it back before it caught up with him. He was only half way back when the wind struck, whipping the fine powder on the surface into a ground blizzard. He gave up the trail, knowing that to continue was futile. He sought shelter amid the stand of spruce, seeking out the inner cone of one of its giants where he could wait out the storm. It would not be the first time he had done so. He hoped that Jenny would remember that he had told her that this sometimes happened and that she would not grow restless and afraid. Such things concerned him now.

He found his tree and crawled into its dark, tent-like interior. For a moment he waited, until his eyes adjusted themselves to the gloomy light. Then he unshouldered his pack and broke the lower, dry limbs off the tree for a warming fire. He had saved back a little of the lunch in case he was unable to get back, but he was also secure in the knowledge that the pack contained the bodies of ermine and fox. If need be, they would sustain him for the time he would have to spend cooped up. The biggest problem he faced would be to keep the opening clear so that his oxygen would not be depleted. Many a man had suffocated under such circumstances and they were not to be taken lightly.

The first several hours passed pleasantly, the fire lit the temporary home and kept it comfortably warm. The wind outside howled with increasing intensity, blowing the small opening full with snow. Each time Jed cleared it, it began to fill again. Jed poked his head out of the hold periodically to check the progress of the storm. Already there was an accumulation of snow nearly a foot deep new laid over the old. It was not a good sign. The storm showed no sign of weakening. Whiskey looked up from his bed near the fire and whined as Jed returned from the opening.

"Yeah," Jed grinned, "I know son. I wish I was home too. We don't have a choice, though, so I guess we'll just have to make the best of it."

The clock that Jed kept in his head told him the approximate time that had elapsed. He knew that twenty four hours had gone by and still the storm showed no sign of blowing itself out. The inside of the cone of spruce had started to become less hospitable. Body heat from Jed and Whiskey along with the heat of the small fire had begun to cause a constant rain to fall from the roof and walls. Jed spent the better part of two hours digging a well at the low end to collect the excess water. He then dug channels in the icy floor to carry the main part of the flow. Even that did not stop the constant drip from the roof. There was no shelter from it and he was soaked by the end of the second day.

Jed knew the consequences. He had to dry his clothes. He built a small rack near the fire and stripped off the wet garments, draping them over it. He took care to keep the fire small but constant. He squatted close to the other side, hugging Whiskey tightly to him, unable to stop the shivers that racked him. It wasn't working, the constant drip would wet one side of the clothes as soon as they were turned. Jed gave up the meager comfort of the blanket that he squatted on and rigged a shelter over the rack that held the wet clothes. Finally they began to dry.

Naked and cold, he still had to make sure that the opening to the shelter remained clear. The storm was beginning to abate. It was late afternoon. He had been confined here for almost fifty five hours. There was blue sky beginning to open behind the gray-white shield of clouds. The night would be clear and bright, the temperature would drop abominably. There was no choice, it would have to be tonight. He returned to the fire and impaled a frozen weasel on his knife, holding it over the fire to thaw and perhaps cook a bit. He ate it half raw, accustomed now to the strong flavor. He wished he had a cup of coffee, it sure would have gone good.

He dressed quickly, hoping to exit the cavern of snow and branches before the freezing rain wet him once more. He scrambled out the entrance, followed quickly by Whiskey. He dug out his snowshoes and secured them to his boots. Now came the trail and the cold. It took only a short time after sunset for the mercury to dip below minus thirty. Before he had gone three miles it would be forty below, sixty below by the time he reached the clearing. He stopped to wrap his face in the heavy scarf, choking on the smoky smell of the filtered air. It was just another inconvenience to be endured. Temperatures this low could freeze a man's lung tissues if breathed directly long enough.

Freezing is not an unpleasant death, at least not after the initial pain of cold has passed. You simply grow drowsy and never wake up. Jed shook himself and stumbled on, pressing the thought from his half-numbed mind. The moisture that crept through from the inside of his mittens froze as it came into contact with the outside air, welding his mitten to the steel of the thirty-thirty. He was tiring rapidly and his eyes began to play tricks on him. Snow fire, those lights that might be reflected moonlight or starlight on distant mounds of snow, began to dance invitingly. Jed forced his mental compass to stay on course. If he followed the path to those lights that looked so much like those of the cabin, they would lead him to certain death.

He did not know how long he had been on the trail when the real lights of the cabin came into view, just that it seemed like forever. He tried to hurry and fell heavily into the deep snow. It was pure anguish to get up and steel discipline that made him do so. He was seeing only through one eye now, the lashes of the other had been frozen together by the escaping steam of his breath. Whiskey whined nervously as Jed slowly got to his feet, looking anxiously toward the cabin that held salvation for his master.

The last few yards were agonizingly slow and Whiskey was at the door, scratching and barking, before Jed gained the porch. Jenny threw open the door and rushed out, terrified by what she saw. Jed was an apparition of ice, like some frigid monster that had been delivered up from the bowels of a frozen hell. Jenny had never seen anything like it, even in the documentaries of the arctic regions she had seen.

The heat in the cabin hit Jed like a wall of pain. He was unable to stifle the groan that escaped past his cracked lips. The pain intensified as he began to warm, the iciness of the storm leaving his body with stabbing messages. Jed welcomed the pain, the signal that he had survived, that he had beaten the foe, that nature had not finished with him yet. He let go a rough cough and recognized the tight pain in his chest. It wasn't over after all, he thought.

Jenny fussed over Jed like a long lost child. It gave her the first feeling she had had of being needed here. She was no longer an intruder in Jed's life. She talked to him constantly, even though he did not appear to hear her words. It didn't matter what she said, just as long as she kept him in touch. She pried off the stiff clothing from his body and worked the patches of frostbite from his fingers and toes, feeling the cold of it against the warmth of her own skin. She put Jed to bed and watched over him as the fever rose in him.

Suddenly it was the midwest again, Jed's mind was reeling back in time as the fever burned and festered. The lightning flashes that broke across the horizon of his blurred vision breached the chasm of his memory as he relived the tortuous moments of that last savage storm.

ANOTHER TIME, ANOTHER PLACE: Jed had seen the black cauldron brewing far in the west all day, pushing the ground fog just ahead of it. He breathed the heated, water laden air, his body sweltering and wet. The vast black thunderheads stacked thicker and higher, snuffing the brilliant afternoon sun as if it were a mere candle, rendering it impotent, turning day into night. The reflections of an endless series of electrical outbursts lit the clouds like muzzle flashes from giant cannon, thunder rolling towards him in an almost continuous wave. Hot wind had blown ceaselessly all day, but now there was an ominous calm in the atmosphere. He picked up the tools he had been using in the garden.

It was a lot of work, that garden, but by God if he did

not get anything else from this job, he was going to get a good harvest of vegetables from the garden plot he was allowed to keep. The lightning flashed again, closer and hotter this time. The heat in the house was almost unbearable as he walked in. He had no more shut the door than the wind was back, slamming into the house like an unseen wall. The violent cauldron began its advance from the southwest, boiling and overflowing onto the passive fields that lay in its path. The rain began with a few innocuous drops and turned rapidly into a furious downpour that obscured the barn a short hundred feet away. The lightning was suddenly vicious, lashing earthward in white-blue bolts, searing the atmosphere as oxygen was fractured into ozone. The house shook under the onslaught of thunder.

Jed watched as the garden plot was flooded for the twelfth time since its planting. Some of the seed he had just planted would wash away and become lost in the rows of field corn that bordered the garden, some would probably rot in the moisture laden ground. He suspected the melon seed already had. there was still a little time left in which he could replant.

The fury of the storm grew as Jed watched uneasily. If it were possible, it had gotten even blacker outside. It grew calm without warning. The leaves on the maple in the back yard quivered and there was a faint roar. From the kitchen window, Jed searched the sky anxiously. He couldn't see anything but rain, black sky, and buildings. He was searching the horizon to the south when the windmill tower that now served as a perch for the mercury yard lamp was wrenched from its moorings and thrown violently to the ground in a tangled mass of steel and electrical sparks.

Unable to move, he stood in terror as he watched the roof of the barn disappear. Only when the giant funnel skittered across the yard, bypassing the house, and began plucking tender young plants from his garden did he find his legs. Without thinking, he ran screaming to the back door.

"Noooo!"

The blinding light of winter streamed through the window as Jed sat up slowly, feeling empty and sick. His eyes shut against the hurt of the brightness and his mind struggled to collect his thoughts and his bearings. He slowly swung his legs over the edge of the bed, remembering the last parts of the return trip. He didn't remember much after that and he wondered how he had managed to crawl into bed. Gradually he became aware of the heat in the room and remembered Jenny.

When Jenny heard the noises inside, she hurried through the door. She had gone to feed the horses, as she had for the past two days since Jed's return. He had been resting quietly, and the scream she had heard had traveled across the clearing to the far side of the corral. It was Jed's voice, and yet it wasn't.

Jed looked startled when she came bursting through the door. He managed a half hearted smile. "Hullo," he croaked, and then was racked by a tight cough. "Damn!"

"Hello yourself," Jenny smiled in relief. "How do you feel?"

"Lousy." He looked down at his naked knees and grinned. "We're even, aren't we?"

"Huh?" Jenny replied, and then blushed a deep red. "I . . . I . . ." she stammered.

"'S okay," Jed smiled. "Thanks."

Jenny turned her back and used an uncommon amount of energy in removing her coat. Jed coughed a couple of more times. "I've got some soup heating, it will be ready in a few minutes. I was so worried, I didn't know what I should do. I just tried to take care of the chores like you did . . ." She was talking too fast.

"Shut up," Jed said, "and come sit down."

Jenny looked around sharply at the command and then saw the twinkle in Jed's tired eyes. She crossed the room and sat heavily next to him. He put an arm around her shoulders and gave her a squeeze. Jenny found herself looking at his chest, there were four rows of long white scars. She reached out with a forefinger and traced down the length of one of them and looked up with questioning eyes.

"Lynx," Jed stifled a cough. "My second season. I don't think he had much sense of humor about winding up in one of my traps. He had even less when I went to whack him with the baton."

"What happened?" Jenny asked, wide eyed.

"He whacked me and then I whacked him." Jed looked at Jenny and saw the seriousness in her face. "It doesn't happen much anymore. My real problems are the ones you can't predict, like the longevity of that storm. I thought that might be the end for me, but I thought of you and was afraid that you wouldn't make it without someone to show you the ropes."

It was a rough attempt at humor to relieve the moment that didn't work. Jenny looked away and was silent. Jed wrestled with his emotions for a few minutes, not sure that he wanted to commit himself to anything absolutely. He felt the tension in her shoulder muscles.

"All right," he said almost gruffly, "I wasn't quite ready to let the world go. It takes more than a storm to beat me. And, God help me, I'm growing fond of you. There, I've said it. Your turn."

Jenny looked at Jed. His face no longer held the stony appearance she had become accustomed to. There was almost a tenderness of expression, and there was a definite softness in the eyes. She could not reply, her throat was choked with emotion and her eyes misted a bit. She wiped a hand across her eyes and turned away from him. Jed waited for her to find her voice. She finally did.

"I'm glad you're back," she said quietly.

"Yeah, so am I."

The bonds were growing, they were in the voices of both of them, and in the glances they exchanged. Jed grew stronger and returned to the business of trapping within a few days. More and more, his thoughts were of Jenny when he was out alone. He still thought of Cassie, and asked her forgiveness for thinking of what was real and alive and waiting for him when he returned each night. He remained faithful to Cassie, he was not yet ready for that kind of a commitment. If he had thought about it realistically, he would have known that Cassie would have been the last person in the world to hold him to such a bond. No, the bond was his, and when the time came he would understand and go on.

CHAPTER 21

Two weeks had brought the grizzly in almost a full circle. Kills had been spare and he had felt drawn back to the little narrow valley where the big, dumb beasts had fallen so easily before his attack. He skirted the north end of the valley and ambled through the deep snow to its southern end. The sweet smell of livestock drifted up lazily from the corrals of the Diamond Bar. He savored the odor and made a bed beneath the fallen trunk of an old pine. There he would wait until darkness came to mask his movements.

Bob Price moved stiffly in the cold weather, attending to the needs of his string of horses and mules. Cold weather always brought problems for Bob. His arthritis kicked up and slowed the completion of his chores. Something was always breaking down, the trucks, the plumbing, always something. He looked at the seam of the water trough, the electric heater had failed and the pressure of the ice had burst the seam. He kicked the solidly frozen trough and cursed the pain that coursed up his shin. Damn it, now he'd have to go get a new trough and heater. This one was beyond repair.

He stomped back to the house and told Louise that he was going to town. "Goddam weather . . . gets worse every year."

"Now Bob, you know that ain't true. Yer just gettin' older is all. Why don't you let young Sam stay home from school when it gets like this an' give you a hand?"

"You know why, honey, I don't want him to wind up like this, dependin' on a uncertain way of makin' a livin'. Let me finish this cup an' I'll be off. Probably take a couple of hours to get everything taken care of in town. I'll be

153

back as soon as I can."

"You want me to pack you a lunch?"

"Naw, I'll get a bite at the cafe."

"Just don't get stuck there jawin' with the boys," Louise admonished.

Bob grinned broadly at her, waved, and went out the door, letting the screen slam behind him. The old pickup coughed and sputtered before the engine caught and turned over. As he drove, Bob listened to the satisfying slap, slap, ching of the chains as they bit into the smooth glass surface of road ice. The winter had reduced the wide dirt track to a single, slippery lane. It took half an hour to negotiate its twists and turns to the main road that led to town, and another fifteen minutes to reach the Emporium. Bob creaked open the stiff hinges of the pickup door and got out, stretched, and went inside.

"Hello," Pete hailed him from near the warm stove. "Is there somethin' I can get for ya?"

"Yeah, Pete, I need me a new stock trough."

"How big?"

"Hunnert gallons, if ya got one."

"I think we do. Hey John! Check the back for a hundred gallon stock tank."

"Okay, Pete . . . give me a couple of minutes," John shouted back.

"Yeah, yeah," Pete waved a hand. "Well, Bob, how's things up to the Diamond Bar?"

"Oh not so bad. Things breakin' down as usual, but nothin' outta the ordinary. Sure will be glad to see spring back again."

Pete laughed. "Hell, we gotta get winter outta the way first, and it's just gettin' started."

"Yeah, I know, that's what bothers me. Listen, if you can have John put that tank in the pickup, I'll go over to the cafe and grab a quick bite. And hey, get me one of them tank heaters too. Mine's busted."

"Sure, you go ahead. We'll take care of it. You want this on your tab?"

"Yeah, if you don't mind. I'll be gettin in the advances on the fishin' season pretty soon and then I'll be able to settle up the account," Bob said apologetically.

"I don't worry about you, Bob, we've done business too long."

Bob wandered over to the cafe and ordered the noon special while John loaded the trough for him. The meal was hot, if not as tasty as Louise's. He washed it down with four cups of steaming coffee. Ordinarily he would have dawdled in the cafe, but today he was in a hurry. There was that trough to set up and his old mare was having hoof trouble. She was carrying a foal and he didn't want anything to cause him to lose the old girl. Her colts always brought him good money.

He was about half way home when the right front tire gave out and he skidded to a stop, swearing at the tire. It took almost an hour to get the bald, blown out piece of rubber off the wheel and replaced with an equally bald spare. The day was slipping away, he'd be working in the dark again. He swore at the weather, he swore at the truck, and he swore at himself. It didn't do any good, the time slid by and paid him no attention.

The chill of the evening shadows crept in the bear's hiding place and pried him from sleep. He roused himself and dragged his rump along the surface of the snow. Worms. He stretched his hind leg and, with a huge, hairy back foot, raked his itchy ribs in satisfaction. Lice. With a mighty yawn, the bear rose and tested the air. That tantalizing smell of horse and mule still drifted up from below. He began a deliberately slow approach that would bring him to the outskirts of the Diamond Bar just after darkness had fallen.

Bob had just returned to the barn after a quick dinner to tend to old Buttons when it happened. He'd heard the other horses in the far corral milling, but had seen nothing from the barn door and returned to tend the hoof. It was that ungodly shriek that had sent him bolting from the barn, yelling for Sam to bring the rifle. He figured wolves, or maybe a cat. He was not prepared for what waited in the shadows.

The bear had felled one of Bob's best pack mules with a single, savage blow to the neck. Before the mule's eyes had stopped rolling, a great raking slash had split his belly and the bear was at the entrails before he'd breathed his last. The sight of it stopped Bob in his tracks. He had no weapon with which to defend himself and the scene lay only a few yards away. He could hear Sam's running boots on the hard snow of the driveway. The bear heard them as well. He charged the sound, he would not be deprived of another meal.

Bob was directly in the path of the charging bear. He threw himself to one side, yelling to Sam, "For God's sake shoot!" He felt the pain of the blow, saw a shower of sparks in his mind, and slipped into darkness.

Bob had taught his son well, there was no hesitation. The blast of the magnum shook the night air. The bullet went wild and the bear still bore down on him. There was no time for a good aim, Sam simply raised the rifle and pointed it instinctively. The bear dived to the side, the charge was broken. Sam chambered another shell and sent it after the fleeing animal, then ran to the spot where his father had gone down.

Bob was still alive, but he had taken the brunt of the bear's bulk as the animal had unwittingly slammed into him with his shoulder. When the doctor examined him, he found that Bob had four broken ribs, a compound fracture of the right arm, and a broken collar bone. Bob was a very lucky man, the bear had been intent on Sam and that was what had spared him.

While the grizzly fled to the north and west, the people of the small valley gathered in town to plan their strategy. This was the second major attack on their community by the bear. Something had to be done before the bear killed one of their number. The crowd in the Blue angel swelled and the noise level increased. Finally Jim Raudsep mounted a table and demanded silence. When the room became quiet, but for an occasional cough, he began his speech.

"Now listen," he said with authority in his voice, "we all know we have a problem that isn't likely to go away. If none of you have any good suggestions, I'd like you to hear mine." He looked across the concerned faces and continued when there was no reply. "All right, what I propose is that my men, with as many of you other men who would like to, begin a systematic search for the bear. We can follow his trail on snowmobiles and maybe catch up to him. Then maybe some of the others can fan out and try to get ahead of him and force him into a corner. If we can do that, we'll get him and all of us can sleep a little easier. Otherwise, we'll have to wait until he comes back, as he surely will, and we might have a repeat of tonight," he paused for effect. "It might even be worse . . . nobody got killed tonight."

There were murmurs of approval that coursed through the room. MacKelvy leaned against the bar, nursing a drink, with a sour expression on his face. By "we" MacKelvy knew that Raudsep meant him and the other guides. Raudsep would never risk the cold and harsh conditions unless he knew the kill was at hand. The he'd swoop in in a rented helicopter and steal as much of the glory as he could. He saw one of the men staring at him. The sour look was quickly replaced by his brawling sneer. It was his turn now.

"Awright! Listen up! I want everybody that's goin' to meet at the ranch at six thirty tomorrow mornin'. You'll need five days' provisions an' all the firepower you can carry. We'll make the assignments then. See you in the mornin', boys."

The party might have caught the bear if they had started out right away, but there was a lot of wasted time spent in arguing over who was going to do what when. It was ten thirty before they got going. By that time the bear had traveled far. The bullet that had broken his charge had split the skin along his shoulder and he had run from the sting. Finally the cold had worked its way on the wound and reduced it to a minor ache. It wasn't serious. Still, the bear was intent on putting as much distance between himself and the valley as he could. While the hunting party stopped for lunch and liquid encouragement, the bear continued to move. He was making a beeline for the center of his territory. Only there would he rest.

It took MacKelvy's party two days to reach the camp they had used for the fall hunt. MacKelvy grinned in satisfaction when he saw the track that skirted the camp. It was the same bear he had wounded earlier that year after all, he was sure of that now. The bear had been run to home, he'd not leave here without a fight. MacKelvy knew that, and counted on it. Tomorrow they would get the bear, tonight they'd have a party. No sense in wasting a good winter outing.

He got on the portable walkie-talkie and called in the chopper that was spotting for them. No sense in having Tom return tonight, he carried enough spare fuel. They'd gas up the chopper in the morning. MacKelvy had the men set up the tents and get everything for the morning before he announced his plans for the evening. His suggestion was met with a rousing cheer. Tom wandered over after having landed on the far side of the clearing.

"What's all the hullabaloo?" he asked quietly.

"We're gonna have ourselves a little party," MacKelvy grinned. "Then tomorrow we're gonna go get that bear. We've run him to ground."

"You sure?" Tom asked excitedly.

"Damn near certain. This is the same place I wounded that one last fall. I'll bet you money he's the same one."

"Damn! Maybe' I'd better try to get Raudsep and bring in the others."

"You leave off that radio!" MacKelvy turned on the pilot viciously. "I ain't gonna have that overstuffed bastard steal what belongs to me an' the boys this time!"

Tom put his hands up, palms turned outward. "Okay, it was just a suggestion. It doesn't matter one way or the other to me, eh. I don't want to be the one to steal your glory."

MacKelvy relaxed his glare. "All right then, here, have one on me."

Tom took the glass of whiskey. "On Raudsep, you mean," he laughed.

"Yeah, Raudsep . . . aw what the hell, he's worth something I guess."

Darkness fell and the men enjoyed their party. While they huddled themselves around the tables in tents warmed by propane stoves, playing cards, the night cloaked the intruder. In the deep shadows around the perimeter of the camp the bear stalked. His eyes were shot with the blood of hate. The pursuer was here once more, the hated scent told him so. Once more his territory had been violated. No more would he run. Here he would stand and fight, but it would be on his terms, not the pursuer's. Here he was master, he knew every inch of ground, every tree, every rock. The advantage was his. The blackness of night gave him patience. When no more sound came from the three tents, he would strike. He paced and waited.

CHAPTER 22

JED AWOKE early, darkness still crowded the cabin. He could hear Jenny's deep breathing in the stillness. There was a storm brewing outside, Jed could feel it in his right knee. Whenever the bad weather came, the old injury gave him sharp reminders. He worked the joint deliberately, massaging the stiffness away. Whiskey whined and slipped off the bed where he had kept Jenny's feet warm through the night. Jed heard him coming and reached out to scratch the dog's ears.

The cabin still held the warmth of the banked fire, but Jed knew that it would not be long before the balance shifted in favor of the cold. He added new wood to the fireplace, resting the pieces of split spruce on the glowing embers and blowing gently to encourage the flames. The dry wood caught and demon's shadows danced on the walls. Jed grinned in satisfaction as the heat drove the pain from his knee. He rocked back on his heels, immersed in the quiet. This was his time alone in the cabin, before Jenny woke, the time of silence when he could be alone with his thoughts.

As he walked toward the window, Jenny stirred in her sleep. He looked out the window and was not surprised to see the heavy drifting from the sky's gray-white clouds. He would not run the trapline today. It did not bother him much, he had completed the line yesterday, and there were some things he needed to talk over with Jenny. Despite her outward cooperation and acceptance of his way of life, there were little things that told Jed that Jenny still held to her idealistic views of the wilderness. Even the bear had not been enough to drive them from her mind. He was but a single animal, the exception to the rule. It many ways that was true, but Jed also knew the truth about predators. They do not merely prey on the weak and the sick, they will take whatever they can without hesitation. Sooner or later the subject would have to be brought into the open, they could not dance around it indefinitely. Jed preferred to pick the time, it would give him an advantage in the discussion.

He pulled his jeans over the long thermal underwear and buttoned his heavy wool shirt as he wandered into the small kitchen. He thought about how best to open the subject as he built up the fire in the stove and started the coffee. It would not do to take a direct approach, that would only cause a confrontation. He didn't want that. No, he would have to slide into it and try to keep it on a friendly basis. He did not want to risk losing the relationship he felt was just beginning, but he didn't want it built on false premises either.

He heard Jenny beginning to wake, becoming restless in the gray light of dawn. The coffee was boiling happily on the stove. He dumped a half cup of cold water into the pot and watched the grounds sink to the bottom before filling his large mug with the steaming liquid. He swirled a mouthful around, savoring the rich, bitter taste. Jenny called sleepily from the other room. He moved sideways and leaned against the rough doorway.

"Mornin' sleepy," he said cheerfully.

"Mornin'," Jenny yawned. "How long have you been up?"

"Not long. I won't be going out today, we've got a storm going."

"Really?!" Jenny turned and parted the crude curtains to look out the window. "Oh, isn't it beautiful?!"

"Yeah, it is, isn't it? There's nothing quite like big, heavy snowflakes drifting in the air. Winter is the one time of year when nature hides all the ugly things it the world."

"Goodness, you're in a philosophical mood this morning, aren't you?"

Jed laughed and slipped back into the kitchen. "Why

don't you get dressed while I fix breakfast?"

"What if I want breakfast in bed?" Jenny teased.

"You came to the wrong establishment," Jed rejoined wryly.

Breakfast came and went, and with it the passage of time by way of small talk. Jed still had not broached the subject with Jenny. He gauged the conversation, looking for an opening, anticipating the opportunity. When it became obvious that Jenny was deftly sideslipping his attempts to steer the conversation, he went to the bookcase and searched the shelves. He found what appeared to be a bound volume and pulled it out. He opened the cover and looked casually at the contents within its hollow cavity, and then looked across at Jenny. She returned his gaze curiously.

"I was hoping to approach this subtly," he said tentatively, "but I guess that it won't be possible. I know that you have . . . how should I put it . . . well, a Walt Disney perspective of the wilderness." He paused, looking at the lines of consternation on Jenny's face as she knitted her eyebrows. "I don't want to be critical, but I think that a relationship is beginning here, and I don't want any false impressions to slip by."

"What do you mean by false impressions?" Jenny demanded.

Jed crossed the room, sat down opposite Jenny, and placed the fake book on the table between them. He looked at her with a seriousness in his eyes that she had not seen before. "This is hard for me," he explained. "I hope that it will not be too hard for you. The last thing I want to see is us drift apart and wind up where we started. I know that you have been trying to see things from my perspective and that helping with the furs is difficult for you."

"I never said that," Jenny replied quietly.

"You didn't have to, I could see it in your face."

"It was that obvious, huh?"

"I'm afraid so," Jed said gently. "The closest you ever

came to feeling like I do was when the bear came, and it didn't last. Even then, our feelings weren't exactly the same. You wanted the bear dead, you said, because he directly threatened you. That's a gut reaction, and a valid one. Self preservation is a strong and necessary motivation for survival."

"So, does that mean I was wrong?"

"Yes and no,"

"That's a definitive answer."

Jed smiled. "You have to keep things in perspective. You were right so long as the bear presented a direct threat, you reacted in the correct way, but when the threat was no longer direct, I got the distinct feeling that you dismissed the situation. I got the feeling that you were questioning the way you reacted, the way you felt when it happened."

"I don't see anything wrong with that. You can't go around killing everything that threatens you, especially when its an endangered animal. Even you said he was endangered."

"Yes I did. But, I didn't change my reaction to the attack. If he comes back and I'm here, I'll kill him. Before you ask why, I'll tell you. This is his territory, and mine. We both claim it. It's obvious that he won't hesitate to protect it, and neither will I. If I expect to remain here, that is a fact. You might argue that because I have a mind that I must take it upon myself to protect this defenseless animal. That's bull. His habits have made him a marked animal. If I don't kill him, then somebody else will. What you must understand, if you intend to preserve your own life in this environment, is that there must be no hesitation in your decisions. If you question your reactions, your response will be delayed. Out here that can spell death."

"That might be," Jenny replied evenly, eager to pursue a philosophical argument, "but because you have a brain, you should realize that it is not necessary that you intrude on what is left of the wilderness environment. What I mean is that we must recognize other animals' rights to exist. We have to protect them."

"I've heard that argument before," Jed mused.

"Well, don't you agree with it?"

Jed stroked his beard, lost in contemplation for a moment. When he spoke, it was with earnest deliberation. "Jenny, I once had to speak to a group of environmentalists, the reason I had to is immaterial. They didn't like to hear what I had to say, it offended their sensibilities. Now, I'd like you to listen to what I told them." Jed paused for effect. "People are the most selfish animals on the face of the earth, environmentalists are no exception. There may be truly altruistic individuals in the environmental movement, but they are far overshadowed by the selfish ones. Listen to them when they speak. They use terms like 'posterity,' 'primeval,' and 'pristine.' Whose posterity? Certainly not the animals', they want to protect the wilderness for the enjoyment of their children and their children's children. Admirable, but selfish. Primeval and pristine? Nebulous terms at best, and certainly not applicable to any of our wilderness, or any on the North American continent. Those terms imply an absence of the hand of man and that simply does not exist here. I doubt that many of those environmentalists would get much enjoyment from those areas if there were no trails carved in them, and I doubt you would find many who would support a wilderness environment where man was strictly prohibited.

"In Montana the Sierra Club tried to buy up some tracts of land to, quote, preserve them. The deal fell through when the land owners found out that they were to be excluded from access to the land for hunting, fishing, or any other outdoor recreational purposes. Access was to be strictly limited to members of the Sierra Club. That's elitist as hell, preservation in the name of enjoyment for a few. It didn't gain them many followers back there."

"Now wait a minute," Jenny interrupted, "the Sierra Club has done a lot of good. If it weren't for them and other groups just like them, the big corporations would have ruined a lot of wilderness and a lot of species would not be around today."

Jed looked at her and nodded. "They are a counter balance to the big corporations, of course, but I think you're
giving them more credit than they deserve. Besides, I
wasn't picking on Sierra Club, just using them as an example. Personally I think there is a balance between exploita-
tion and extremist environmentalism, but that's getting
away from the point I'm trying to make.

"Both sides are rife with scientifically trained individuals who are prostituting their training. It is not the job of a
scientist to project a point of view, merely to study and as-
certain the facts. Individually he may hold opinions, but it
is not his right to use his position to justify his *opinions* and
try to force them on others. Again off subject, but a point I
wanted to raise.

"Let me illustrate my point. I asked the people to whom
I was speaking whether they owned land or lived in towns.
Most of them owned land, most of them were involved in
the back to nature movement. The land holdings varied
from one to twenty acres for the most part. I asked them
what single thing most influenced the animal populations.
There were a lot of answers, but none that was satisfac-
tory. What do you think it would be?"

Jenny looked across at Jed, playing with a string that
she held in her hands. "I suppose habitat destruction."

"Close, but be more specific."

"You know, cutting down the forests, building roads,
draining swamps . . . things like that."

"All right, but you're not touching on the root cause."

"Damn it! You're playing word games!"

"That's how they reacted, but it's not true."

"Well then, suppose you tell me!"

"Fine. It's the ever expanding of the human population.
His drive to have his own little space. You see, all those
environmentalists wanted their own little area of wilderness to enjoy. What was already designated for the use and
enjoyment of the general public was not enough. Simply
by their selfish need for that personal possession of a piece

of land they made hypocrites of themselves. If you sug-
gested that they combine their resources and construct a
central building complex while preserving the large bulk of
the land as open space, they had innumerable arguments.
And so they became contributors to the pressure of human
population on the wilderness populations. They bought
scenery and cut it into thousands of little pieces, obliterat-
ing natural corridors for the migration of elk, destroying
habitat merely by their presence. Except for those species
compatible with the presence of man, the animals retreated."

Jenny looked at Jed in shock. For once all of her arguments seemed empty. If what he said were true, then the
wilderness had little hope of survival, except for those
small parts already set aside by governments. And what
were they but little living zoos? The thoughts ran through
her mind with rapid abandon and she seized on the only
argument that made sense. "What about you? Aren't you
guilty of the same thing? Doesn't that make you a hypocrite?!"

Jed smiled, his point had been made and he recognized
the futile attempt to point a finger, a justification of her
beliefs in the denouncement of the opposition. He was
prepared for it. "Guilty of the same thing? In a way I suppose, but I don't own this land, merely occupy it. It does
not pass on to another automatically. As for being a hypocrite, I don't think so. I told you before that I'm a predator, I have freely admitted it and have made no excuses,
claimed no altruism. I accept the realities and live within
their boundaries. I practice what I preach, if you will. I
don't think that fits the definition of a hypocrite."

Jenny looked at him and then down at the table. There
was a silence that hung over them like a dense fog. Jed
had been prepared for the exchange, she had not. She had
wanted to avoid just this kind of discussion that would
highlight the conflict she had tried to keep hidden. It was,
she had felt, the sort of conversation that would finally
burst the bubble of illusion she had about Jed. Jed watched

her closely for reaction, letting what he had said sink in. Jenny's fingers toyed with the book that was a box and Jed reached to touch her hand.

"Open the box, Jenny. Open it and look at what it holds."

"What is it?" she asked with a touch of hurt in her voice.

"It is my world, or at least pictures of it. In there you will find photographs of the beauty of it and the brutality of it. Both wait out there, Jenny. To appreciate one, you must understand the other. That is the reality of it. The system must be taken as a whole, you can't pick and choose when you live in it. If you stay you will see both, perhaps even experience both. If you want to stay and not live under the shadow of fear, you must understand how the system works. If you do not wish to stay, the knowledge will not harm you. It might even help."

"Do you want me to stay?"

"I can only answer that selfishly. I don't think that would be fair at this point."

"I don't care whether it's fair or not. Do you want me to stay?!"

Jed looked across at her and there was pain in his eyes. "I've been alone for a very long time, Jenny."

It was not a direct answer, but it was answer enough. Time was weaving its web, spinning the silk of emotion, binding the two together, ending the isolation of one, awakening the mature feelings of another. This was no longer a game, no longer play-acting.

CHAPTER 23

" . . . NEARLY THREE FEET
of new snow, total accumulation near six feet. Wind died
down late last nite. Jed running the line again this morning." Jenny laid aside the pen and reread the entry under
December 15 of her diary. She looked at the date once
more. There were only ten days before it was Christmas.
Normally she would have been planning the festivities,
buying presents, and attending parties. Here it was difficult
to imagine those things, they seemed far away, so far
away. Still, she was not willing to abandon all of the things
she had known. Christmas was a tradition in her family, a
time to lay aside petty quarrels, a time to give and receive,
a time of joy. She thought of the Christmases past and
vowed to make this one a memory of something more than
an experience in an alien world.

Jenny had been working on a present for Jed for almost
a week now. She used the skills she had, finding that she
could be resourceful when she had to. The boxes beneath
the bed had contained a quantity of wool socks whose feet
had been holed by use. Jed was a pack-rat, he threw away
nothing that might be of future use. Jenny had taken those
socks and had carefully unravelled the yarn until she had a
sizeable ball of it. Two actually, one gray and a smaller one
of red from the tops of the socks. She had hoped to have
enough for a sweater, but soon realized that it would take
more than a collection of old socks for that. Very well, a
scarf then, but what was she going to use for the needles?
She had searched the cabin from top to bottom and had
found nothing suitable. It was when she was in the shed
checking on the horses when she solved the problem. A
box of ten inch spikes lay half-hidden under the harness,

two of them became her knitting needles. They made a curious metallic clicking sound as her fingers manipulated
them, forming yarn into fabric. She felt happy and
matched the rhythm of the needles to the melodies of the
carols she was singing.

On the trail, Jed too was thinking of the Christmas that
was coming. It had been some time since he had shared
the holiday season with another person. He thought of the
deerskin shirt-dress that lay hidden in the horse shed, and
of the moosehide moccasins that were almost finished. He
had made excuses to Jenny to steal the time that was necessary to make them. These, along with a moosehide coat
that Jed had altered, would give Jenny a suit of trail-wor-
thy clothes. Perhaps she would join him one day to check
the trapline, or perhaps they might take a walk into the
quiet world of winter simply for the joy of doing it.

He was almost half way through his run on the south
trapline when he spotted the congregation of ravens
flocking toward Moose Ridge. Whiskey's nose twitched at
the smell of death when a freak ground wind stirred from
the southeast. He rose and began trotting in that direction
to investigate. Jed whistled to him, but when the dog
paused and whined, still looking in the direction of the
wind, he decided to follow along. The path carried him
away from the trapline, across a small valley, and up
Moose Ridge. He paused at the crest of the ridge, digesting
the scene below him. There must have been a hundred
ravens bickering and fighting on the frozen mounds down
there. Jed shifted the weight of his pack a little and proceeded grimly down the hill with Whiskey guarding his
flank.

The first body he came upon was unrecognizable, pock-
marked and faceless from the ravages wrought by the
ravenous black scavengers. One after the other, he checked
the six bodies that lay scattered across the snowswept
clearing with a growing sickness. In the ramshackle remains of one tent he found one more body, a rifle clutched
in the death grip of the decapitated man. Less than a hun-

dred yards away from the tent he found the last member of the party frozen in his own blood to the seat of the battered Bell helicopter. He had not even been able to get the switch on to start the helicopter when his chest had been caved in. It was Tom Phillips. Jed recognized the well known bush pilot.

Jed felt the bile churn in his stomach, but choked back the impulse to be sick. With difficulty, he forced his eyes away from the dead man to study the blurred impressions on the ground. The clearing lay in the path of the prevailing winter winds, and much of the dry snow that had fallen in the last storm had been blown into large drifts on the far side of the clearing. Carefully, Jed brushed away the surface snow from the nearest print. Jed looked back inside the chopper suddenly. Tom's snow encrusted feet were clad only in a pair of socks. The gashes in the aluminum skin of the chopper told Jed most of what he wanted to know, but he uncovered yet another print for confirmation. There it was, unmistakable, as if it had just been made.

"Grizzly," Jed grunted. He had struck in darkness, mercilessly and deliberately. The positions of the bodies told him the rest of the story. The men must have been sleeping when the attack came. They had run in panic, only to be cut down by the slashing claws of the enraged animal, one by one. Only the pilot and the man in the tent had tried to do battle or make a sensible escape. Jed reached into the cockpit and picked the rifle from the passenger seat. He opened the bolt and caught the spent shell as it left the chamber. It was a .300 magnum. There were two live rounds left in the magazine. He chambered one, slipped the safety on and returned to the tent.

For a moment Jed studied the shred of canvas that fluttered from the tent pole like a banner on the scene of a massacre. Resolutely he stepped inside the tent's tattered remains. He brushed the snow from the right hand of the body, where it was frozen to the rifle stock, the forefinger tightly squeezing the trigger. There was a jagged scar that ran to the wrist and Jed knew that he had found MacKelvy.

It took him almost five minutes to find the head, and it still took him by surprise. He recoiled from the vision of it as it stared open eyed from the corner of the tent, ten feet from the body. The claws of the grizzly had destroyed the left side of the head, but that savage, twisted grin remained beneath the reddish moustache.

Jed was no longer able to contain the boiling cauldron in his gut. He rushed out and spent its contents on the frozen ground. Whiskey came to him, nuzzling his face and neck. Jed reassured the dog and he sat quietly beside his master, surveying the grisly scene.

Whiskey's low growl snapped Jed back sharply. He picked up the rifle quickly and brushed the snow from the lenses of the scope. Slowly he scanned in the direction of Whiskey's gaze. It was several minutes before he heard the dull drone of the search plane. He ran to the 'copter, quickly surveyed it, and found the radio and instruments damaged irreparably. In the cockpit he found the flare gun still in its compartment. He removed it along with several ground flares.

Jed listened to the sounds of the aircraft. It was clear that the plane was flying a pattern, slowly zig-zagging in the general direction of the clearing where he stood. He waited until the plane began its return run, using the time to set the ground flares and soak the pile of firewood near the center of camp with fuel from the jerry can that had been strapped to the chopper. As the drone of the plane grew louder, he fired the flare into the air, touched off the gas soaked woodpile, and ran from flare to flare, lighting them as he went.

The pilot spotted the brilliant red flare soon after it reached its zenith. He was already banking the plane sharply when the smoke of the fuel drenched fire billowed black into the clear sky. Immediately he radioed for the chopper in the next sector, giving him the location. In this timber he would not be able to land the single engined Piper. He wagged his wings at the lone figure that waved to him on his second pass.

It was a few short minutes before Jed heard the approach of the large chopper as it skimmed the trees. The heavy thump, thump of its rotors told him that it could only be a search and rescue type employed by the service. He turned away when the downdraft of the giant rotors whipped the surface snow into a stinging blizzard. There was no urgency to tell the story to them, they would know as soon as the rotors stopped. He was left with a feeling of emptiness.

Jim Raudsep stepped from the cockpit of the chopper, stopped to look at the scene, and strode towards Jed. He'd recognized Jed the instant he'd seen the lone figure when they had cleared the fringe of trees. 'Damn him!' Raudsep had thought, 'he moves through these woods like an animal, alone. Eight good men die, and that bastard comes away untouched. How the hell does he do it?!' Raudsep didn't like Jed, he never really had. He thought about the first time he'd tried to offer Jed a job as a guide. Jed had spat to the side, looked him in the eye, and turned on his heel. The man hadn't even been civil. Then he thought about their last meeting. Jed had come riding into the hunting camp on that big bay of his, dragging the headless carcass of an elk. How the hell had he known that the warden would be in camp to check on Raudsep's operation, Jim would never figure out. Taking only the heads was a piece of stupidity on MacKelvy's part that had damn near cost him his outfitter's license.

Even now, as Raudsep rapidly approached Jed, he shivered at the cold gaze that looked through him. "Marsh," he said flatly.

"Jim," Jed replied coolly.

"God this is horrible," a sergeant of the R.C.M.P. said as he hurried towards Raudsep and Jed from the helicopter.

"Murder . . . cold blooded murder," Raudsep spat viciously. He looked at Jed who had raised an eyebrow above a cold gray eye. "What do you think of your damn wild friends now, goddam it?!"

Jed's short, tight laugh startled the sergeant who

opened his mouth to speak, but was cut off by Jed's bitter words. "You talk of murder, Jim, but only when it happens to men. I think no more or less of the beasts than I ever did. It's a system you never could understand."

"You sonofabitch!" Raudsep exploded. "You dare to defend them with the souls of dead men still hovering over this bloodbath?!"

"Your grief is touching," Jed said sarcastically. "I didn't know you'd got religion." He turned and picked up his pack, preparing to leave.

"Hey there, hold on a minute, man," the sergeant called. "You can't go just yet."

"Why not?"

"I have to get a statement from you."

Jed turned and looked at the man. He shrugged his shoulders. "All right, it's short and simple. I was working my line when I spotted a congregation of ravens. I investigated and found them feeding on carrion."

"Carrion?! My God man, you call this carrion??"

"Man or animal, when it's dead and laying around it's carrion."

"That's sick . . ."

"That's fact. Sentimentality doesn't change it," Jed replied unemotionally.

"But how," the sergeant rejoined, "can you look at this and not be bothered."

"Who said I wasn't bothered? Death in any form is frightening . . . This . . . this can't even be described."

"You don't make sense."

"So I've been told. Do you want the rest of the statement?"

"Yes, go ahead."

"I heard the plane," Jed continued, "and gave the signal. You know the rest. Now, I have a question. What the hell were they doing out here?"

"Tracking the bear. He hit Simpson's place a while back, and Bob Price's last week. Busted up Price a bit."

Jed's eyes narrowed in concern. "How bad?"

"Just a few ribs and his arm. His boy, Sam, drove the bear off."

"Anyone killed by the bear before now?"

"No, at least not that we know of. But you know about these marauders. Anyway, some of the men decided that he'd better be stopped before he did . . ." the sergeant faltered.

"Something like this?" Jed finished.

"Yeah, something like this."

"Fools at a fool's game," Jed muttered.

"What?" the sergeant asked, looking up.

"Nothing. Mind if I get going? It's two and a half hours back to my place."

"I'm afraid we're going to need you . . . Raudsep!" he shouted and waited until Jim rejoined them, red eyed and angry. "You tell mister Marsh what you told me just before we landed."

Raudsep shot the sergeant a hard look. "I'm not so sure anymore."

"Tell him, dammit. There's eight men dead out here. Leave your personal feelings out of it."

"All right, all right." Raudsep looked at Jed through squinted eyes. "I told him that you are probably the best tracker in the territory."

"You see we . . ." the sergeant began.

"Forget it," Jed said flatly.

"I told you!" Raudsep shot at the sergeant.

"Just hold on a minute . . ."

"I said forget it, and now I'll tell you why. Everything's against it. Wind, snow, and the bear. With all this commotion he probably headed for the center of his territory. With the timber, there's no way to spot him from the air. The odds are with him and against everybody else."

"Hell," Raudsep cackled morbidly, "you're probably glad the bear did to MacKelvy what he did."

"What in hell is that supposed to mean?" the sergeant snapped.

"They hated each others guts . . . Ask him to deny it. Go

on, ask him!"

"The way MacKelvy and I felt about each other was never any secret. He was the one who always came looking for trouble, and a death like that," Jed gestured at the remains in the tent angrily, "I wouldn't wish on anyone."

"All right! That's enough from both of you," the sergeant shouted. "There's death all around us and you two are acting like asses."

"You do your duty, whatever the hell you think it is, sergeant, I've done mine," Jed replied caustically. "But you go after that bear now and you're as big a fool as I've met."

"You won't help us?"

"No."

"I'll put that in my report, Marsh."

"You do that, sergeant," Jed said and turned away. "Whiskey, take the point." He looked back at the two figures and added, "If that bear hits again, chances are that it will be at my place, assuming he keeps to his pattern. If and when he does, I won't hesitate to kill him."

"I hope the sonofabitch catches you in the open and does to you what he did here!" Raudsep shouted as Jed began the trail home.

Jed stopped and turned. There was a half-frozen smile on his face. "I expected better out of you, Jim. I try not to judge a man by the help he hires, but I guess I was wrong this time."

"Damn you to hell."

"Probably already am," Jed said and picked up the trail. When he reached the top of the ridge, he looked back down. The detail was loading the last of the plastic bagged bodies aboard the helicopter unceremoniously, like garbage collectors cleaning up a messy campsite. He looked to the north, where he knew the bear waited. He shook his head, knowing that the world was closing in on the both of them. Soon there would be no place left for their breed, for he and the bear were wild and independent, and the world of man was intolerant of such things.

CHAPTER 24

JED CLEARED the ridge and set a course that ran straight toward the cabin where Jenny waited. He felt an urgency to get back and check on her and the horses. He made no effort to conceal his presence, Whiskey would give him ample warning if the bear was near. He was reasonably sure that the animal would not chance another meeting in the open, but he had struck the cabin and come away unscathed. Jed was certain that the bear would try again. The questions was when? He remembered the bear in Montana, it had taken him eight nights of patient sitting before he had killed it.

Jed paused in a small clearing to get his second wind. He still had about four miles to go and he would have to recross the river soon. Ahead he could see the lumpy landscape that marked the brush along the river's banks. He would have to find a path through that brush. In his mind he pictured the landscape as it had been last fall. There was a path, he remembered, to the south and not more than a half mile away. He motioned to Whiskey and they continued.

To the north in the wreckage of a deer yard, the grizzly stood amid the carnage. He had come upon the yard on the way back from the campsite where he had done battle. The victory there had done something to the animal, he had changed from predator to killer. There had been no need to slaughter five deer and yet he had done so. He had eaten his fill and kept the hungry pack of wolves at bay. Their smell was still close and the bear growled ominously. The wolves were patient, knowing that eventually the bear would move on, leaving them with plenty. But they did not test his anger any more, they sensed the danger he represented, and lurked in the shadows of the mantled forest.

Desire for sleep had left the bear and he was beginning to feel the urge to travel. He paced the edge of the yard nervously, wanting to go and yet wanting to stay. The day was growing old, shadows putting a beard on the clean face of the snow. Finally the bear settled down. Tomorrow he would begin the trek to the south.

About the same time, Jed broke the clearing that held the safety and warmth of his cabin. It was almost an hour ahead of his usual arrival time. Jenny heard the whinny of the bay and looked outside in time to see Jed approach the corral. She opened the door and called to him with a wave. He returned the greeting and disappeared into the horse shed. Jenny knew that he would not come to the cabin for a while. She knew that he had been spending time out there for the past two weeks, but had been unable to find the reason on her daily trips to pet the horses. She dismissed the thought of going out now, knowing that it would probably displease Jed.

Jed quickly skinned and fleshed the few animals that had been yielded by his trapline before Whiskey had drawn him away from his work and to the horror beyond Moose Ridge. Tomorrow he would bring in the traps. It would no longer be safe to work the line, he would have to be satisfied with the catch he already had. After the new pelts were on the stretchers and hanging, he looked over the pelts that were suspended on a wire in the shed. The take was good, but it didn't approach what he could have taken. He would have to hope that the prices did not decline. This was all he was going to get. Before leaving the shed, he retrieved the moosehide moccasins he had been making for Jenny and put the finishing touches on them. At least he would have something for her come Christmas.

Jed decided that he would avoid telling Jenny about the incident on Moose Ridge. There was no reason to cause her any undue alarm. He knew that she didn't have any knowledge of what constituted a good catch, so he would simply give her that as the reason for pulling in the traps.

He decided that he would have to tell her that he had run across the grizzly's track in order to justify his command that she stay inside the cabin at all times from now on, unless he was with her. She would not easily give up her daily trips to see the horses and wander around the little clearing. Jed was still absorbed in his thoughts as he approached the door to the cabin. He looked at the deep gashes that remained in some of the boards of the door. He had little doubt that the grizzly was the same animal that inflicted the damage at MacKelvy's last camp.

The door swung open and he looked up to see Jenny smiling at him as he mounted the steps to the porch. "Hi there," she said cheerily. "You're back early."

Jed tugged off the heavy fur hat and smiled wearily back at her. "A little, I guess. Got any coffee on?"

"Ready and waiting. I'll go pour you a cup."

Jed stopped to stomp the snow from his boots. He turned to whistle at Whiskey. "Get in here dammit. It's cold out there."

Whiskey looked up amiably from the bird track he was investigating and trotted to the door. When the dog was safely inside, Jed pushed the door closed and slipped the bar in place. He hung up his cap and shrugged off the heavy coat, placing it on a peg. He leaned the .300 magnum he had *borrowed* from Tom Phillips' cockpit against the wall and he reached out to touch the cold steel of its barrel before he deposited the extra box of shells he had liberated on the table. He could return the rifle to Phillips' widow next spring . . . if there was a spring.

"Where did you get it?" Jenny asked. She had stood near the kitchen doorway watching Jed, holding the big coffee mug and waiting for him to speak. He was unusually quiet tonight.

"What?" he asked, suddenly looking up.

"The rifle . . . where did you get it?"

"Oh that. I've had it out in the shed. Just decided that I'd better bring it in," he lied. "I ran across the bear's track again. I don't think it would be a good idea for you to be spending any time outside for a few days."

Jenny looked at him as he took the cup of coffee from her. She noticed that he hadn't looked at her when he explained about the rifle and there was something that didn't ring quite true in the account. She didn't pursue it. "How close were the tracks?" she asked.

"Close enough to be of concern," Jed answered steadily. "I wouldn't be surprised if he pays us another visit. I've decided to pull the traps, I've made a pretty good catch and I'm afraid that the bear might steal anything I catch from now on. No sense in giving him reason to stay around here."

"Would you be doing this if I weren't here?" she asked quietly.

Jed caught the implication and answered immediately. "Probably. There's no sense in taking careless risks."

"Then why didn't you pull the traps after he hit the cabin the last time?"

"Because that might have been an isolated event. Now that I've spotted his tracks again, I know that it's not. He's included us in his travel pattern."

"Does that mean he'll be back for sure?"

"It's a reasonable assumption."

Jenny saw something in Jed's eyes. It wasn't really worry, more like concern. As the evening passed she watched his face, noting the changes in the lines, the way he seemed to drift off when she was talking. Jenny suspected that Jed had seen more than just track and was not telling her. He wanted to spare her from the worry of it. Not so long ago he would not have been so cautious about her feelings, she thought. It was one of the many signs that she had picked up on over the past few weeks. She was sure that he was developing some feelings toward her and she wanted to reinforce them at every opportunity.

"I saw a bird I couldn't identify today," she said. "He was at the suet for a while." She waited for a response. "He was as big as a house and must have weighed at least three hundred pounds . . ."

Jed snapped his head up. "What?"

Jenny smiled at him. "Well, at least I finally got your attention."

Jed grinned sheepishly. "I'm sorry, I guess I wasn't paying much attention. Just tired, I guess. Maybe I'll turn in early."

"Yeah, me too," Jenny agreed.

Jed stretched, rose, and walked slowly to the door to look outside. His wilderness had taken on a less friendly atmosphere. He was out there somewhere, just waiting for another mistake to be made. But Jed was waiting too, for he knew bears to be creatures of habit, and sooner or later he'd use that knowledge to eliminate the threat the bear posed. When the fires were banked and all was secured, he crawled into the sleeping bag near the fireplace. It took longer than usual for him to fall asleep.

In the darkness MacKelvy came at him, the pipe falling in pieces from his huge hand, the evil grin on his face. In slow motion, Jed's right hand reached out and made contact with the red-haired man's jaw. The head went spinning off the shoulders and skidded to a stop against the far edge of the tent, its left side torn and bloody, the eyes staring. Jed stared at it and screamed.

Suddenly he was awake, cold sweat pouring down him. Jenny cradled his head in her lap and he was holding tightly to her waist. He realized instantly that he must tell her. She must know now that something had gone terribly wrong on the trail. Had she not been here, he would have endured, just as he had endured and finally conquered the dreams that had plagued him after Cassie's death. Had she not been here, there would have been no scream, for there would have been no one to hear it.

Slowly he sat up, relinquishing his hold on Jenny's slender waist, wiping his forehead with a callused right hand. "I'm sorry," he said, "I didn't mean to wake you."

Jenny looked at him with softness in her wide, brown eyes and ran her soft hand across his weather hardened face, stroking his beard. "It's all right. Do you want to tell me about it? I know something must have happened out there today."

Jed looked at her and then away. She looked so damn young, so wide eyed and innocent. A contradiction, a piece of loveliness in a savage world. And yet, she was a reflection of his world, for there was unbounded beauty that dwelt side by side with the savagery. Without delving into the gruesome, brutal details, he told Jenny of the devastation at Moose Ridge. She sat silently, listening as he spoke, always maintaining physical contact with him. He did not move away from her touch.

"It must have been horrible," Jenny said upon the completion of his story.

"It wasn't exactly pleasant," Jed agreed grimly. He looked into Jenny's eyes and reached out to touch her cheek. "I didn't even tell them you were here," he said hesitantly. "I should have told them. I guess that with everything that happened, I forgot. I'm sorry."

Jenny studied him for a moment. He suddenly seemed so tired, as if he'd lost the reserve he always seemed to have. "I'm not," she whispered softly and leaned forward to kiss him on the mouth. She drew back, letting the gentle light of the glowing embers silhouette her figure. "I'm most certainly not."

"Jenny, are you sure you know what you're letting yourself in for? Are you sure you won't regret it later?" Jed asked, knowing full well that her words and gestures could mean only one thing.

"I'm sure," she replied, moving closer to him. "I'm very sure."

"I make commitments for life, Jenny. For life. You must understand that."

Jenny's arms encircled his neck and her body pressed hard against his. "I love you," she whispered in his ear. "That's all I have to understand right now."

These were words that Jed needed to hear. The time for bitterness and hate was gone. It had been gone for almost a year and a half now, but there had been little to fill the void left by it. But now there was Jenny, with her many moods, her girlish laughter, the velvet of her voice, the allure of her feminine figure. All the things that Jed had shut out, or at least had tried to, flooded his mind. The obstinacy, the quarrelsome idealism, the depression she had manifested now seemed petty and insignificant, things of the past. Now there seemed to be a foundation on which to build. Each of them had suffered pain and shared it, each of them had felt joy and had touched each other with it. Such are the maneuvers of the mind, the ability to selectively perceive when necessary, the necessity dictated by want, that have kept the human race viable over the years. The human race has been given the gift of reason and feels compelled to justify with reason what other species do as a matter of course. That is what Jed was doing now, and he knew it. He smiled, as much to himself as to Jenny, and took her to himself.

In the small hours of the morning, Jenny lay basking in the warmth of the man who lay beside her, wondering at the curious twists and turns of life's pathway. Not so long ago she would have considered a man such as Jed an adversary to be dealt with, an opponent worthy only of uncompromising antagonism. Jed had shown her another side to the story, another vision of a way of life that she would have otherwise persisted in believing to be wrong and base. She understood now that categorizing led to depersonalization, and that made it very easy to condemn another's way of life. It was a mistake that she would not be likely to repeat. She had learned that compromise was a necessary part of existence, that it could open doors that would otherwise remain forever closed. But she did not sell herself short either. Left to his own devices, she was sure that Jed would have continued to reject all of mankind in the name of those few who had done him harm. She knew that that was not a healthy situation and gave herself some measure of credit in proving that not all were against him.

She looked at Jed, studied the small scars on his chest, the lines in his relaxed face, the minute details that might have gone unnoticed. She had already looked into the part of him that could not be seen, that part that had been revealed to her in his writing. She was glad now that she had trespassed, that she had opened the box, for indeed, she knew more about him than he did about her. If he had not said that he loved her, she knew that he eventually would, for she understood him to be a man of depth and feeling. As he came to know her better, his love would grow. For now she was content to love him, to satisfy his physical needs, and build on the foundation of what he termed a "commitment." She nestled close to him, resting her head on his chest and listening to his breathing, feeling the strength of his work hardened muscles against her soft skin. Soon she slept, an arm thrown carelessly across his chest.

Jed awoke before she did. In the half light of the morning he touched her hair and ran his hand lightly down her back. He sighed to himself and looked at the ceiling. In his mind, he saw Cassie smiling and smiled back. She would not leave his memory, but she would no longer be ever present in his mind. A man had to go on, he knew that now. He bade Cassie farewell and thanked her for finally showing him that there was an eternal spring. A spring that did not come with the turning of the seasons, but one that dwelt within the mind and the soul.

CHAPTER 25

JED PAUSED at the edge of the clearing. He appraised the tops of the small spruces that rose above the drifts. Finally he spotted the one that he wanted and walked over to it. Using the bow saw, he made short work of cutting it. It made a perfectly symmetrical Christmas tree. Christmas was now only five days away, according to Jenny's calendar. He had pulled the traps without incident and nothing had occurred since then. He was beginning to wonder if his judgement about the bear had been wrong. If it had, then he had given up part of his income needlessly. Well, maybe not, the time he's spent with Jenny was certainly worth whatever he might have lost in money.

He laughed spontaneously. He just felt good and it came from deep within him, rumbling out with rich tones. He grasped the tree by its trunk and dragged it back to the cabin where Jenny was stringing berries and rose hips together to form a garland for the tree. Jed thought about all the time he had spent gathering and drying those fruits for future use. Well, they could be salvaged.

Jenny was singing carols when Jed opened the door. She looked up from the collection of berries and string on her lap and smiled at him. He grinned back and began fashioning a base for the tree. Jed burst out in a chorus of "Joy to the World" and was joined, in off-key harmony, by Jenny. It formed the sort of scene that nostalgic producers like to portray in film, but without the contrivance of a production. Outside the horses milled in the corral, pawing at the scattering of hay left on the ground.

That night the two of them admired the tree they had decorated and languished in the warmth of the fire. They made love and slept in each others arms, oblivious to the world around them. Day followed day in a familiar pattern and Christmas came, bringing with it that special joy of giving. Jenny greeted the day like a child, rising early with anticipation. Jed, although more reserved, joined in the revelry. He was truly happy, but there was a nagging feeling in the back of his mind. A feeling that had nothing to do with his relationship with Jenny.

In the woods, five miles to the north of Jed's clearing, the grizzly was on the prowl. He'd hunted in his wandering way for over two weeks, killing as he went and leaving a wide swath of destruction in his path. The forest had grown even more quiet with every mile of his passage. The tight knots of deer dispersed, taking with them the wolf packs, moving further and further away from the deadly presence of the winter bear. Only the ravens followed his progress with active and raucous interest, filling their bellies with the leavings of his formidable brutality.

The cold of the Arctic pressed down in the first week of January, increasing the bear's restless nature. He moved on, southward, closing in on the small clearing. It was a cold and dark night when the smell of Jed's horses drifted up to him. In the stillness he could hear them milling in the shed. The human odor that mingled with the others no longer concerned the bear. He no longer associated that odor with fear. He had met the creature and conquered him. He began the approach carelessly, moving directly toward the corrals. He heard the barking of the dog and ignored it.

Jed rolled over in bed, shaking the sleep from his mind. Whiskey was barking urgently, there was something out there. Jed called softly to the dog and went to the window to investigate. The snow was lit only with the light of the stars and Jed could see nothing. Still, Whiskey was not given to falsely warning his master. Jed reached for his pants on the peg. He did not have a firm grip on them when the silence of the night was split by the sound of breaking timber. Jed dropped the pants and grabbed for his boots. In an instant he heard the screams of agony from the shed. He grabbed the rifle, threw open the door, and sprinted for the corral, a dark figure crossing the silvery expanse of snow. He saw the splinters of the smashed pole and knew immediately what it meant. It took his eyes a moment to adjust and when they did he swallowed hard.

The monster stood in all his glory, over seven feet tall, the scimitar claws glinting shiny black at the end of massive paws, his nose blowing enormous plumes of breath that hung frostily in the air. Jed remembered the scene of MacKelvy's camp and retreated, bringing the scope of the magnum to bear on the bulk of the animal. Just as he pulled the trigger, the bear dropped to all fours and the slug splatted harmlessly on the poles behind him. Jed did not feel the powerful kick of the rifle, nor did he seem to hear its sharp report. Quickly he chambered another round.

The bear was on the move, he'd cleared the break in the corral and turned northward before Jed had locked down the bolt. Jed sighted through the scope, found the target, and squeezed the trigger again. Nothing. A little click that marked the progress of the firing pin and nothing more. The hand loaded shell had misfired. Why the bear had not charged, Jed did not know, but he was thankful. In another instant the bear was gone, leaving a wide rumpled trail in the heavy blanket of snow. Jed stood there, sweating heavily in the subzero temperature, steam rolling off his body, making him appear a wispy apparition. He moved toward the corral, straining his every sense to the limit. Unthinkingly, he chambered the last shell in the rifle's magazine, uncertain of its performance. It, too, was a hand load.

The bay lay on his side just outside the shattered door of the shed. He was kicking feebly in the throes of agony. Jed saw the shiny shaft of bone that pierced the skin of the bay's right foreleg and the dark spreading stains that spotted the unsoiled surface of the light covering of fresh snow. Without ever losing the slightest consciousness of the surrounding environment, Jed knelt beside the bay, his old friend with whom he had begun the trip and his adventure to the north. He laid a hand on the silky cheek of the animal and caressed it lovingly. Even in pain, the bay quieted at his touch. It wasn't meant to be this way, Jed thought. He'd always envisioned the steadfast old horse living out his last days in quiet pasture, retired from life's labor.

Only a few moments had passed and, despite the animal's stillness, Jed knew its suffering must be ended. He said a quiet goodbye, stood, and, holding the muzzle of the rifle an inch from the bay's ear, pulled the trigger. The crash of the rifle shook Jed to the bone, letting the chill in. He shivered and a transparent tear slid down his face. He shook a fist and shouted hoarsely, "Now it's personal, you son of a bitch!"

Jenny watched from the doorway, holding to the thirty-thirty as Jed calmed the remaining two horses and hammered strong boards across the splintered opening. She waited as he walked slowly back to the cabin, his shoulders slumped in grief. She knew how he felt about the big, gentle horse, and she remembered how the bay had brought them safely home when it seemed certain that that first strong storm of winter would end their lives. She had showed the horse an extra measure of affection on her trips to the corral. She felt the pain of loss almost as intensely as Jed.

Jed did not sleep that night, nor would he sleep for the next few nights. He had begun his patient wait for the bear to return to the kill. Each morning he would pull on his coat and fix the snowshoes to his packs and check the perimeter of the clearing. Each time he would come back without having found new sign. It became apparent that the bear had drifted away from the clearing. Jed's patience began to wear thin. He waited quietly by the window each night, checking the clearing beyond as far as he could see, sleeping restlessly during the day.

Jenny noticed the change in him before it became obvious. The tightening of the bonds between them made her more sensitive to the changes in his moods. She knew when he began prowling the interior of the cabin during the day that something was brewing in his mind. She knew that soon he would not be content to wait, that something would send him out after the beast. It gave her reason to be afraid, but she held it in and did not let Jed see the fear. She was awake the night he stepped quietly out on the porch, rifle at the ready.

What it was that told Jed the bear was back, he did not know. Perhaps it was that sense that had served him so well in the past. Whiskey confirmed his suspicion with a low growl. The moon was almost full and there was an electricity in the stillness of the night. Jed knew the bear was out there waiting, but he could not see him, there was not even any eye shine. The bear stayed well within the shadows of the trees. The bear knew Jed was there, his nose and ears fed his brain the information. His dull eyes caught the glint of the moon on the rifle barrel. So they stood, two adversaries, each unwilling to meet the other on open ground in the night.

Finally Jed came back in to keep his vigil, he wanted to lose no more horses. Jenny was waiting in the darkness, sitting up on the bed with the blankets drawn close around her. She was feeling the same chill of fear that had been with her the first time the bear had come. Jed saw her huddled there and came to sit by her side. He leaned over and brushed her hair with his lips.

"Did I wake you?"

Jenny shook her head, "No. He was here, wasn't he?"

Jed smiled in the darkness. Jenny was beginning to sense things too. That gave him a measure of comfort. If something were to happen to him, it would give her a better chance. "Yes," he said, "he was back."

"You're going after him, aren't you?"

"I have to. We can't let him keep us prisoner, and that is exactly what he'll do . . . even when he's not around."

"I wish you wouldn't."

"I know, I know," Jed replied.

"But that won't change your mind," she said with resignation in her voice.

"No. It must be done. He's a creature of habit, even with his idiosyncrasies. That will be his undoing."

"You sound very sure."

"I am. Besides, I'll have Whiskey with me. There's no way he'll come on me without my knowing that he's coming."

Jenny understood the finality of his decision, but she no longer viewed his decisions with hostility. "You had better get some sleep then," she said. "Whiskey and I can finish out the night for you."

Jed held her close, realizing the fear that she must feel, aware of the strength she had to exercise to keep it hidden from him. It pleased him that she could do so when she knew that he might not come back from this hunt. It took a strong woman to live under these circumstances and his admiration for Jenny grew. "I love you," he said haltingly.

Jenny knew how hard those words must have been for him to say, it was the first time he had said them to her. "And I you," she whispered back. "Please now, get some sleep. I'll wake you if anything happens."

Jed changed places with Jenny, curling up in the blankets. He was soon asleep, as if the decision let the fatigue overtake him. Jenny listened to the deep breathing she had become accustomed to. She leaned over and kissed him on the cheek and whispered those words women have whispered to their men for centuries. "Be careful, my darling . . . be careful."

CHAPTER 26

IT WAS GOOD to be back in the woods again. Good to feel the trail beneath the ungainly looking snowshoes. Good to see the track and know the feeling of the hunt. It was Jed's world, a world he knew and understood. It was the grizzly's world as well. That gave this day a flavor of challenge. Jed had put Jenny out of his mind, It was necessary. Only the hunt must occupy his thoughts today, and that must be pushed far back, for the senses had to be in the forefront. Sight, smell, and touch the only realities, the only information that must feed the brain for instantaneous reaction.

The track was fresh. Jed had found the bed that the grizzly had made not six hundred yards from the cabin. The bear had not moved until Jed had started across the small clearing. The path that led from the bed headed north and west, a deep plowed furrow in the quilt of snow. The spacing of the footprints in the bottom of the furrow told Jed that the bear moved quickly. He would be far ahead of him. It was a good sign, for the pace would tire the animal. Sooner or later he would stand and fight. Jed pushed the pace, giving Whiskey encouragement as the dog struggled in the deep snow.

Jenny sat in the chair by the fire, recalling the morning. She had watched Jed dress with the meticulous care of a warrior about to go into battle. It was almost a ritual, the way he had done it. She was mildly surprised that he chose not the heavy wools that he had worn while running the trapline, but the fringed elkskins he had made himself. He had disdained the leather and rubber packs for the boot-style moccasins of moosehide. He had laid all the incidental things such as rope, matches, cartridges, and a small first aid kit on the bed, checking and rechecking the items. The whole kit weighed less than ten pounds and could easily be carried in the pockets of the wolverine and elk-skin coat. He would not be slowed by having to carry a pack. She thought about the running conversation that they had carried on.

"Why," she had asked, "are you going to wear the moosehide moccasins? Won't they be cold?"

Jed had smiled. "A little colder than the packs, I guess, but they're also lighter. I'll be able to keep a faster pace without tiring so quickly. By leaving the hair on the out-side, I made sure that they will turn water. My feet won't get wet."

"Are the elkskins lighter too?"

"Not really. They do stop the wind better than the wool and they are not as bulky. That's a real consideration when you have to react quickly. Besides, I like them and I'm com-fortable in them."

It was only when Jed went to the window box that Jenny suspected there was some other, deeper reason for the way Jed was dressing as he did. She watched as he re-moved a small nylon bag from the box and opened it. With quiet deliberation, he removed the bear claw necklace and the beaver skin hat that had lain within, untouched, for many months. The necklace was simple in design, six large claws from the front paws of a large black bear separated by blood red beads. The hat was adorned with two feath-ers, their shafts protected by red felt wrapped with black yarn at each end. He went to the box once more, with-drawing a small fringed buckskin bag. This he fastened to his belt just in front of the huge, Bowie style knife that al-ready hung in its sheath on his hip.

Jed looked up into Jenny's questioning eyes. "Tradi-tion," he said simply as he drew the necklace over his head and positioned it on his chest. "And a little superstition perhaps. The tribes that used to live in this area would call it religion, and I guess my beliefs run pretty well the same. Maybe with less conviction, but close."

"All of this has some meaning then . . . I mean beyond the utilitarian meaning?" Jenny inquired.

"Yes, yes it does."

Jenny now reflected on the explanation Jed had given. Each of the items he wore or carried with him held a special significance to him. Each piece of apparel was in harmony with his environment, for each was from it. If you believed the legends, man drew his strength and wisdom from the spirit above as manifested in the creatures below. Thus Jed carried traditional totems as tokens of his faith in his way of life. Jenny thought about it, and came to the conclusion that if these beliefs helped to keep Jed alive there must be something to them. Even if it was a sort of manifestation of self-confidence, she could accept it. She did wonder if there was something that had turned him away from the traditional Christian religion, or if this was simply an addition.

Jed stopped at the top of a wooded rise to survey the territory that spread out below him. The bear had led him onward for over three hours now. Still he had not shown himself. Jed looked at the meadow beneath. The furrow that marked the grizzly's passage was plain even at this distance. Jed studied it from where he stood, retracing it to where he was at this moment. On the hillside was a long skid mark where the bear had temporarily lost control in the drifts. Whiskey sniffed the air and whined softly. Jed patted the dog's head. He knew as well, the beast was beginning to tire. At the far end of the meadow the trail began to curve slightly back to the east. The bear was trying to quarter, to gain an advantage.

Jed squinted at the sun in the clear, dark blue of the January sky. He unwound the scarf that Jenny had made for him, letting it drop from his face, and squatted on his snowshoes. He would break for a quick lunch and allow the bear to complete his maneuver. He would take the chance of losing the grizzly, cut back to the northeast, and try to intercept him. If the tactic did not completely succeed, it would still place him between the bear and his clearing. He mapped his strategy while he ate and fed Whiskey bits of sandwich. Going away from the bear's trail would mean that the dog would have a harder time traveling. He would have to leave the trail plowed by the bear and follow in the prints of his master across expanses of deep powder. Jed took that into account in his calculations and still felt that they could at least reach the safety of the rock cavern that lay in the heart of his trapping territory.

Whiskey's yip in the clear, cold air had carried quite clearly to the bear that morning. For a few moments he had stayed in the den beneath the spruce, listening and testing the air. The man and dog were coming his way. As the scent became stronger, it became plain that they were zeroing in on his resting place. Of course, this was not a thought process as such, merely a sifting of messages fed to his brain by his acute senses. He was once again being pursued, and he moved from the comfort of his bed to the deep snow, cutting a new trail. All morning the odor of the man and dog carried to him, never falling behind, always gaining. His breath was coming in short, tight gasps when he reached the top of the hill and tumbled down the side to the meadow. A splinter of copper jacket had found its way to an anterior horn of his spinal column that day long ago when Sam Price had turned his charge with a burning reminder of the strange power held by the two legged creatures, and it caused him pain.

He stopped abruptly in the center of the meadow, the blood of madness coloring his eyes. The scent carried to him once again and he began a wide sweeping turn to the east. He would run no longer. He gained the cover of the brush at the edge of the meadow and stopped. The odor of Jed's sandwiches carried to him and still he waited. Only when the odors began to grow fainter did he move out of the cover, emerging carefully from the snow-laden brush, ready for an instantaneous retreat. Nothing. He waited a bit more. Still nothing. He began retracing his steps, moving more easily through the path already established. At the top of the hill he investigated the site where Jed and

Whiskey had stopped. The scent was powerful. In a hole next to where Jed had squatted the grizzly detected the hated smell of gun oil. the odors of the trail to the north were there, but growing fainter. The wind caught the bear full in the face when he turned toward that trail and, with only a moment's hesitation, the pursued became the pursuer.

Jed paused, waiting for Whiskey to catch up and rest a bit. He could see that the soft snow was taking its toll on the big, gray dog. The sun told him that he had been on this trail for almost an hour now. He still had not seen any sign of the bear. It did not disturb Jed, he had not expected to cut his trail just yet. While Whiskey lay panting, Jed used the scope of the rifle to scan the landscape ahead. He saw nothing. Reslinging the rifle, he knelt to check on the bindings of his snowshoes and then reached out to pat his dog.

"Well, son, you about ready to give it a try again?" he asked Whiskey.

The dog answered with a lolling tongued "smile" and rose to follow at his master's heels. Where Jed went, he would always follow. The way Jed felt about Whiskey was manifest in the way he looked at the dog, his eyes held that special affection reserved for but few in his life. Jed smiled at Whiskey and turned to pursue the trail.

It was another half hour before the chill coursed down Jed's spine. He stopped suddenly. There was no wind and no perceptible drop in the temperature. By the sun it was only around two in the afternoon. Since early this morning he and Whiskey had come almost twelve miles, four since the change in direction. Jed recognized the feeling and knew that it came not from physical effects. He should have cut track or caught a glimpse of the bear. At least Whiskey should have smelled the bear, but he had given no indication as yet. Something was wrong . . . something was seriously wrong.

The sensation stayed with Jed and he was sure of its meaning. The bear had doubled back on him. That meant one of two things, either the bear was well on his way back to the cabin, or he was at this very minute stalking him. Jed looked at his surroundings. He was at an extreme disadvantage. He was in heavy timber now, the wind was in his face and that meant it was in the bear's face as well, if he were following. Whiskey would not be able to give him much warning. He took stock of the situation, running the terrain over in his mind. If he turned sharply to the south, he would be able to reach a large meadow in fifteen or twenty minutes. It was a meadow he knew well, he cut hay from it in the summer for his horses' winter feed. The only problem that such a turn presented was that it would put him on a semi-parallel path to the bear, moving through heavy timber. And if the bear was indeed back there, it was certain that he would sense the change in direction and a good chance that he would alter his direction to intercept.

There was no time to dally over the decision. If Jed stayed put, his field of fire would be extremely limited, and the range short. The bear's charge would certainly carry him into Jed even if the wound was fatal. Jed snapped his head up at the chatter of a nuthatch, whistled sharply to Whiskey, and began the push for the meadow. If he could just make it in time. The leering grin of MacKelvy's dead face surfaced in the back of Jed's mind and Raudsep's voice danced jeeringly . . . "I hope the sonofabitch catches you in the open . . ."

"Yeah, me too, you bastard," Jed grunted through his teeth. "I'd prefer that to heavy timber." He unslung the rifle and placed a finger on the safety, ready to fire if necessary.

The bear sensed the change in Jed's direction of travel almost immediately and altered his own course. As yet his keen nose did not detect the fear that had been present that night at MacKelvy's camp, so he did not blaze a trail that would intersect Jed's. He was more cautious than he had first been in his contact with man. He did not have the cover of darkness and he still feared the strange weapon that could hurt without touching. He rambled on, clawing his way over some of the deadfalls, sliding under others, closing the gap between himself and his quarry slowly. He reached the brush line at the edge of the meadow, knowing that the enemy was still to the north and still moving. He cleared the brush and turned sharply.

Jed was in the meadow at the same instant. Whiskey struggled through the deep snow and saw the bear immediately. Jed heard the deep throated growl and turned to face the south and saw him for the first time of the day. He was a little over two hundred yards away and already beginning a fast charge through the deep snow. The speed the grizzly was capable of under these conditions was awesome. Dropping quickly to one knee, he slipped off the safety and, using the sling to steady his aim, found the target and fired. The hit was solid, but not fatal. The bear dropped his right shoulder and came on. With smooth action, Jed chambered another shell without taking his eye from the scope. He fired a second time. Spray flew from the bear's head and he faltered. He was close enough that Jed could see the blood flowing from his nose and mouth. Whiskey charged through the snow toward the bear.

"Whiskey! No! Dammit no!"

Jed's call caught up with the dog just in time and he turned aside, escaping the full blow the grizzly aimed at him. It still rolled him several feet and opened gashes along his ribs. Jed heard Whiskey's yelps, but the bear was not yet finished. The force of his own strength in delivering the blow had flung the bear on his side. His vision was growing clouded, he tasted the salt in his mouth, and his brain burned. He struggled to get up, floundering in the snows of the meadow. He found his legs and lumbered forward briefly.

Jed steadied the rifle and waited for the shot that would finish the bear. As the animal lifted his massive head from the snow a second time, and staggered like a drunk, the crosshairs of the scope found the space between the huge canines of the upper jaw and the drooping lower jaw. Jed fired. The shock of the bullet lifted the grizzly's head up and back. He dropped to the ground, death spasms jerking at his legs and shaking his mighty shoulders. Then it was over. The winter bear was no more.

Jed started to stand and found that his legs were shaking so badly that he could not. The sweat was pouring down his face and he felt weak. He called to Whiskey and the dog came limping back to his side. Jed inspected the gashes the bear had opened on Whiskey's rib cage. The skin was split and would have to be sewn, but the wounds were not too serious. Finally Jed stood, swaying slightly. He looked to the bear that lay a mere fifty feet away. What a magnificent and horrible beast he had been. Jed raised his rifle in salute. The victory was not hollow, this had been a worthy opponent.

CHAPTER 27

THE SPRING came softly, almost like a whisper on the gentle breath of nature's awakening. The snows receded slowly, sinking deeply into the forest soils and, when the soils could no longer hold their volume, running first in tiny rivulets, then in streams that fed the river that swelled with each passing mile. The waters fed as well the tiny flowers that braved the chilly nights, the crisp mornings. The mosses seemed to burst forth, sending their tiny shafts from the logs and rocks skyward. And with the return of the warmth that melted away the snows came the chatter of the wild that had been cloaked in the sleep of winter.

A broad smile lit Jed's face as he stood in the stirrups and pointed with wide sweeping motions across the valley that marked the river's passage. Jenny sat with a serene calm aboard the pack horse that Jed had bought last fall from Bob Price. Her cheeks held the bright glow of the spring sun, her mind the bliss of growing things. She was not the same young woman she had been before, nor was Jed the same man. The beauty that spread before them reflected their growing love in the persistent green blades of grass that shoved up through the dreary brown carpet that had been lost in the abyss of winter. Jed felt in his soul the coming of a new spring of life as it emerged from the cold bitterness of the past. Jenny felt a contentment she had not known before, in tune with the growth of things as she laid her hand across her belly where the child that would be born in late October grew.

It was mid April and Jed had put off the trip he usually took to town for almost a week. As he sat astride the Paint and looked over the vastness and beauty of his world, he knew that it could be put off no longer. He looked across the valley once more and turned the Paint away from the vision of it. It was a scene he would never forget. He had seen it time and time again, but never had it had the significance that it did now with Jenny by his side. It was something of him that he shared with her. Not just the sight, but the feelings as well. She had understood in a way that would not have been possible before the events of this past winter. His world was at peace once more and the winter bear that had threatened their world was but a memory stored with the other furs that were ready for market.

Jed looked back at Jenny, who still faced the valley as if unable to free herself from the sight of it. "It's time," he said softly. "We must go."

Jenny tore her eyes away. "Just a moment longer," she pleaded.

Jed smiled to himself. He knew the feeling. "Of course, a moment. It will be here when we return," he added gently.

"But will it be the same?"

"No, but that's the beauty of it. It is never the same, it always changes. You will never grow tired of it."

The next morning Jenny was astride the Paint as Jed secured the cabin for their absence. Whiskey waited impatiently near the head of the trail, barely able to contain his eagerness to travel. Jed returned from the cabin and took up the lead rope of the big pack horse. He would walk the trail, leading the pack horse, with Jenny following behind on the Paint. He looked around the clearing one last time, wondering if things would ever be the same, if he and Jenny would in fact return.

Jenny looked down at his strong back, the broad shoulders, the slim waist. She knew what he was thinking. "It won't be forever, Jed, we'll be back soon."

"Only if you're sure. There's the baby to think about."

Jenny could not answer. She had no doubts now, but that could change and she was aware of it. She remembered what Jed had said about leaving this place when she had been here but a short time. She knew that Jed would ultimately return, with or without her. She vowed to herself that it would not be without her.

By pushing all day at a steady pace they made it to Jed's old camp. He kept Jenny amused throughout that first day's hard trip with tales of past passages. He pointed out the blazes on the trees that marked his first passage of it, and he laughed when he told her of his lack of confidence when he had first come. He was deliberately filling out some of his background for her so she would have something of substance to tell her father about him when the time came. He wove facts into the fabric of his stories so that she would not realize his true purpose. He had had contact with midwestern fathers before, and he was guessing that her father's reaction would not differ substantially. He hoped that the reunion would not be too difficult, but he wanted to be sure that Jenny was prepared.

That evening Jenny sat on the bank of the stream watching Jed fish the swirling waters for their supper. She had shaken her head in disbelief when he had shed his shirt and boots to wade waist deep in the frigid snow fed stream. He constantly surprised her, and yet she was learning not to be surprised. She had learned that he was a man of immense physical strength for his size, and strong in mental discipline. They were qualities necessary for his way of life and he took great pride in them. She laughed at herself as she swatted at the blackflies that buzzed around her face, noting that Jed ignored them as they gathered on his back and shoulders. She wondered if she would ever have the strength to disdain the irritating little beasts.

The pole bent sharply and Jed began working in a trout to the shore. As soon as he had the fish in his grasp, he freed the hook from its mouth and nonchalantly tossed it high on the grassy bank next to Jenny. With a broad grin, he shouted, "He's all yours . . . get busy, there's more to come."

"Oh you rat!" Jenny squealed as she hurried to catch

the flopping, slippery form. she whacked it against a rock, grimacing as she did so. "I suppose you want me to clean it too?"

"Knife's in the top pocket of my shirt," Jed called as he flicked the fly toward another calm pocket of water.

They savored the end of the day together, each taking a turn at slipping Whiskey a bit of their supper. Jenny ran her hand along the dog's shiny coat, feeling the ridges of scars where Jed had sewn the gouges made by the grizzly back together. Whiskey responded to her touch by sitting up and licking her wetly across the face. She hugged the dog close to her. He was as much her dog now as he was Jed's. The moon rose slowly above the horizon and Whiskey cocked his head and listened to the mournful call that floated to them from the distance. He walked to the far side of the fire, sat down with care, pointed his nose skyward, and returned the call of his ancestors.

The morning found Jed up early, nervous and anxious to be on the move once more. The anxiousness was normal, the nervousness was not and Jenny sensed the change. It seemed to increase with each mile they traveled, each step that brought them closer to the small village. Jenny held her peace and gradually became aware that she was beginning to feel the tension as well. Each time her thoughts about her father had surfaced, she had suppressed them. When they topped the final rise and looked down on the village below, she could no longer do that.

"I wonder if I should send him a wire, or phone him?" she mused.

The words hit Jed like a wall falling. Each of them had been with their own thoughts and now the silence was broken. "I don't know," he said softly. "You know him, you'll have to decide."

"I know." Jenny looked down from the saddle. There was a twitch in the corner of Jed's eye. "You're not afraid of what he might say, are you?"

Jed looked startled. "Good God no . . . I just don't have any idea of how he will react to the fact that you're alive. I imagine that he's probably given up hope by now."

"Yeah, I thought about that too. I'd better send him a wire, that probably wouldn't be so much of a shock. Knowing Daddy," (Jenny used that almost mockingly), "he probably just buried himself in work and has forgotten all about me by now," she laughed nervously.

"I doubt that," Jed said tersely.

"Well, no matter, he'll find out soon enough. Gee that's a pretty valley. Can we get married down there?" she pointed at the village. "I mean, that is, if you haven't changed your mind about it . . . I mean, I know that things might change now . . ."

Jed looked up at her and took both of her hands in his. "Will you shut up," he said with a gentleness in his voice. "All this chatter is going to drive me nuts."

"You haven't changed your mind?"

"Of course not. Will a J.P. do, or do you want a church wedding?"

Jenny thought about the vows they had exchanged beneath the starry winter sky as the Aurora Borealis shimmered in the north. "A civil ceremony will be fine. I don't think we'll find a church as beautiful as the one at home."

"We can have a church wedding there, if you like."

Jenny smiled mysteriously and bent to kiss Jed. "I don't mean my father's home, I mean *ours*," she whispered.

Jed ran his fingers through Jenny's hair. "You're beautiful. Come on, I want some special people to meet my bride."

Bob Price was leaning against the barn when he saw them coming. He rubbed his eyes and looked again, as if his sight was deceiving him. "Well I'll be damned . . . I'll be damned! Louise . . . damn it Louise! Jed's a comin' an' he's got a woman in tow! I'll bet ya anything it's that girl that come up missin' last fall. Damn it, woman, are ya listenin'?!"

Louise emerged from the kitchen door, wiping her hands on her bright blue apron. "I ain't deaf yet. I'll be, I'll be. Better get ahold of O'Malley."

"There's plenty of time for that. We don't want to go jumpin' to conclusions."

"You're the one that jumped . . . I was just agreein'."

Bob grabbed Louise's hand and pulled her after him up the lane to meet Jed and Jenny. Jed's reunion with the Prices was warm, and Louise took Jenny under her wing like a mother hen, fussing over her like a long lost daughter. Jenny looked back at Jed helplessly as Louise dragged her toward the house.

"You'll be wantin' a good hot bath, child . . . and then a good hot home cooked meal. I got a nice new perfume . . . Bob bought it for my birthday. It'll suit a pretty young woman like you," Louise rattled, running all of her words together.

Jed smiled after them and turned back toward Bob and the horses. "Heard you had a run-in with a bear this winter. Hope he didn't hurt you too bad," he said.

"Naw, just a busted arm an' a couple a ribs," Bob replied.

"Well then," Jed said as he reached into one of the fur filled panniers, "I've got a present for you." He pulled the huge bearskin from the bag and draped it over the corral fence. "He's all yours."

Bob stared at it. "You got him," he stammered. "By God, you got him!"

"I didn't have much choice, he was starting to make a pest out of himself."

"Yeah, I'll bet he was," Bob said, narrowing his eyes. "I heard about you findin' MacKelvy's party . . . Was it as bad as they say?"

"Probably," Jed answered. "I don't like to think about it much."

"No, I s'pose not. Well, nobody really misses MacKelvy, but that damn fool took some good men with him from town. We oughtta donate this to their memory. Maybe get it tanned an' hang it in the school or the Emporium, or somethin'."

"Whatever you want to do. Speaking of the Emporium,

I better be getting down there and unload these furs. How
are the prices this year? Down again?"

"Some yes, some no. You know how it is."

"Yeah, I know. Listen, tell Jenny I'll be back in time for
supper. With Louise taking charge, I won't see her for an
hour at the least anyway."

"Hell I will," Bob said forcefully. "When we get done
unloadin' these animals, we'll get an early meal an' take
ever'body in my pickup. I'm gonna call ol' Pete an' we're
gonna throw you two a party!"

"Come on now, Bob."

I mean it . . . an' don't you argue with me. Ain't ever'
day we get to go to a weddin' an' a homecomin' all at once.
Come on now, let's load this stuff in the back of my
pickup."

Pete could turn out quite a party when he wanted to,
and tonight he'd pulled out all the stops. It would be a cel-
ebration to remember. He'd called in all the favors that
were owed to him and, with all the people that had
showed up, the large back room of the Emporium had been
cleared and turned into a regular dance hall. The preacher
had donated the use of the church piano and Sam Price
was banging away at the keys while Bob sawed the fiddle,
and the preacher picked a guitar. The justice had started
off the works by marrying Jed and Jenny. It was official
now.

Jed stood off to one side, giving O'Malley the details of
Jenny's rescue and the killing of the bear for his report,
while Jenny accepted the congratulations and good wishes
of the townspeople. Pete looked on like a proud father, and
was glad that Raudsep wasn't here to spoil the whole affair. He had gone to the States for a vacation before the
spring season got under way.

Three thousand miles away, John Peters sat in the
leather chair in the livingroom of his empty house. It was
dark outside and only a small table lamp lit the room. In
the grip of his white-knuckled hand was the telegram he
had received this evening. It was lined with crumple marks

and he'd read it over and over. At first he'd felt a sort of joy, and then the anger had set in. How dare she?! After all these months . . .the memorial service . . . the fund he'd set up in her name at the junior college she had attended, not to mention all the people that would have to be told, all the donations that would have to be returned. He read the telegram once more.

DAD

AM ALIVE AND WELL STOP AM MARRIED NOW STOP JED AND I WILL BE HOME NEXT WEEK STOP WILL EXPLAIN EVERYTHING THEN STOP MEET US WED O'HARE 1:30 P.M. STOP LOVE JENNY END

"How dare you?!" he screamed and wadded up the telegram once more and threw it across the room. "Alive . . . married?! Not even ask? Not even tell me before?! How dare you do this to me?!" He grabbed his jacket and stormed out of the house, releasing his anger in the power of the big Lincoln as he sped toward the lounge. He needed a drink, and some company.

CHAPTER 28

JED SHIFTED in the comfortable seat and looked out past the wing of the plane, scanning the ground that sped past far below them. Jenny slept quietly, her head against his shoulder, spent from the excitement of the party and exhaustion from the long trip to Glasgow, Montana by bush plane. Jed thought about the packed suitcases that Pete had presented them just before their departure, and smiled. What a friend the old man was. He already missed him. It was odd, he thought, he'd never really missed old Pete when he was in the woods, but this trip was like going to a foreign land and it was somehow different.

The Western Airlines plane banked and began a descent as it approached the high, flat plateau of Billings' airport. Jenny opened her eyes and yawned. Jed was glad that they were on the milk run and not a direct flight. It meant changing planes in another hour, but having the extra time to prepare himself was welcome. Anyway, Glasgow had been closer than Spokane and the only direct flights to Chicago went out of the Washington state airports.

Jed brushed the hair from Jenny's eyes. "Feel better, sleepy?"

"Ummm, yes. Where are we now?"

As if in answer to her question, the captain announced the location over the intercom.

"Good timing," Jed chuckled. "Now you know."

"You're awfully calm for someone who's only flown once or twice before."

"I said only once or twice on commercial flights . . . these big birds. I've been aboard a lot of small aircraft."

206

"Oh. Well chalk one up for your side," she teased, making a pantomime motion in the air with her finger. "How much longer do we have to go?"

"You should be telling me," he chided. "You're the one with all the airline experience."

"Yeah, but I've been sleeping," she laughed.

"Okay then, I'd guess about three hours."

"Ugh . . . g'night."

The plane touched down and Jenny did not drop off again until a few minutes later after the plane was once again airborne. Jed held her hand in his lap, wondering what sort of man her father was, if they would get along or not.

In Rockford, John Peters was just about to leave his home, and there was no doubt in his mind, he already disliked Jed, whoever he was. He thought angrily about his visit to the lawyer, an old family friend. He sure as hell hadn't given him much ammunition. All that crap about Jenny being of legal age and there wasn't anything he could do about it. Well, the hell with him then, John would have to handle matters himself. He looked to the driveway where the bright red sportscar waited for Jenny. If that didn't do it, he would find another way. What was that one glimmer of hope the lawyer had given him, something about diminished capacity? Yeah, that was it.

He arrived at the gate just ten minutes before the United flight that Jed and Jenny had transferred to touched down. He strode towards the window to icily watch the plane taxi in. There was a cold set to his square jaw and he jammed his hands into the pants pockets of the somber suit he had worn to Jenny's memorial service. Jenny would come with him, and Jed . . . well as far as he was concerned, this Jed could damn well get back on that plane and go back to where ever the hell he came from. He waited, coldly watching, searching the faces of the passengers as they deplaned, looking for his Jenny. Then he saw them, walking arm in arm as they emerged from the walkway. He felt the color rising in his face.

Jenny spotted her father and mistook the bright color of his face for excitement at seeing her. She waved at him and said to Jed, "There he is . . . that's my dad!"

Even at this distance, Jed could tell that John Peters' eyes did not hold a welcome look. Jed was used to telling what was on a man's mind by the way he used his eyes, and the look they held. He was sorry now that they had decided to return to Jenny's home immediately and not wait for the Wednesday that they had decided on first, but at the urging of O'Malley and Pete, Jenny had wired the new arrival date as soon as the reservations had been confirmed. Jed had wanted Jenny to phone home with the news, but she had been reluctant, feeling that talking face to face with her father would be better. As Peters drew near, Jed extended a hand in friendship. It was frigidly rejected without so much as a glance.

John Peters grabbed his daughter's arm and brusquely chopped his words. "Come on, Jennifer, we're going home."

Jenny's eyes held that startled fear that Jed had seen when he had come home after that first bear attack. "Dad!"

"Don't 'Dad' me . . . let's go." He turned viciously on Jed. "Whoever the hell you are, get out of my daughter's life and mine!"

Jed's voice held that stoniness that Jenny recognized as cold fury. But Jed didn't lose it, he held it in with all the self-control that had been built up over the years of practice. "Excuse me, she might be your daughter, but she's my wife. And unless you relax your grip on her arm, I'll relax it for you."

John was taken aback. He turned to more closely study this man's face. He'd expected a younger man, and had not even looked to be sure. Jed had to be in his thirties, thirty three, maybe thirty four. He still wasn't ready to give in, all his life he'd made his decisions stick. "You damn well better watch your tongue . . . and if you have any physical ideas, there's a cop right over there."

"You'd better call him then, because if you don't let go

of Jenny's arm . . . " It wasn't necessary for him to finish the sentence.

Jenny wrenched free of her father's grip and reached for Jed's arm. Her voice was tight, "Maybe Jed and I ought to find a room in Chicago until we go back. I can't believe you're acting this way, Father."

John looked at Jed with anger, and then at Jenny. "What the hell do you expect?!" he demanded. "You disappear and I think you're dead . . . for six months I think that, and now you show up married to some man I don't even know. You send a goddamn wire, for Christsake, you don't call. You don't say, 'Hey Dad, I'm getting married, why don't you come to the wedding, we'll wait.' Oh no, you just go ahead and do it. What the hell do you want from me?"

"You could at least be civil," Jenny shot back. "I thought you'd at least be glad to see me, to know that I was alive. There were reasons, really there were. I hoped for some understanding."

"That's the trouble with all you young people, you want the understanding, the consideration. And why not? All that your parents wanted to do was to give you a better life. We spoiled you rotten. Now it shows. 'I want . . . I want . . . ' Well fine, you got, that doesn't mean I have to take it."

Jed ignored the people that stared as they passed them on the concourse, but the tone of the meeting was beginning to grow tiresome. He had always hated family squabbles. "I think that is about enough," he said firmly. "If you want to pursue this, I suggest you do it elsewhere, Mr. Peters. Jenny and I are going to find a hotel room."

Peters watched as Jed steered Jenny away from him. All his planning had gone wrong, it wasn't supposed to have worked out this way. He was losing it, he immediately changed tactics. He couldn't work on Jenny if she went to some damn hotel room with Jed. "All right, all right. Let's drop it. Maybe I was too hasty. Give me some time, I'm just tense, that's all."

Jenny cast a furtive look at Jed and hesitated. She

wanted to believe that nothing had changed between her and her father, that there was still room for discussion and compromise. Jed thought about all the things Jenny had said in bitterness about her father and his friends, and he thought about the good things she had said about him. Maybe there was a chance, after all, they had just met and Jed could understand some of what Peters might feel. Peters' eyes were still calculating, but Jed felt that Jenny had the right to make the decision.

"It's up to you," he said. "You know him."

A brief discussion ensued between Jenny and her father, and it was decided that they would journey to Rockford. Jenny postponed the decision as to whether she and Jed would stay with her father. It would depend on how things went during the trip. John Peters left them to go get the car. Jed and Jenny claimed their bags and went to meet him outside the airport. Near the entrance they were approached by a clean cut youth.

"Hello," he said with smooth self-assurance, "I represent the Temple of Light and I would like to give you a book that explains our mission on earth."

"Judas!" Jed exploded. "That's all I need!"

"It will take only a moment of your time, sir, and all we ask is a modest donation of twenty dollars . . . "

"Will you get lost?" Jed did not mean it as a question.

"Oh no, sir, I will never be lost again, not since . . . "

"Beat it! Scram! Leave us alone. That ought to be plain enough."

When the young fellow retreated and turned his attention to another unsuspecting target, Jenny giggled. "Guess you told him."

It momentarily broke the tension. Jed grinned back and said, "Yeah, I guess I did. I'd forgotten about all the religious freaks at airports. At least this one wasn't hitting us up in the lobby."

"I don't think they can anymore. If I recall, they were to be limited to booths or else not disturb people inside the terminal."

"I hope my other memories of civilization aren't still around, the bad ones anyway. But," he sighed, "I suppose they still are."

John Peters arrived with the car and Jed loaded the bags into the trunk while Peters opened the front door for Jenny. He started to close the door after her, but Jenny put out a hand to hold it open and shook her head at her father. Peters reluctantly went around the other side as Jed slid in beside her. Jed said little on the trip to Rockford, choosing to look out the window, trying to shut out the memories this area held from his past, his suspicions about the future.

If Jenny noticed the bright sports car in the driveway, she didn't mention it. Peters was disappointed, but she was home now and he had time. He felt his confidence coming back, but was smart enough to avoid a confrontation just now. He let Jenny wander around the front yard, absorbing the memories that still hung in the boughs of the maples waiting for her return. Jed leaned against the car, watching Jenny with intense interest. This would be the final test. They planned to stay two weeks and then return. Jed was keenly aware how rapidly time passed and he wondered if she would be ready when the time came. He knew what was necessary to get everything ready for the fall season, that it took almost all of his time during the warm months to get it done. At the end of two weeks he would have to return or give up his way of life, and he wasn't sure that was possible.

"Well," Peters said roughly, "I guess we'd better go inside. Jenny, I kept your room just the way it was when . . . well, when you left."

Jenny turned around and said brightly, "I thought that Jed and I could use the guest room upstairs."

Peters gave her a hard look and said harshly, "I want you to stay in *your* room. Jed can use the guest room." He looked at Jed and added quickly, "Just for a couple of nights."

"No Father, it wouldn't be right."

"Just a couple of nights. I need time to get used to this. Please."

"It's all right for a couple of nights," Jed said, "if you think it will help your dad, Jenny."

Jenny bit her lip and looked at Jed. "Well, all right."

That night Jed tossed and turned in his bed, unable to get to sleep. He'd forgotten the noise that a city makes at night. There was a rush of automobiles on a nearby thoroughfare, the sirens of police cars, and a number of other noises that he did not care to decipher. Only the wailing of a cat in heat came close to any of the sounds he was used to now. He was still awake when he heard the sounds of muffled voices coming from downstairs. Gradually they became louder and Jed realized that an argument was in progress. He was tempted to go down, but something told him to stay out of it. He clamped a pillow over his head and tried to go to sleep.

At dawn he was up, dressed, and prowling around the spacious guest room. Finally he could contain himself no longer. He crept out of the room and stopped to peek inside Jenny's room. She was asleep, her dark hair spread over the pillow and an arm thrown over her eyes. Jed closed the door quietly and slipped out of the house. The damp morning air greeted him refreshingly. The city was quieter than it had been all night. Jed could even hear the call of a small owl in the distance, and the chirrups of the robins as they greeted the new day. He closed his eyes and imagined what it was like back at his clearing. He thought about Whiskey, laughing a bit when he thought of how old Pete would spoil the dog, stopping a tear when he thought of the look in his dog's eyes as he had left.

Jed wandered down the block and back, aware of all the eyes that peeped out from behind slightly parted curtains. Well, it would give the neighborhood something to talk about. Such small minds, he thought, that have to find something constantly to gossip about. Perhaps he was being too harsh in his judgment, but he remembered about the time on the farm when a neighbor had come and recounted for him each move he had made during an entire week, and he didn't think so. Finally he mounted the steps to the porch of the Peters house, opened the door, and went in. He'd been gone an hour. Jenny was up and making coffee in the kitchen. Peters walked in just after Jed had said good morning to Jenny. He was wearing pajamas, a terry cloth bathrobe, and slippers.

"You might have locked the door when you went out," he said roughly.

"Sorry, I didn't think about it."

"You better next time, there's criminals out there just waiting for an opportunity such as this."

"All right," Jed said, "I'll remember that." He walked around to where Jenny stood and put his arm around her, unconsciously laying his other hand across her belly as he was accustomed to doing since she had told him of her pregnancy.

"Take your hands off her!" Peters shouted suddenly. "I will have no obscene suggestions in my house!"

Jed threw back his head and roared with laughter.

"Father!" Jenny protested.

"Don't you talk back to me, young lady! I'll take care of this, you'll see! I'll get this ridiculous marriage annulled!"

Jenny stared at him and her words came hard and fast. "Can you have our child annulled as well?!" She hadn't meant the news to come so harshly, but she felt cornered and fought back the only way she knew how with her father.

John Peters sank heavily into a kitchen chair, the shock of the statement obvious on his face. For a moment he was totally unable to speak, and after unwilling to. Throughout the morning, Jed felt the strain of silence. He knew that he would have to leave them alone to work it out. If they had not by the time he returned, then he and Jenny would have to leave.

"I think I'll take a walk, maybe go buy some tobacco," he said. "Know any good shops?"

Jenny came to him and walked him to the door.

"There's a drug store five blocks away. Thank you, darling."

"Yeah. Well, if you don't have it worked out by the time I get back, I think it would be a good idea if we found someplace else to stay. I'll be back in a couple of hours."

Jenny watched Jed stride away. She would try to reason with her father, but if it didn't work, she knew her life was with Jed now. The decision would be easy.

CHAPTER 29

JED WALKED slowly, taking in the sounds and smells of the city, remembering what they were like from the past, comparing them to the clean odors of the forest. He passed a small park and stopped to watch an old man feeding the pigeons. There was still time to kill and Jed decided to go sit beside the old man and pass the time of day for a short time. The old man looked up as Jed approached and said nothing as he sat down on the bench beside him. A passerby would have thought them an odd looking pair, for the old man wore neatly pressed sports slacks, a bright plaid jacket, and tweed button down sports cap while Jed wore the comfortable jeans, plaid flannel shirt, and heavy western boots, topped off by the broad brimmed, high crowned Stetson that Pete had given him before the trip.

"Nice mornin'," Jed offered.

"Huh? Oh, sure is." The old man scrutinized Jed and decided that he meant no harm. You had to be careful these days. "Never seen you before, you're not from around here, are you?"

Jed laughed easily. "No, I'm not."

"Colorado, maybe Montana?" the old man guessed.

"Close. Originally Montana and Colorado. Now I live in the Canadian Rockies."

"Never been there." The old man spoke with the rapid midwest accent typical of the area. "Farmed most of my life up to Boone County. Always was cold enough to suit me, don't need no place colder. Are you here on vacation?"

"Sort of. We came down to visit my wife's father." There was a tightness to Jed's voice in the statement.

"I always tried to get along with my in-laws, paid off in

215

the long run. Doubled the size of my farm when they died. Yes sir, when I sold out I had enough to buy a place here in Rockford and a small place in Florida, plenty to live on. If you think about it, it pays to get along with the in-laws if they have money."

"I have money of my own, that hardly seems to be a good reason to base a family relationship on."

"Well now, I didn't say it was the *only* reason, but it is a good one. The others will come along. Can't have enough money these days with inflation and all."

"All the money in the world can't buy what I have," Jed said slowly. "Well, I guess I'd better be getting along. It was nice talking to you." It hadn't changed, he thought, money, or the pursuit of it, was still the main criteria of life here. Nothing else matters quite as much. Those who didn't have it conspired to get it, those who had it connived to get more. They missed, he thought, half the beauty of life, maybe more.

The old man shook his head as Jed walked away. "Strange sort of fellow," he muttered. "Don't know what he's talking about . . . well, he'll learn." He clucked to the pigeons and scattered crumbs to them.

Jenny sat across from her father at the chrome and glass kitchen table. Her eyes were red from crying. He just did not want to understand. His mind was made up. She listened to his words, but that was all they had become to her, just words. There was no room for compromise, he demanded that she do things his way and that was not possible. What he said to her made no sense at all. He sat there with his fists planted firmly on the glass top of the table.

"I'll buy him off, by God! You'll see what kind of man he is when I offer him a chunk of money to disappear. You'll see what his interest is then! Maybe then you'll understand how this old world works! I've kept you too sheltered all your life is all."

"Go ahead and try," Jenny returned. "It won't work, you don't know Jed."

"I know men. I know that some guy who squirrels him-self away the way he does has got to be just a little bit nuts. Hell, he's got to be plain crazy! And as far as that kid you're carrying goes, don't expect me to help with anything but an abortion!"

"Abortion?! Boy, you're really jumping ahead! You ac-tually think I'd have an abortion? You think after all the crap you've thrown I'd even want to stay here? You're ab-solutely blind, you can't see that Jed loves me, can you?"

"Love! Ha! Sex is more like it. First thing a man like him would do is latch onto the first woman that came along. It wouldn't make a damn bit of difference if she was the ugliest thing in the world, just so long as she had someplace for him to put it!"

"Damn you! How dare you talk to me like that?! How in hell did Mother ever stand it with you?!" Jenny jumped up and ran toward her room.

"Don't you dare bad-mouth your mother!" he shouted after her. "She was a good woman! She sure as hell would not have given me the trouble you and your brother Phillip have!" He heard the door to her room slam. "You get back here! You can't run off like that!"

Jenny turned the lock on her door to keep her father out. To shut out his bellows, she turned on the small tele-vision set on her dresser and turned up the volume. She looked past the set and out the window at the new leaves on the huge old maple. God, how she wished she hadn't come home. She had ignored the noise on the set until she heard that harsh, bitter laugh. Good Lord, was that Jed? She looked at the set. Police and news people were milling around in front of the drug store she had directed Jed to. A reporter was talking into a microphone in the foreground. Something about a robbery. In the background she caught sight of Jed's Stetson lying on the floor of the store. Next to it was a sheet-covered body.

"Oh my God!" she cried and ran from the room with the keys to the new sports car. The door banged behind her and she was gone before Peters could react.

Jed had come to the drugstore a half an hour earlier. For a while he had just browsed, flipping through the magazines on the rack, looking at the headlines on the various newspapers, and searching the shelves for a little something that he could take back for Jenny. He whistled softly to himself as he shopped. He found the tobacco rack and looked over the various brands before finally making a selection.

"Good morning, sir," the clerk from behind the counter said. "Is there anything else?"

"No," Jed replied, "that ought to do it." He thought for a moment. "Well, if you have a small makeup kit, I might be interested." He thought it might make a nice surprise for Jenny when they got back to the cabin. He had not failed to notice how just a small application of makeup underscored her natural beauty, and how it seemed to make her feel.

"Sure thing, let's just go down to the cosmetics counter and see what we can do."

For fifteen minutes they discussed the merits of the varied kits and the possibility of making up a special one. Jed did not know very much about the things Jenny liked to use. He did know that she favored a fragrance called Tabu, and made sure that he included a small bottle of that. Finally they settled on a small kit the clerk recommended. They went back to the front of the store and the clerk punched up Jed's purchases on the register. He had just put the items in a bag and handed them to Jed when a black car screeched to a stop in front of the store. A figure clad in black slacks, turtle neck, gloves, and ski mask burst through the door waving a small caliber handgun.

"All right! Nobody move! Nobody!" he shouted. He turned the gun on the clerk and handed him a small bag. "You . . . . fill this up. Hurry up! Nobody moves, nobody gets hurt."

Jed's eyes narrowed, but he remained still, not five feet from the gunman. This was like a scene out of an old B-grade movie, right down to the dialogue. The gunman looked at Jed nervously, bringing the pistol to a point halfway between the clerk and Jed. The clerk was stuffing the bag with cash from the register, sweating profusely. Jed saw the police cruiser approach the intersection. When it suddenly turned and blocked the car outside, the gunman turned the pistol at the clerk again.

"You called them! You hit the alarm!"

"No I didn't . . . I . . ." the clerk never got to finish the denial.

The gunman jerked the trigger and the pistol responded with a sharp pop. A hole opened in the clerk's forehead and he dropped spasmodically, bounced off the counter, and came to rest on the floor. Almost instantly, the robber turned toward Jed, but Jed was already moving. Just as the man brought the gun around, Jed's right foot shot out and made contact with the man's hand. The gun went off and Jed felt a sharp pain in his left arm. No time. His right hand shot out, a hammer of a fist catching the gunman square in the throat. Jed felt the hard cartilage give way and heard the gasping sounds. He let the man fall and slapped at the pistol, sending it flying down the aisle. He knew there was no hope, but he still rushed to the clerk. It didn't take a second look, the clerk's wide, staring look of surprise was one of finality. Jed turned away from the sight of it as a second patrol car pulled up out front.

The officers approached the door cautiously, guns drawn, and entered in a rush, covering each other. Jed leaned back against the counter and touched the sleeve of his left arm. It was soaked with blood, but there was still mobility in the arm despite the pain. He stood by as the police checked the corpse behind the counter and pulled the mask off the criminal in the front and handcuffed him. He was still alive, but just barely. His eyes bulged and his tongue was thick and blue. It was his youth that surprised Jed, the young black couldn't have been more than sixteen or seventeen. A policeman stepped in front of Jed.

"Let me look at that," he said, pointing at Jed's arm.

"It's nothing," Jed winced, "just a scratch."

The officer ripped open the sleeve. The bullet had entered the biceps and passed completely through, leaving an exit hole the size of a large pea. "Just a scratch, huh? I think you better sit down until an ambulance gets here."

Jed looked at it and probed the wound site. "At least it didn't hit the bone."

"An X-ray will tell the tale on that. Hey Joe! Get me the first aid kit."

"Okay Frank. We just lost the perpetrator, he's dead."

The cop that stood beside Jed shook his head and said, "You're damn lucky, you know that don't you? You could have been killed pulling a stunt like that."

Jed returned the man's look. "Maybe, but I would have been for certain if I had done nothing. I was his next target and your boys were a little busy outside." Jed looked out the door at the commotion. A camera had been set up and there was a crowd gathering. He laughed and there was a bitter irony to what he said. "Here come the vultures and scavengers for their little bits . . . just like the ravens following the bear."

"What?"

"Nothing. You wouldn't understand."

"Well, here comes the ambulance, let's get you out of here. We can get your statement at the hospital."

"As you wish. Grab my hat, will you?"

At that moment Jenny had come to a screeching stop just outside the barricade set up at the end of the block. She jumped out of the car and ran toward the drug store. An officer grabbed her by the arm as soon as she got past the barricade.

"Hey miss! Hold on there, you can't go any further. Now please, get back behind the barricade."

"You don't understand," she screamed, "my husband is in there!"

"All right, all right, just calm down and let's sort it out."

By the time Jenny had calmed down and told the police her story, the ambulance had left with Jed. The officer in charge told her what had transpired and that Jed was going to be all right. He arranged for one of his men to go with her to cut through all the crap at the hospital. One of the reporters got wind of what was going on and led the charge to interview Jenny. Jenny held to the arm of one of the policemen and fought through the crowd, refusing to talk to the reporters. By the time they got to the hospital, Jed was sitting on the edge of an emergency room examining table, listening to the droll instructions of the doctor who was finishing the dressing on the wound.

Jed looked up and saw Jenny. "I'm okay," he called to her.

"Oh thank God! I was so worried. They told me you were okay, but I wasn't sure I could believe them. They always say that," she was crying.

"Excuse me, Doc," Jed said and went to put his arms around Jenny. "It's okay, it's really okay."

"No it's not," she sobbed. "We should never have come back here. Let's go home. Please, let's go home."

Jed held her and rocked her gently. "What about your father? Did you get things worked out?"

"No, hell no! He will never understand. He thinks he can still run my life, that everything can be the way he wants it to. Do you know he even thinks he can buy you off?"

Jed laughed bitterly once more and thought about the conversation on the park bench. "I'm not for sale, you know that. I think we *had* better go home, at least I understand the animals there."

...........Please Cut Along This Line...........

Wilderness Adventure Books
320 Garden Lane P. O. Box 968
Fowlerville, MI 48836

Please send me:

_____ copies of *PREY FOR SURVIVAL* at $10.95

(Postage and sales tax will be paid by the publisher.)
Send check or money order—no cash or C.O.D.

Mr./Mrs./Ms. _____

Street _____

City _____ State/Province _____ ZIP _____